A PRISONER OF THE LORD
The Story of Gaius of Derbe, A Stalwart Layman
in the Early Christian Church

By

Kurt H. Starke

Copyright © 2001 by Kurt H. Starke
New Testament Scripture is from the New King James Version.
© 1979, 1980, 1982 by Thomas Nelson, Inc.,
Nashville, Tennessee.
Used by permission. All rights reserved.

No part of this book may be reproduced, stored in a retrieval system, or transmitted by any means, electronic, mechanical, photocopying, recording, or otherwise, without written permission from the author.

Published by Accent Publications Inc.
P.O. Box 1171, Bay City, Mi. 48706

PREFACE

Most books logically fall into appropriate categories: be they biographies, novels, mysteries, or whatever. Such is not the case with this book.

This book began as a study of the books of the New Testament – when and where they were written and by whom. This study was also done to enhance one's understanding of Holy Scripture. Some of the books can be fairly well placed while others cannot be placed in any way whatsoever.

There is a varied array of opinion on all of this. As one reads and studies available material on these things, the conclusion is reached that much of this is somewhat of a guess and nothing more. Likewise, one senses ambiguities and inconsistencies that make one wonder. Second thoughts are that this is an adventure one would like to join.

The primary starting point as a source of information is The Book of the Acts of the Apostles. However, Luke does not always supply us with all the facts for a total picture. Paul's letters must also be taken into account. Here, too, we are often left with an incomplete picture. Finally, one tries to coordinate all the New Testament books into one framework in the hope of piecing together a fairly accurate picture.

This means getting involved in a story. This story will have to be a delicate balance between the inviolate Word of God and pure fiction. Events recorded in the Bible cannot be changed. However, if one wishes to proceed, creative imagination must be used to fill in the blank spaces.

These are some of the questions for which answers are sought:

Were the Scriptures taught by Eunice and Lois to

Timothy confined to Old Testament books, or were some New Testament writings included?

Why did Mark leave Paul and Barnabas so suddenly to go to Jerusalem?

When and where do Paul and Mark become reconciled?

Where was Paul when he told Timothy to stay in Ephesus?

When and where did Paul first meet Titus?

Where was Titus from the time of the Apostolic Council in Jerusalem in 49 until the time of his appearance in Corinth in 55?

When does Paul go to Crete?

Why did Apollos come to Ephesus?

Where were Apollos and Zenas the lawyer coming from when they delivered Paul's letter to Titus, and where were they going?

When does Paul go to Dalmatia?

When does Titus go to Dalmatia?

Where does the door opened by the Lord for Paul lead?

When was Paul overtaken in a trance in the temple at Jerusalem?

Where was the place 'far from here' referred to by Jesus when Paul was in that trance?

What did Paul notice which caused him to declare, "For the mystery of lawlessness is already at work"? (II Thess. 2:7)

Did Timothy succeed in getting Mark to go with him to Rome as was requested by Paul?

When did the confrontation between Peter and Paul take place?

Did Peter abandon ministering to Cornelius and his family?

Under what circumstance did Silas find his way to

Rome so that he was able to assist Peter with his first letter?
When and where did Paul first meet Luke?
Who were the Syrians that brought their sick to Jesus for healing? (Matt. 4:24)
Who were the men who helped Paul escape from Damascus by letting him down in a basket through a window in the wall?
Why did Luke include the governor of Syria in his story of the birth of Christ?
Why the seemingly abrupt end to Luke's story of the Acts of the Apostles?
What was Gaius of Derbe doing in Macedonia with Paul as he was about to leave for Jerusalem in 56?
Why did Paul leave his cloak, the books, and the parchments with his friend Carpus in Troas?
Who was with Luke when he stayed behind at Philippi as the rest went ahead with Paul to Troas, and where was the other party coming from?
When did Epaenetus (Romans 16:5) move to Rome?

These unanswered questions leave the door open for speculation and conjecture. Some of the speculation and conjecture that has occurred has come to be accepted as near fact. Indeed, some has been promoted as fact. This is especially true of the last years and death of Paul.

Did Paul, in fact, visit Rome twice? Did he, in fact, die in Rome? It has been noted by some that the tomb in Rome supposedly containing the remains of Paul holds a beheaded corpse of a man of goodly stature. Paul writes about himself in his second Letter to the Corinthians: "'For his letters,' they say, 'are weighty and powerful, but his bodily presence is weak...'" (II Cor. 10:10) Is this a case of mistaken identity?

In the process of filling in various blanks, it is not

intended to add to or diminish what is written in Holy Scripture. Some items do present a problem. The multiple closing in Paul's letter to the Romans is an example.

Now the story grows larger and becomes a small book, with the original study added as an appendix. In this book, the element of time is transcended. No attempt is made to present an accurate picture of the way life was lived in biblical times. For instance, currency is measured in dollars, language encompasses present day speech and jargon, the works of Luther and others are quoted, names of characters are localized with modern names, etc. Having characters speak and act in this manner blends with the tenor of the book, namely, that it is a mixture of fact and fiction.

It has been said that Christianity is the only truly historically documented religion. However, opponents of such a claim counter: "If this is really so, why cannot a date for the crucifixion and the resurrection of Jesus be accurately established? Some say that it happened in the year A.D. 30, and others say that it was A.D. 33." To help shed light on this subject, Appendix, B, "Observations on The Works of Josephus," has been added.

Although much of what is written in this book is pure fantasy, one must recall that the primary purpose of the original study was to search the Scripture. That means that we must forevermore be trying to hear what God is saying. And in trying to hear what God is saying, the Bible is the only source of truth and doctrine.

In summary, the Holy Writers left many gaps in their tale of the early church as recorded in Holy Scripture. In our searching of the Scripture we are, to some extent, compelled to try to fill in these gaps with our imagination. What would it have been like if the story had been complete in every detail?

Not much incentive would be left to search the Scripture. We must reiterate, however, that the Holy Scriptures do give us all that is necessary for us to know of our salvation in Jesus Christ.

This book, then, is my imagination of these things captured on the printed page.

This work could not have been completed without assistance of one kind or another. That help is sincerely appreciated.

DEDICATION

This book is dedicated to the memory of

    The Reverand Theodore Stiegemeyer
    and
    The Reverand Martin A. Bertermann

CONTENTS

Chapter 1	Jerusalem A.D. 33	Page 1
Chapter 2	Galatia-Derbe 33	10
Chapter 3	Galatia-Derbe 36	15
Chapter 4	Galatia-Derbe 37	22
Chapter 5	Pontus 40	30
Chapter 6	Galatia-Lystra 47	36
Chapter 7	Galatia-Lystra 49	48
Chapter 8	Antioch 52	54
Chapter 9	Jerusalem 56	66
Chapter 10	Ephesus 58	77
Chapter 11	Syria 59	90
Chapter 12	Ephesus 60	95
Chapter 13	Rome 59	107
Chapter 14	Pontus and Cappadocia 61	119
Chapter 15	Gaul 63	127
Chapter 16	Sisalpine Gaul 63	135
Chapter 17	Rome 64	148
Chapter 18	Ephesus 64	158
Chapter 19	Ephesus 67	165
Chapter 20	Ephesus 68	171
Chapter 21	Ephesus 72	185

APPENDIXES

Appendix A — Page 188
   A Chronology of the New Testament Books of the Bible
Appendix B — Page 214
   Observation on the Works of Josephus

ADDENDUM

Addendum 1 – Page 234
   Early Church History and Projection
Addendum 1 - Page 240
   St. Paul's Third Missionary Journey and Projection
Notes - Page 246
Supplement – Page 254
   The Antichrist Puzzle

Chapter 1
Spring 33

What began as a quiet heart-to-heart talk had turned into a shouting match. Suddenly, Gaius realized that people in the lobby of the inn were staring at them. Trying to gradually withdraw from Barak, he spoke more softly, saying, "Okay, okay, so I bungled the job. What's done is done. All I can do now is try to patch things up."

That was not good enough for Barak. Still speaking loudly, he told Gaius, "You are not the man your father was. You will never amount to anything."

Upon hearing that, Gaius wheeled about and left him, returning to his room. He needed time to unwind. Most of the business for which he had come to Jerusalem had been concluded. The weeklong sessions of trading, bartering, buying and selling had tired him.

This was his first trip to Jerusalem since his father's untimely death, and there was so much more to operating this part of the business than he fully realized. It was true that Barak, his father's chief steward, shouldered the majority of the responsibilities, but that was not his primary job. For now, Barak was trying to teach Gaius the art of running the business, making decisions, and assuming control.

Until this time, Gaius' father Nerius had done most of that work himself. He had been reluctant to have Gaius overly involved in the details; details that he could much more easily handle himself. Since his death, however, all that changed.

The room at the inn faced west and as the sun sank lower in the sky, Gaius' mood turned to one of melancholy. That may not have been so strange, but this was spring, the season of new life. What was happening to him was not what Gaius had desired. He felt that somehow he was being saddled with something that would stifle him. Gaius really wanted to get out to see something of the world.

His father's successful business was now his; his education was about the best that could be had; he had read most of the Greek scholars and was well-versed in literature, and money was not too much of a question; the problem was – he was just not quite ready to settle down – period.

What loomed larger in his mind, however, was that he would be doomed to a life of routine. Gaius contemplated with the philosophers – is this all there is to life – birth, eating, working, sleeping, death? For the present, yes; Gaius resigned himself.

Tomorrow morning before keeping a few last minute business appointments, he would leisurely stroll the streets of Jerusalem. There was so much to see, and the customs of the Jewish people interested him. And then next day he would head back to Derbe.

At breakfast in the east room, the spring sun shone brightly through the window. A freshness permeated the air. It penetrated Gaius' gloomy spirit of last evening. Gaius told Barak of his plans. He would meet him at Levi's shop at one o'clock.

Gaius had not gone far before he entered the residential section of the city. This was unfamiliar territory to him. In previous visits to Jerusalem, he was more or less confined to the business community, although once he did inspect the massive Jewish temple, with which he was thoroughly impressed. Barak was a Jew and there were other Jews among his friends in Derbe so he had a little knowledge of their history. He had also read portions of the Torah and some of their prophets, most notably the prophet Isaiah.

The calm of the quiet of the morning suddenly vanished with the sound of a mighty rushing wind. Gaius was astonished because the weather was so pleasant. He headed in the direction of the sound, and soon there was a great many other people doing the same thing.

He found a crowd of people gathering in front of a house, a fairly large two-story dwelling. The men who were in the house came out and began to speak in various languages. As Gaius stood in amazement in the background, clusters of Jews gathered around the man who was speaking in their tongue. He could hear at least a dozen different languages being spoken. Above all the clamor, Gaius heard shouts and insults as some in the crowd ridiculed these men as being drunk.

Eventually, one man with a ruddy face gained the attention of the whole crowd. He spoke vigorously concerning a certain Jesus of Nazareth. He explained what the prophets had written, and how Jesus was the fulfilling of such prophecies.

He finished his exhortation by saying, "Therefore, let all the house of Israel know assuredly that God has made this Jesus, whom you have crucified, both Lord and Christ."[1]

When he finished, the people were cut to the heart and said to him and his friends, "Men, and brethren, what shall we do?"[2]

Then the man who had just finished speaking said, "Repent, and let every one of you be baptized in the name of Jesus Christ for the remission of sins; and you will receive the gift of the Holy Spirit. For the promise is to you and to your children, and to all who are afar off, as many as the Lord our God will call."[3]

The last sentence of this speech intrigued Gaius. Here was a Jew, speaking to a group of Jews, seemingly inviting people outside their community to be a part of their religion. From his knowledge of Judaism, he knew that the Jews were, for the most part, a closed society. Anyway, that was the impression he received from his friends who were Jews. Yes, indeed, his curiosity was piqued.

Forgetting entirely about the time, he elbowed forward to have a closer look. He noticed that almost all of the men who came from inside this house were fairly young, near the same age as himself. There were several exceptions, however, and he thought to himself that in order to find out more about this group, he should approach an older looking man. He did this and soon he was in a position to introduce himself.

"Good morning," he said. "I wonder if I might introduce myself and have a word with you?"

"By all means," was the reply.

"My name is Gaius and I am a Greek merchant from Derbe in Galatia. I am in Jerusalem on business."

"I am pleased to meet you, Gaius. My name is Matthew."

Gaius continued with a few amenities, but then proceeded to tell Matthew how impressed he was with what all he had heard. "I would be very grateful to you if you could tell me a little more about this Jesus and your group."

Matthew immediately recognized the opportunity Gaius had given him, and he put his arm around his shoulder, in a welcoming gesture. "To ensure a slightly more private atmosphere," he said, "shall we seek a more quiet location?" Gaius agreed.

Matthew began by telling Gaius about the family history of Jesus Christ, and the circumstances of his birth. He then tied this event with the prophecies of the ancients, concluding with the narrative of John the Baptist. Gaius listened intently, but finally asked, "Is this baptism the same as what your friend was talking about?"

"It is related," Matthew replied. "For John did indeed baptize with the baptism of repentance, saying to the people that they should believe on Him who would come after him, that is, on Christ Jesus. Baptism is a gift of the Holy Spirit."

Gaius suddenly realized what time it was and explained to Matthew that he must keep a business appointment. He implored Matthew to meet with him again a little later, although he had no idea how long his business would take. Matthew suggested that they perhaps could have dinner together at his home. Taken by surprise that Matthew would do such a thing, Gaius stuttered his acceptance of the invitation, and Matthew gave him directions.

During dinner, Matthew and Gaius exchanged more information

about themselves. Gaius was surprised to learn that Matthew knew Greek fairly well. He saw that Matthew knew more Greek than he knew Hebrew. Gaius noted, also, that he had made a fortunate selection in his desire for more information.

As they became better acquainted, Matthew sought to put Gaius more at ease. He told him that his profession as a tax collector had placed a certain stigma on him, as it had on all tax collectors. His association with the Jewish community had considerably diminished before he became associated with Jesus. He had, in fact, not entered a synagogue for over ten years. His work was not the only thing that caused this. The sect of the Pharisees, with pretentious show of piety and their boastfulness, had turned him off early in his life.

Because of these things, Matthew told Gaius he was not as concerned about observing all the Jewish customs as were the rest of the disciples of Jesus. He was accustomed to entertaining non-Jews in his home. And he was more than pleased when Jesus had accepted his invitation to dine with him. Many thought this was a strange thing for Jesus to do, since he was a tax collector.

Matthew resumed his story of Jesus by telling of the beginning of Jesus' ministry and the choosing of His disciples. "Most of the men chosen by Jesus," Matthew related, "were simple fishermen. None of them had much schooling of any kind.

"To my knowledge," Matthew said, "only three of the other original eleven disciples are literate. They are, however, a very zealous group and faithful to their Lord. They left their jobs and families and friends and followed Jesus when they were chosen by Him."

Matthew explained that those called first were the brothers Peter and Andrew, and James and John. "Peter was the one who spoke to the whole assembly," said Matthew.

"As for me, I was sitting at my tax office one day when Jesus came and said to me, 'Follow Me,' and I did. When I invited Jesus to dinner together with some of my friends, the Pharisees, who were becoming antagonistic toward Jesus, complained that He was breaking some of their laws. They asked, 'Why does your Teacher eat with tax collectors and sinners?' But when Jesus heard that, He said to them, 'Those who are well have no need of a physician, but those who are sick. But go and learn what this means: "I desire mercy and not sacrifice." For I did not come to call the righteous, but sinners, to repentence.'4 This is the sum and substance of the purpose of His ministry."

Matthew continued, "The more I learned of His ministry, the more I felt 'at home' in it. His teaching was one of freedom and liberty. The restrictive teaching of the Jews that 'the Torah always and in all time is inseparable from the ceremonial laws'5 was repressive, and Jesus came to lift this burden on the hearts of men. He came to free men from the yoke of the law, the ceremonial law, that is.

"For the Jews, the time for observance of these ceremonial laws is over. They were given in ages past solely as a sign, similar to many other signs.

"Jesus Christ's message of the Love of God might well be called the perfect law of liberty. This law of liberty sets men free from the bondage of sin. And God was in Christ reconciling the world unto Himself. Christ died for the sins of all mankind, and not solely for the Jews."

Matthew explained to Gaius what Jesus' teaching meant and told of some of His miracles. Likewise, Matthew described Jesus' suffering, death, resurrection and ascension. Gaius listened carefully, but, nevertheless, many of the things that Matthew revealed left more questions that needed answering.

As the hour grew late, Gaius had to excuse himself, and explained that tomorrow he was leaving early for home. Upon leaving, Gaius thanked Matthew more than once for having fulfilled his request, and for having been such a fine host.

Gaius went to bed immediately, but could not sleep. A thousand thoughts thundered through his mind. How differently the day turned out from what he had anticipated. He was thoroughly impressed with all that he had seen and heard. How was he to remember all the things that Matthew told him? A new spirit seemed to pervade his being. He determined that he had to see Matthew again before he left for home. First thing in the morning he would see Barak to tell him that the time of departure would have to be delayed. For how long he could not say. He would stand firm.

He had made the first decision in regard to his involvement in the running of his father's business. It was that the business would not always demand first priority in his life. Only after making this decision did he fall asleep.

At dawn, Gaius arose and went to tell Barak. Upon hearing the news, Barak hit the ceiling. "What in blue blazes do you think you are doing?" he asked. "Everything is ready and the servants are waiting. You can't run a successful business by making these last minute contrary decisions. That is no way to operate!"

"I know how you must feel," Gaius asserted, "but something happened yesterday that has made things different for me. If you are willing to listen, I will explain this on the journey. But for now I must see this man I met. I will try to make it as short as possible. Tell the servants to leave ahead of us. As we can travel faster than they, we can catch up to them."

Not sure about getting to Matthew's home too early, Gaius wondered when and how to make his approach. When he got there he hesitated. However, he did see some sign of activity, so he rapped on the door. Matthew looked noticeably surprised when he opened the door, but bade him enter. Gaius apologized for this early intrusion. He then explained the multitude of thoughts he had last night as he tried to get to sleep.

Matthew listened patiently as his wife Leah prepared breakfast. As Gaius also partook, he finally said what he had come to say. "I was really inspired by what you revealed to me yesterday, and I would like to learn more. But I simply cannot assimilate everything after hearing it just one time.

"May I make a suggestion, Matthew?" he added.

"I think I already know what it is, and I have already given it some thought. You want me to put what I told you yesterday on paper, right?"

"Right," said Gaius.

"I have never tried my hand at writing," Matthew replied, "but as I said, I have been thinking of it. I have already made a few notes. Perhaps, I thought, that was one of the reasons the Lord chose me to be one of His disciples.

"Something else that has been on my mind since Jesus ascended into heaven is what Jesus spoke of concerning His coming again. He said, 'All authority has been given to Me in heaven and on earth. Go therefore and make disciples of all the nations, baptizing them in the name of the Father and of the Son and of the Holy Spirit, teaching them to observe all things whatever I have commanded you; and behold, I am with you always, even to the end of the age.'[6]

"This statement was the cause of much discussion among the disciples. The consensus of opinion was that Jesus' second coming would take place fairly soon. I argued against this idea because Jesus also told us to eventually go unto the uttermost parts of the earth with His story. It seemed to me that this might take some time. I was unable to convince any of them. Your interest and enthusiasm might just convince me to do what you ask."

"Let me urge you, then, to make a positive commitment," Gaius stated firmly. "It doesn't have to be done in a hurry, and from the impression you gave me yesterday, I believe you are eminently capable."

"All right," Matthew said, "I will do my best to provide what you are looking for."

"I – I have another request to make," Gaius said hesitantly. "I will not be in Jerusalem again for a few years, and I was wondering about how I will receive a copy of your – er – writing; I almost said good news."

"That is a very interesting thought," Matthew exclaimed. "What I shall write is indeed good news – the good news of salvation through our Lord Jesus Christ. In short – your word – GOSPEL."

Matthew continued, "I have no way of really knowing how long this project will take me, but I shouldn't think that it will take longer than two years. Because there is such uncertainty about the timing, I will take it upon myself to deliver your copy in person, if that meets with your approval."

"Oh, yes," was the reply.

"And if I am not there in two years, rest assured that I will come eventually," Matthew added.

"My life has been pretty well confined to Palestine," Matthew said. "I haven't ever been north of Damascus. I would welcome a chance to go to Galatia. In fact, Jesus himself said that we will be His witnesses in Jerusalem, and in all Judea and Samaria, and to the end of the earth – not that Galatia is at the end of the earth."

Gaius chuckled. "Everything sounds great," Gaius said with a note of happiness. "I will write down some directions for you if you have paper."

Chapter 2
Spring 33

Barak did not say much when Gaius returned. He acted displeased and anxious to get the convoy moving. He muttered something about they would not be able to stop at the usual places on the return trip.

As they moved on, Gaius focused his thoughts on the things at home. His father had begun an association of merchants in Galatia. A meeting was to be held after his return. That meant he would be going to Iconium. Hosts of this meeting were to be Nestor and his wife Eunice. They were a friendly couple; this in spite of the fact that Nestor was Greek like himself and his wife was Jewish. Gaius did not mind in the least. This would be the first chance to see their young son, Timothy.

Although he did not particularly relish the job, yet because of his father's role in them before he died, Gaius would make an appearance. He was glad that his good friend from Lystra had assumed more of a leadership role. Philemon, he was sure, was more suited for that job than he. Besides, he thought, it was something to help keep him occupied because of the troubles Philemon was having at home. There was unhappiness over the fact that Philemon and his wife were unable to get a family started.

The one thing about his own home that occupied a good deal of Gaius' thoughts was the welfare of Apphia. She was the young slave girl his father had acquired to be his cook about a year before his death. Her baby surely would have been born by the time he arrived home. Usually the slave's personal affairs meant very little to him, but this was something out of the ordinary. He had every right to believe that he was the father of the child.

His father insisted that the cook stay in the main house; whereas, the other slaves had their own quarters. Apphia came to their household after being purchased from men who operated caravans to the east. Gaius' mother had died some years earlier.

Apphia was lithe and spirited. Gaius was physically attracted to her from the outset, and even though such things were strictly forbidden in their house. The fact that she stayed in the main house placed a great strain on Gaius. Apphia was so much different from the other slaves. The difference seemed like night and day.

And the inevitable happened. What amazed Gaius the most when he seduced her was that Apphia did not resist in any way whatever. After the episode, Gaius was able to constrain himself, but it was a struggle. At times it almost seemed as though he consciously avoided her. His father once commented about it.

The easiest way for Gaius to solve the problem would be to sell Apphia. But that meant finding a replacement for her. He decided to keep her and play everything by ear. He would distance himself from her, but with his close association with her now, this was almost impossible.

Gaius had come to know Apphia as a person with a warm and outgoing personality, and had gradually accepted her presence. But she, however, went quietly about her business in the kitchen and kept mostly to herself. Her association with the other slaves was remote. Most of them, in fact, resented her.

As the convoy continued and approached the end of the journey, Gaius and Barak began to be a bit more civil to each other. Gaius especially tried to reach out to Barak and showed more concern about running his father's business.

Gaius debated with himself continuously whether he should share with others his experience with Matthew in Jerusalem. He had privately committed himself to what Peter and the others preached, but for him to make an outreach at this time was, he thought, asking more of him than what could be expected. After all, this was all so new, and he was so ill equipped. Anyway, he reasoned, who would believe what he had to say? Such a radical change in his outlook on life would not be accepted by his friends. For the present, he finally concluded, everything would have to remain as it was.

The convoy's arrival at home was a joyful occasion, as usual. Nothing much in the way of change had occurred in the business affairs. It was a matter of clearing away details that had piled up, and getting back into the swing of things. Barak had everything humming smoothly again in no time. He worked efficiently with Gaius and did not mention to anyone in Derbe what had taken place as they were getting ready to leave Jerusalem.

Apphia had given birth to a healthy baby boy. She named him Onesimus. Gaius expressed his delight that everything had gone well with her delivery. Other than that, he did not pay any inordinate attention to her or her son. Apphia's new responsibilities in taking care of her child did not immediately seem to hinder her greatly in the performance of her regular tasks. All in all, Gaius was glad to be home again.

After the business association's meeting in Iconium, however, a distinct change in Gaius' personality appeared. He seemed to be somewhat troubled. Apphia noticed it, but did not discuss it with anyone, not even Barak. But with the passing of a few more weeks, Apphia became increasingly concerned.

At length, she went to Barak to ask his advice. Barak then told her of the spat in Jerusalem between himself and Gaius, and added that he, too, had noticed the difference in Gaius' behavior.

They exchanged thoughts and ideas.

"I think it would be better if you would say something to him rather than I," Barak commented.

"Wouldn't it be out of place for me to say anything?" Apphia asked.

"Since he has no one close in his family here to look into it," Barak replied, "I feel that we must take the initiative."

"But," Apphia tried to interrupt.

"From what I have observed, you are definitely more suited to this sort of thing than I am," Barak asserted. "I tend to be brusque and impatient. Suggest that you could perhaps get something for him. From there, depending on what he said, express your concern for his health, and then, if appropriate, inquire into the nature of the trouble."

"It seems to me that it is easier said than done."

"You are right, but I think it is our duty to try, don't you?"

"Yes, yes I do, but…" Apphia trailed on. She had run out of excuses. "If you really want me to try, I'll try," she finally conceded. "Wish me well."

"I most certainly do," Barak assured her.

Selecting the right opportunity to say something to Gaius was not as difficult as Apphia imagined. Gaius was tired and irritable that very evening. He ate very little. Afterward, Apphia began saying everything Barak suggested. The most she got for her efforts was a couple of grunts.

"Master," she finally said in a more resolute tone, "you are not helping yourself one bit by not talking about what is troubling you."

"So what?"

"I am not the only one who is worried about you – Barak, too, is concerned."

"Leave Barak out of this," he snapped.

Apphia asked him if something happened on the journey to Jerusalem, and added, "Barak has no intention of interfering in any of your affairs," she said, not really knowing. "But, he is as concerned about you as I am."

"Look," he finally relented, "if you must know, and I suppose sooner or later you must, I had a very unusual experience in Jerusalem. I met a man named Matthew, and he will be coming to Derbe some day. It probably won't be until next year sometime. He and I became friends. That is all I'll say right now. Tomorrow I will tell Barak myself, because I have given Matthew instructions to go to the shop.

"And now, if you would, please, bring me a cup of hot tea," he said, sounding somewhat relieved.

Apphia happily obeyed.

Chapter 3
Spring 36

More than two years passed and Matthew still hadn't come. Gaius convinced himself that Matthew was having more difficulty in writing his Gospel than he foresaw. When another six months elapsed without any word from Matthew, Gaius became increasingly concerned.

Meanwhile, Gaius received word that his uncle (his mother's brother) had died in Ephesus in Asia. Gaius had been there only one time. His uncle was a widower like Nerius, but he and his wife did not have children. Gaius was the sole heir.

A communication from officials in Ephesus stated that it would be necessary for Gaius to come to Ephesus to claim the estate. Although Gaius knew that the property was extensive, and on the seaside, and therefore, of considerable value, he hesitated in immediately going. He wanted to be in Derbe when Matthew arrived. Not wishing to disinherit himself, though, he finally made plans to go.

He called Barak and Apphia together for a meeting, giving them instructions to make Matthew feel entirely welcome and at home if he arrived. He suggested that perhaps Matthew might be interested in improving his Greek, and asked them to make sure his library was at his disposal. In the event Matthew was interested in writing, he showed Apphia where the materials were. He told both of them that although he might be a while, Matthew should be urged to stay until he returned.

Gaius had been gone for two months when Matthew and Leah, his wife, finally came. Matthew was sorry to hear that his host was not present to welcome him. However, he and Leah thanked Barak and Apphia for their welcome and accepted their hospitality. He then added that a number of reasons kept him from coming sooner.

Apphia was in a more favorable position to host Matthew and Leah than was Barak, and she did so very graciously. It did not take long for them to become friends on a first name basis. Although Apphia explained that she was a slave, Matthew and Leah accepted her warmly. She acted happy for the opportunity of relative freedom of character that their visit afforded her. She became more open to them than at any time since she became a slave.

Matthew sensed Apphia's openness, and did not feel that he would be amiss to inquire into her background. Apphia told him that she came from an eastern country. Her father was the chief in their small village. She was the oldest of four children, having two brothers and a baby sister.

On a quiet day some years ago when she was fourteen, a group of marauders entered their village and began to make a nuisance of themselves. As chief of the village, her father protested vigorously. He paid very severely for this protest, because the intruders became enraged. They proceeded to kill their entire family, sparing only her. They sped off taking her with them. They obviously wanted her body. This was only the beginning of a series of horrifying and debasing experiences for her.

Not wanting to intrude on Matthew and Leah with any more details, Apphia shifted the subject of conversation. Soon Matthew was telling about himself. He told Apphia that he was brought up in an ordinary Jewish family. As a youth, he was an apprentice to a tax collector. In time he became one himself.

Tax collectors, he explained, were not the most popular people in the country. In fact, he said, they were downright despised by most people. Many of them were notorious cheats.

Matthew then told Apphia that suddenly a great change came into his life. "Do you know anything about the Jewish people?" he asked.

"Very little," she admitted. "And only a very few words."

"The Jewish people are a very religious people," Matthew started. "They have a covenant with God that says that they are His special people, and that through them God would send a sin bearer (a Redeemer) to atone for the sins of the people. For generations, the Jews have been waiting patiently for this Messiah to appear. Many prophets throughout the long history of the Jewish people have written about Him.

"In waiting so long for someone to come, though, many people, myself included, became indifferent and skeptical. Religion for many of us was a sham. Then there was some talk about thirty-eight years ago that a child was born in Bethlehem in Judea who was supposed to be this promised Messiah. It was reported that angels were singing in the sky announcing His birth to some shepherds."

The mention of Bethlehem brought a look of added interest to Apphia's face.

Matthew continued, "Very few people paid attention to it, and it was largely forgotten.

"About eight years ago, I was sitting at my tax office one day when this man came by and said to me, 'Follow Me,'[1] and I did. This man's name was Jesus, and He was the same person as that baby who was born in Bethlehem."

"Was this Jesus a king?" Apphia excitedly asked.

"Most assuredly," answered Matthew. "He was the King of the Jews, the long awaited Messiah."

Astonished by the question, Matthew asked Apphia to explain.

She began by stating that her grandfather was an astrologer. He lived in a city not too far from the village where her family lived and they visited fairly often. Her grandfather welcomed every opportunity he had to become better acquainted with the children, and many times told them stories of one kind or another.

The story he particularly liked to tell was of the time he and two of his colleagues made a trip to Jerusalem. They had seen a star belonging to the newborn King of the Jews. Upon their arrival in Jerusalem, they were surprised to learn from the king of that country that he did not know of any newborn King of the Jews. After the king, named Herod, consulted the chief priests and scribes of the Jews, he directed them to Bethlehem, a small town five miles south of Jerusalem. There they found the baby Jesus with his parents, Mary and Joseph. They worshipped the baby King, and presented to Him gifts of gold and frankincense and myrrh.

Matthew was utterly amazed and speechless. Regaining his composure, he managed to say, "Apphia, coming to Derbe and meeting you and talking with you has to be the happiest coincidence in my life.

"I have something I want you to see. But before I show it to you, I would like to tell you the story behind my coming to Derbe." When Matthew finished relating everything about his encounter with Gaius in Jerusalem, he said, "The scrolls I brought with me are the beginning of my story of the life and ministry of Jesus Christ."

"I was wondering what they were," Apphia interjected.

"There are eighteen of them, but I particularly want you to see the second one. This is written in Hebrew so I will read it to you." Matthew began, "Now after Jesus was born in Bethlehem of Judea in the days of Herod the king, behold wise men from the East came to Jerusalem, saying, 'Where is He who has been born King of the Jews? For we have seen His star in the East and have come to worship Him.'[2]" Matthew then read the entire scroll.

"I am fascinated," exclaimed Apphia. "I now see why this story was my grandfather's favorite. I am as excited about this Jesus as I know that Gaius must be.

"I would like to learn as much about Him as I can, but, of course, I cannot read Hebrew," Apphia continued.

"I have thought about such things a great deal," Matthew said. "Since Gaius and I did not have an understanding about which language I should write in, I thought best that I should do it in the one that is best known to me.

"I am sure he will be disappointed that I did not write the story in Greek. But that will give us something to do when he returns. I intend to ask him to work together with me in translating it into the Greek language."

"He will be glad to," Apphia assured. She paused a bit and then asked, "Is this the only copy of your story, Matthew?"

"Yes, it is," he said, "for the story is not yet finished. I still have much to write."

Apphia remembered Gaius' instructions to offer Matthew materials in case he wanted to write. She did so, and Matthew happily welcomed the opportunity to resume writing.

A short time later, Apphia summoned enough courage and remarked, "I would like to help you if I may. My mother taught me many things, including reading and writing. Maybe I could start to copy what you have already written."

"Do you think you can handle Hebrew lettering?"

"I practiced copying letters quite often at home. My mother complimented me on my work."

"In that case," said Matthew, "there seems to be no reason for not giving you a chance. As long as it doesn't interfere with your duties."

"I promise, I will do it in the time I have free from my duties and from looking after my son."

"I can help you with him, if you'd like," said Leah, who was sitting nearby. "We were never able to have children of our own."

"Good," said Matthew.

A month went by before Gaius returned. Matthew finished writing another scroll while Apphia copied two of the others.

Gaius and Matthew embraced, shook hands, and then embraced again. Gaius was highly elated to see Matthew, and was equally as happy to learn that he had been made to feel at home. For the first time since she came to their home Gaius openly expressed approval and thankfulness for all that Apphia had done.

Matthew apologized to Gaius for any inconvenience his delayed arrival might have caused. He then went on to explain all that took place while Gaius was gone. When Gaius found out that Apphia had been helping Matthew by copying the scrolls, he remarked that he had never heard of such a thing – a woman doing what was thought to be a man's job. He inspected her work, and thought she had done a fine job.

Matthew then gave Gaius a detailed description on the progress of the gospel. "The conditions at Jerusalem and my illness kept me from writing as much as I would have liked to. Persecutions of the followers of Jesus by the Jews, especially by a Pharisee named Saul arose, and became increasingly intense.

"When one of our evangelists, whose name was Stephen, was stoned to death, other evangelists and disciples left Jerusalem for Samaria and Judea and the countries to the north. But the Apostles remained in Jerusalem. Many people in Samaria received the Word spoken by the evangelists, so Peter and John visited them. They returned and reported what was happening.

"It was then that I told Peter and also James, the brother of Jesus, that I was attempting to write the story of Jesus. I showed them what I had written, and both of them marveled, expressing their approval. James, in particular, was very interested, and offered his support and suggestions.

"When I became sick, the work on the Gospel was suspended. It took several months before I regained my health, and I then suggested to Peter that perhaps I should leave Jerusalem, and he agreed. Before I could tell him of my plans, Peter also left Jerusalem again. I then explained my plans to come to Derbe to James, and he gave his blessings on the trip. He made it plain to me, however, that when I had completed my writings, he wanted to receive a copy of the book."

Gaius wanted to know if there was anything that he might possibly do to help. Matthew said that the work was about two-thirds complete, and that as soon as it was finished, they together could start to translate it into Greek. Gaius consented.

It was another ten months before Matthew finished his work. He then reviewed it completely and made minor adjustments and changes. Meanwhile, Apphia continued copying the Gospel. Gaius saw to it that she would be relieved of her kitchen duties as much as possible. Apphia now realized more fully the magnitude of all of Gaius' various affairs.

Chapter 4
Summer 37

Gaius' acceptance of his uncle's estate in Ephesus introduced a new dimension into his life. Besides inheriting his uncle's property in Ephesus, he received property in Achaia, a home in Corinth, and part ownership of a shipbuilding concern in Cenchrea. Yet another enterprise of his uncle was a shipping business whose territory included most of the Aegean Sea.

For the time being, Gaius arranged for his uncle's partners to operate these businesses as they had. He made similar arrangements with the overseers of the property at Ephesus.

During the journey to and from Ephesus, Gaius reflected on the course he wanted his life to take. Aside from the commitment to the cause of Jesus Christ, he thought much on business matters. He discounted the possibility of selling the business in Derbe. After surveying all options, he concluded he should bring Barak into the business as a partner, and gradually phase himself out.

Gaius felt that he could afford to be this generous now that he had received his uncle's estate. Surely Barak would not refuse this offer. Yes, in eight or so years, Gaius would be free of this business.

The week following his return from Ephesus, Gaius presented his proposition to Barak. Just as he expected, Barak was happy to accept, and they worked out a detailed agreement for the partnership, and the eventual takeover of the business by Barak.

As they talked, Barak mentioned that he, too, had witnessed the strange events that day in Jerusalem. He told Gaius that he was among those who thought those men were drunk. Nevertheless, he gave Gaius his word that he would support him in his new avocation.

The time had now come for Gaius to set goals for himself.

First, he would finish translating Matthew's Gospel. Then he must make copies in both Greek and Hebrew for him to distribute to his friends in Galatia, and also for Matthew to take to Jerusalem.

For his far range plans, Gaius envisioned trips to Rome and Alexandria, and perhaps elsewhere. He would take copies of the Gospel with him on his travels. Stops at Ephesus and Cenchrea would also be necessary because of his newly inherited interest. In fact, he would probably have to go there more often than that. Eventually, he would move his permanent residence to Ephesus.

As Matthew proceeded to finish writing his Gospel, Apphia continued making copies, and became more proficient. As a change of pace, she suggested that perhaps she could start copying the Greek translation. She was, of course, eager to understand a little more of what she was working on.

Her wishes were granted, and soon she was overwhelmed by what she was reading. The idea occurred to her that this message should be passed on to her native people. By the time the translation was completed, and she finished making a copy of it, she was firmly convinced.

She told Matthew her heartfelt desire. "That is a lofty and noble idea," he said, but cautioned her that the task would be tremendous. "You would be working alone, since no one else knows the language."

She replied, "Although it has been about twelve years since I was abducted, my native language is still fresh in my mind."

"Gaius eventually would have to be consulted," Matthew remarked.

"In that case," Apphia replied, "I will need your assistance. Will you help me?"

"Yes," Matthew offered, "and if you want me to be your spokesman, I will do that, too."

"That would be most gracious."

One day as Gaius and Matthew were translating and Apphia was copying, Matthew mentioned to Gaius of Apphia's desire. "Apphia has confided in me that she is convinced that my Gospel should be translated into her native tongue, and that it should be passed on to her people."

Somewhat stunned, Gaius asked, "Who will do the translating?" He exclaimed. "I do not even know to what people she belongs."

"Apphia intends to try to make the translation herself."

"I didn't know Apphia could read."

"While you were away, Apphia and I came to know quite a bit about each other," Matthew explained. "Her mother taught her to read and to write. Apphia comes from an eastern country where everyone is taught these things."

At this point, Apphia spoke up, "Master, I have a confession to make."

"Yes?" said Gaius.

"In your absence, I have secretly used your library and with the help from Barak have taught myself how to read Greek."

Gaius held back his anger at the audacity of a slave doing such a thing, to say nothing of it being done by a female. Maintaining his composure, he said, "I greatly dislike things done behind my back! There will be no more of it."

"Yes, master, I understand," Apphia replied.

No further mention was made of the incident as all continued in their tasks.

The next day when Matthew and Apphia were working alone in the library, Matthew said to her, "That was quite a revelation you made yesterday."

"I thought it might help if Gaius knew I could read Greek. However, I am glad to have it off my chest. Has he said anything more to you?"

"No," Matthew answered. "The master-slave complex is engrained in him fairly deeply, but I believe he is struggling to overcome this feeling about you. I also know he admires you – the difference in the stations in your lives notwithstanding. Let's give him more time.

"Gaius told me he wanted answers to two questions. How long would this project take, and who would deliver it when it was finished? I then told him that these particulars had not been discussed."

"Since everything was still so preliminary," Apphia said, "I hadn't given that much thought."

Matthew then added, "Gaius has really not had enough time to make up his mind, and since he has not definitely said 'no,' it is an encouraging sign."

Summer 38

In a few days, Gaius would be hosting a meeting of their business association, and he had to turn his attention to that. He planned to invite those who were interested to stay at the conclusion of the meeting and listen to what he had to say about Jesus, the Messiah. He discussed this with Matthew. "Would you kindly be available for assistance I might need? This is still all so new and unfamiliar to me."

"I would be only too happy to assist you," Matthew consented.

"I will also offer copies of your Gospel to my friends."

Gaius was happy to welcome all of his business friends, and introduced Matthew to everyone. As usual, the latest news was exchanged. Philemon announced that he was finally the father of a son. He named him Archippus.

At the conclusion of the sessions, Gaius announced there was one other item he wished to present.

"My friend, Matthew, whom you all met, is a Jew from Jerusalem. I met him several years ago. He is a disciple of one Jesus Christ of Nazareth. Jesus is hailed as the Holy One of Israel, the world's Redeemer from sin. Matthew is here in Derbe to finish writing the history of Jesus. You are invited to remain to hear more about Him if you are interested."

Only three men were interested enough to stay to hear what Gaius had to say. They were Philemon, Nestor, and Marcellus. Marcellus was from Antioch in Pisidia, a Greek whose parents had come from Crete.

Gaius began, "The coming of Jesus, the Christ, was long foretold by many Hebrew prophets of old. He is the fulfillment of those prophecies." As he continued, he realized that he was not as adept at making the presentation and answering questions that arose as he thought.

Gaius then called on Matthew, "My friend can give you more information." Matthew then related many incidents in his association with Jesus, including stories of His miracles and some of His parables.

After more discussion and more questions and answers, Gaius gave Greek copies to Philemon and Marcellus, but Nestor declined. He did say, however, that if they were inclined, they could come to Iconium with a Hebrew copy, and let Eunice and her mother Lois look at it and talk to them about it. Gaius and Matthew promised that they would.

As the production of more copies of Matthew's Gospel continued, Gaius said to Matthew, "I have decided to allow Apphia to proceed with attempting to translate the Gospel into her native language." His failure, he said, to make an adequate presentation of the Gospel to his friends, made him realize the disadvantage of one person working on his own. The proper method, he thought, is teamwork, and Apphia's efforts required and deserved encouragement.

"That is an important lesson for all of us to observe," said Matthew.

Then Gaius said, "At the appropriate time, I will tell Apphia myself."

He wanted very much to resume a sexual relationship with Apphia. The dilemma of Gaius was that he did not want to give her approval for her project, and then proceed with his amorous attention. By doing so, it would seem as though he would be expecting payment for favors granted. Conversely, if he first made love to Apphia and then approved of her project, it might appear as though he had given permission as a result of Apphia's submission to his sexual advances. Would Matthew approve of this kind of behavior?

"Since there are copies of my Gospel now available," Matthew told Gaius, "Leah and I will undertake a journey to Jerusalem to visit the apostles, and to deliver copies of the Gospel to James, the Lord's brother."

When Matthew told him this, Gaius became inwardly relieved. He thought to himself that this would allow for more privacy between himself and Apphia.

Gaius finally decided that in his relationship with Apphia, the straightforward approach would be the best one for him to use. One pleasant afternoon, he called her into the library. He began by telling her that he loved her very much and had been attracted to her from the first day that she came to their house. He wanted her assurance that his love would be returned.

Surprised, Apphia wondered if Gaius was aware of everything she had gone through. Encouraged by her silence, Gaius assured her that they could be happy together. Finally, Apphia extended her hand saying, "Kindly excuse me for not saying anything before this. My heart is overcome with all sorts of emotions. I never dreamed anything like this could happen to me."

"My darling," said Gaius, "let the past be the past. We have a whole new life ahead of us."

Gaius then said to her that because of the difference of the stations of their lives, this would of necessity have to be a private arrangement. As things presently stood in their society, masters and slaves did not marry.

In regard to his own future, Gaius told Apphia of his business agreement with Barak and of his plans to travel and of his need to tend to the affairs of his property in Ephesus. She must prepare herself for his extended absences. He planned to visit Rome and Egypt. In addition to having adventure, he told her that it was his intention to distribute copies of Matthew's Gospel.

"Apphia," Gaius continued, "I wholeheartedly support you in your efforts to begin translating Matthew's Gospel into your native language. Since you are still producing Greek and Hebrew copies of the Gospel, this work must start on a limited basis.

"In regard to your son, Onesimus will be given every opportunity to receive a good education. When the time comes, he will be permitted to serve as an apprentice to Barak."

"You are most considerate," said Apphia.

Gaius then stressed that Onesimus should be made aware that as a son of a slave, he also was a slave even though he was allowed these privileges. Apphia gave her consent and offered her thanks. From that time they slept together.

Before Matthew and Leah left for Jerusalem, Matthew told Gaius that upon his return, he was contemplating visiting Pontus. On the day of Pentecost in Jerusalem years before, he had spoken with men from there, and had promised to visit them if the opportunity ever arose. "This visit has been delayed for too long," said Matthew.

Matthew and Leah's trip to Jerusalem went smoothly. For them the change of pace and traveling exhilarated them. James was delighted to receive Matthew's Gospel and read it eagerly. He praised it highly and shared it with the church at Jerusalem.

Matthew learned that gradually all of the apostles were leaving Jerusalem. Andrew was in Samaria where he had taken a wife. Matthias, Philip, and Thomas had also left. Of the others, the only ones he saw were Peter, James, and John. Peter was especially impressed with Matthew's work.

When Matthew and Leah returned to Derbe, arrangements to visit Eunice and Lois in Iconium were made. In conjunction with this trip, Matthew decided they would continue on to Pontus, taking along copies of the Gospel to distribute. He could not foretell the length of his absence.

Before leaving on this trip to Pontus, Matthew explained everything about it to Apphia. He told her that upon his return if her translation was sufficiently advanced, he would discuss it with her, and then he would make an attempt to deliver it.

Lois and Eunice excitedly received Matthew and Leah and Gaius, who also went with them. They were deeply moved by Matthew's story, and welcomed his instruction. As they reviewed the entire Gospel, Gaius treasured every opportunity to listen to Matthew as he expounded God's Word. He remarked, "It seems to me that something new can be learned every time it is studied."

The women expressed their gratitude, and promised that they, in turn, would instruct young Timothy, who would soon be of age to also study Holy Scripture.

Chapter 5
Spring 40

Matthew had trouble locating the people from Pontus. He inquired at the synagogue in several cities, but no one seemed to know Aquila or Septus. Finally, at the fourth place he stopped, Matthew was told that these men were itinerant tradesmen. They were tentmakers who did not stay in one place for long and had been recently seen in Amisus, a town on the Black Sea.

Discouraged, Matthew took to the road once more. To him, Amisus seemed like the end of the world. When he arrived there, however, his search was over. Septus had had enough of wandering around and decided to remain in this pleasant coastal resort. Aquila and his wife Priscilla had embarked on a journey to Rome several years previously.

Matthew ministered to the people in Pontus for more than three years. Septus proved to be an invaluable aide. He was acquainted with much of the region, and served as a guide for Matthew. The people of Pontus received Matthew's Gospel gladly, and the church he established there grew and flourished.

Now, Matthew felt he could confidently leave. Relying on Septus, he knew that the church would be in good hands. Matthew was ready to return to Derbe and renew his association with Gaius and Apphia. He wondered if Apphia had translated his Gospel into her native language. Likewise, the possibility of his making a journey to Arachosia occupied many of his thoughts.

Summer 43

Matthew and Leah were happy to be in Derbe. Being around special friends delighted them. But Matthew could not help notice the difference in the way Gaius and Apphia interrelated. When they explained their altered relationship, Matthew let it be known that he was a bit apprehensive about it. In one way, he was happy for them that the master-slave condition was somewhat dissolved, but he told them that they should make it completely free. This, he said, would be pleasing in the sight of God. Gaius demurred. Apphia was happy with this arrangement, and he was content to let it stand as it was.

Apphia had finished her translation. It had been a great struggle for her, and she was not satisfied with the results. The meaning of so many words and events seemed to escape her. Matthew suggested that he and Apphia go over her entire work. At the same time, she could teach him the language.

They went to work immediately. Proceeding slowly at first, Matthew became completely absorbed in the project. "I will definitely make the trip to your homeland to deliver the translated Gospel."

"I am delighted beyond words," said Apphia. "My only hope is that you will be able to locate my people. So much time has gone by, and the changes that are bound to occur might make it difficult for you."

Gaius greeted their plan enthusiastically. He promised that when the time came for Matthew to leave, one of the slaves who had shown an interest in the Gospel would be provided for him and Leah as a servant.

The editing of Apphia's translation took slightly more than one year. In the interim, Apphia told Matthew as much about her country as possible. Gaius was more than helpful in preparing for the mission. Instead of giving Matthew just one slave as a servant, he gave him several. He also provided animals for the journey and outfitted the group.

Knowing that they might not see each other again, the time of departure and farewell was filled with poignancy.

Matthew's departure for Arachosia coincided with the termination of the agreement between Gaius and Barak. Gaius was now busy planning his trip to Rome. During Matthew's stay in Pontus, Gaius had been to Ephesus and Corinth twice, and the thought of extending the distance invigorated him.

A piece of news from Lystra disturbed him, however. Philemon's wife had died in childbirth. The whole community mourned. Philemon now faced the responsibility of raising a six-year-old son and looking after a baby daughter. To his way of thinking, no one in his household was capable of helping him care for the children.

In his grief, Philemon came to Derbe to consult Gaius. They prayed that a solution to the problem could be found. Gaius then said, "The thought struck me that perhaps Apphia might be the answer to our prayer. She would be suitable for the job, and she was no longer absolutely required in my household inasmuch as I will soon be leaving. Yes," said Gaius, "Apphia would make a fine governess."

Philemon replied, "Under the circumstances, there would be no harm in trying to persuade Apphia. I am willing to do what you suggest."

Gaius summoned Apphia and said to her privately, "Philemon and I have prayed for a solution to the problem he is now facing. We thought that perhaps you are the answer to our prayer. We want you to be a governess in Philemon's home while I am on my trip. This would give you something to occupy your time."

"What would become of Onesimus?" Apphia asked.

"Since both you and your son are still viewed as slaves," Gaius said, "I can sell you both to Philemon for a token price. When I am in a position to reclaim you, I will buy you back. Philemon will have to agree to provide the same opportunities for Onesimus that he would receive in my household."

Gaius then returned to Philemon. "I have a proposal for you."

"Are you sure that Apphia is qualified?" said Philemon sounding a bit more skeptical.

Trying to reassure him, Gaius said, "I have every confidence in Apphia's qualifications."

"I don't quite understand this arrangement in regard to Onesimus," Philemon then said.

Gaius then hesitated a bit but then said, "This was one of the conditions agreed to with Apphia."

"I find this strange," Philemon said. "Nevertheless, I will consent to the deal."

Actually, it was not possible for Gaius to tell Philemon that he was really providing benefits for his own son. That is how Gaius had gradually come to see Onesimus privately. An agreement was reached, and the price was set at one dollar.

Apphia and Onesimus moved to Lystra within a week. Now Gaius was ready to do some traveling.

Autumn 46

Gaius returned from traveling after being gone for almost two years. Excitedly, he related everything to Barak about his journeys: "The city of Rome had regained some of its zest for life after enduring the tumultuous rule of Caligula. Roman society was indeed quite different from anything else I have experienced. Their new emperor, Claudius, seemed to be more universally liked."

"What will the change of emperors mean for the rest of the empire?" Barak wondered.

"It can't be anything but positive," replied Gaius.

"I did not confine my visit entirely to Rome. I also took many side trips, including one to Spain and another to Carthage."

"You certainly seem to have enjoyed yourself, and I am happy that many of your dreams have become a reality," Barak said. Turning then to local affairs, he added, "The business, which had started to become quite competitive before you left, had become even more so. Because of the changing conditions, Philemon was investigating the possibility of moving to Colossae."

When Gaius went to Lystra, Philemon confirmed what Barak had told him. Philemon was also eager to hear of Gaius' visit to Rome. "I succeeded in locating the small Jewish colony in Rome. One couple, Aquila and Priscilla, especially gave me a warm welcome. As we became better acquainted, we discovered each other's presence at the coming of the Holy Spirit that day in Jerusalem. I told them about Matthew and his going to Pontus, and the Gospel he had written. The copy of the Gospel that I gave to them made them very happy."

"Were these people very knowledgeable about the life of Jesus Christ?" asked Philemon.

"Priscilla explained to me that they had hoped Matthew would have visited them in Pontus, and were disappointed when he did not come. I then related to them that Matthew found Septus, and that he established a church in Pontus. They told me receiving a copy of the Gospel in Hebrew would provide them the opportunity to study more about what little they knew about Jesus of Nazareth.

"When Aquila and Priscilla revealed that the Romans were not at all interested in the story of Jesus, I gave a Greek copy of Matthew's Gospel to them also. For them and their friends, my visit, they said, would provide the impetus for spreading the Gospel of Jesus Christ to the Romans more zealously."

Philemon had nothing but praise for the services that Apphia was rendering. "She is a perfect governess for my son Archippus and his sister Celeste. But," he added, "I am experiencing a little difficulty with Onesimus. He does not seem to be adjusting to his new surroundings in my household."

Gaius was eager to have a few moments alone with Apphia, but the opportunity never came. He did, however, visit with business friends in Antioch and Iconium.

When Gaius returned to Derbe, he recounted more of his trip with Barak. "I stopped in Cenchrea on my return from Rome, and discovered that the shipping business was not going well. My partners had become discouraged and disinterested, and wanted to be relieved of their commitment. They wondered whether I would be interested in assuming complete control of the business. I was skeptical, but when some of the supervisors assured me that they could carry on the business for a few more years until I could assume control, I agreed to their proposal.

"Despite all that was happening in Achaia, I still plan to go to Egypt. In addition to taking along copies of Matthew's Gospel, I will also look into expanding my shipping interests. I have already done some of that when I was in Italy."

"You are truly making great strides in developing your business acumen," said Barak. "When I told you in Jerusalem that you are not the man your father was, I really underestimated you. I now believe you will become a successful businessman."

Chapter 6
Summer 47

Onesimus, now fourteen years old, worked often with Philemon and Archippus in the store. Today, a shipment of merchandise arrived and they were busy unpacking it. As they worked, a clamoring came from the direction of the Jewish synagogue. The noise grew louder.

Philemon sent Onesimus to investigate. When Onesimus didn't return after a few minutes, Philemon chided himself. He should have known better. Onesimus often slipped away unnoticed.

Some three hours later, Onesimus returned to the store, talking excitedly. "Two men were at the synagogue preaching about a Jesus of Nazareth – the same as Matthew. And do you know the cripple sitting by the synagogue begging? – They healed him so that he was jumping and walking around. The people nearby, mostly Greeks, thought this was great stuff, and they began treating these men like gods, but the men did not appreciate it."

"Hold on, hold on," Philemon interrupted. "Was this what all the noise was about?"

"Oh, no," said Onesimus. "Then some other Jews from out of town came and began to argue. After a while, they began to throw stones at these men. They dragged one man out of the city and beat him severely. When they thought that he was dead, they left, but he wasn't dead. His friend then came and helped him. And I brought them here with me because they needed some place to rest. I guess these men must be friends of Matthew."

Philemon was exasperated. "We will find out," he said.

"This is Paul and his friend Barnabas," said Onesimus as he ushered them into the store.

"I am Philemon, owner of this store. My household is acquainted with the Gospel of Jesus Christ. A man named Matthew came to Galatia to preach Jesus, and to write about His life."

"Although we never met him," said Paul, "we preach the same Gospel as Matthew."

Philemon then welcomed them with open arms. He called Apphia and the other servants.

"Apphia here is a more ardent believer than I am," Philemon admitted. "She worked with Matthew when he was a guest in the house of Gaius of Derbe. Onesimus, the boy who brought you here, is her son. They are slaves of Gaius now in my service. Matthew put the Gospel in writing, and they made copies of it, giving a copy to me also.

"You must be tired after the ordeal you experienced," Philemon concluded. "Apphia will minister to your needs and nurse your wounds. When you are rested, we can dine."

"I am interested in going to Derbe to meet Gaius," said Paul.

"That can be arranged," said Philemon. "We can accommodate you for overnight lodging. In the morning, if you are fully rested, my servant, Onesimus, will accompany you to Derbe."

Philemon then added, "If you care to return here after things have quieted down a bit, you will be more than welcome."

"Yes, we will," Paul and Barnabas replied.

The next day, Onesimus led Barnabas and Paul to Derbe. Paul found Gaius to be a very extraordinary man. His knowledge of the life and ministry of Jesus Christ and of the early years of the church amazed Paul. Gaius explained the circumstances surrounding his encountering the disciples on the day of Pentecost, and his subsequent meeting with Matthew. He gave Matthew credit for everything he knew about Jesus. Matthew's writing of His life and ministry was very helpful to him.

"Philemon said that Matthew had done this," said Paul. "What exactly has Matthew produced?"

"Yes, we would like to hear more about it," said Barnabas.

"He has written a story on the life of Jesus Christ. We call it the Gospel. I have a copy of it right here."

Gaius then showed his copy of Matthew's Gospel to Paul and Barnabas. Paul took it and started to read, handing each scroll to Barnabas as he finished. They did not stop reading until the entire book was read.

"This is really marvelous work," Paul said.

Barnabas agreed and asked, "Is Matthew staying nearby?"

"No," said Gaius. "He has gone to Arachosia, a country in the east. He helped translate the Gospel into Apphia's native language, and is ministering to her people. Apphia, the woman who ministered to you in Lystra, actually belongs in my household."

Gaius then presented a copy of the Gospel to Paul and Barnabas.

In the days following, after Gaius became better acquainted with Paul and Barnabas, he inquired of Paul the history of his association with the church.

"There had been much speculation," said Gaius. And he added, "Matthew called you a persecutor of Christ's disciples."

Paul gladly told his story: "I was, indeed, a persecutor of Christ's disciples as Matthew said. I was born in Tarsus in Cilicia, not far from here. As a youth, my father, a devout Jew, sent me to Jerusalem to study at the feet of Gamaliel, a teacher of the sect of the Pharisees. Hence, I, too, became a Pharisee, and scrupulously observed rules and rituals. I was known then as Saul. While some men have paid great sums to gain Roman citizenship, I was born a Roman citizen.

"As a Pharisee, I was fiercely jealous of 'Jewish national separateness and all the territorial and nationalistic aspirations contained in the Jewish Messianic conception.'[1] God's covenant with the nation of Israel was held in very high esteem by us. We looked for and longed for the day when God would restore His Kingdom to Israel. Only after that was done could the nation of Israel bring peace to the world. Our idea of a Messiah was that God would send a leader to His chosen people to do this.

"Every now and then someone would pronounce that he was just such a leader. They all came and went. When Jesus of Nazareth did the same thing, many thought of him as just another fanatic, myself included. We denounced Him in every way possible, and also tried to beguile Him, but never did succeed. We finally gave up and decided that He must be done away with. We made the elaborate plans for His trial, condemnation, and death. We stirred up the crowds so that they demanded His crucifixion, and thought our efforts were rewarded when this finally happened. Later, the story of His resurrection upset everything, and the story persisted and intensified.

"The appearance of the Holy Spirit on the day of Pentecost was witnessed by us in utter dismay. You see, I also was in that crowd the same as you. This necessitated a change in our strategy. We now had to silence the apostles and the disciples of Jesus. We had Peter and John arrested and made them appear before the Sanhedrin. They were forbidden to speak further about Jesus Christ, but they would not listen. Again the apostles were arrested and brought to trial."

"I must say," said Gaius, "the Pharisees acted with much tenacity."

"We certainly did," said Paul. "Our integrity and honor was at stake. At this second trial, our chief priest asked them, 'Did we not strictly command you that you should not teach in His name? And indeed you have filled Jerusalem with your doctrine, and intend to bring this Man's blood on us!' Then Peter and the other apostles answered and said: 'We ought to obey God rather than men. The God of our fathers raised up Jesus whom you killed by hanging on a tree.

Him God has exalted with His right hand to be Prince and Savior, to give repentance to Israel and forgiveness of sins. And we are His witnesses to these things, and so also is the Holy Spirit whom God has given to those who obey Him.'[2] We were furious when we heard this, and took counsel to kill them.

"But Gamaliel persuaded us otherwise, and they were beaten and let go. They did not relent in their teaching and preaching, however. Then some of us decided that we must begin persecution of the disciples. We followed one of their evangelists around for some time, and when we disputed with him and were not able to refute what he had said, we secretly induced men to say that he had blasphemed.

"At his hearing before the council, he wound up his lengthy defense by saying, 'You stiff-necked and uncircumcised in heart and ears! You always resist the Holy Spirit; as your fathers did, so do you. Which of the prophets have your fathers not persecuted? And they killed those who foretold the coming of the Just One, of whom you have become betrayers and murderers, who have received the law by the direction of angels and have not kept it.'[3] When we heard these things, we were cut to heart, and gnashed at him with our teeth.

"So we took him out of the city and stoned him to death. This man's name was Stephen. From that time on, we continued persecution of the disciples of Christ."

"I was a witness to much of this persecution," said Barnabas. "Fear was in the hearts of many citizens of Jerusalem. I went to Damascus."

Paul continued, "I even was given authority to go to Damascus to do the same thing there. As I journeyed and came near Damascus, a bright light from heaven suddenly shone around me. I was blinded and fell to the ground, and heard a voice saying to me, 'Saul, Saul, why are you persecuting Me?'[4] I answered, 'Who are You?'[5] And the Lord said, 'I am Jesus, whom you are persecuting. It is hard for you to kick against the goads.'[6] And I said, 'Lord, what do You want me to do?'[7]

And the Lord said to me, 'Arise and go into the city, and you will be told what you must do.'[8]

"I was in the city for three days, neither eating nor drinking, when a man by the name of Ananias came and laid his hands on me and said, 'Brother Saul, the Lord Jesus, who appeared to you on the road as you came, has sent me that you may receive your sight and be filled with the Holy Spirit.'[9] Immediately, I regained my sight, and I arose and was baptized.

"I spent some days with the disciples who were at Damascus. It was there that I first met Barnabas. And then I went into the synagogue and began to preach the Christ that He is the Son of God. After a while, the Jews became angry and plotted to kill me. The disciples helped me escape from the city by letting me down in a basket through a window in the wall of the city."

"This is true," said Barnabas. "I was staying at the home of Ananias at the time. When we learned that Paul was in danger, helping him escape the city in this manner was our only choice. A disciple named Luke, a physician, thought of the idea."

"How did you finally become joined to the apostles?" asked Gaius.

"I really then wanted to go to Jerusalem immediately, but I was directed by the Spirit and 'went to Arabia.'[10] I stayed there for forty days and forty nights, and then returned to Damascus. It still was not safe for me to stay there, so I became determined to go to Jerusalem. I went first to visit my sister who had recently married. When I told her of everything that had happened to me and of my intention of going to the temple, she tried to convince me otherwise. 'The Pharisees have an all-out alert for you,' she said. But I did not listen to her.

"I went to the temple and once inside, I fell into a trance. In this trance I saw Jesus who said to me, 'Make haste and get out of Jerusalem quickly, for they will not receive your testimony concerning Me.'[11] I questioned Him about the fact that I was known as a persecutor of the saints, and He answered, 'Depart, for I will send you far from here to the Gentiles.'[12] I quickly left and came to Cilicia.

"Then after three years, I again went to Jerusalem. My sister arranged for me to see Peter, and I remained with him 15 days. 'No other of the apostles did I see except James, the Lord's brother.'[13] 'Afterward, I came again into the region of Syria and Cilicia, and I was unknown by face to the churches of Judea which were in Christ.'[14]

"After another two years, I again came to Jerusalem to try to join the disciples; but they were all afraid of me, and did not believe that I was a disciple. But Barnabas took me and brought me to the apostles."

"This was about seven years after the crucifixion of Jesus," said Barnabas. "I was doing quite a bit of traveling in those days, often staying in Jerusalem. Paul knew where to find me."

"I declared to the apostles how I had seen the Lord on the road," Paul continued, "and that He had spoken to me, and that I spoke boldly in the name of the Lord Jesus and disputed against the Hellenists. 'Then the churches throughout all Judea, Galilee, and Samaria had peace and were edified.'[15]

"'Those who were scattered after the persecution that arose over Stephen traveled as far as Phoenicia, Cyprus, and Antioch, preaching the Word to no one but the Jews only. And some of them were men from Cyprus and Cyrene, who, when they had come to Antioch, spoke to the Hellenists, preaching the Lord Jesus. And the hand of the Lord was with them, and a great number believed and turned to the Lord. Then news of these things came to the ears of the church at Jerusalem, and they sent out Barnabas to go as far as Antioch. When he came and had seen the grace of God, he was glad, and encouraged them all that with purpose of heart they should continue with the Lord. And many people were added to the Lord.'[16] Isn't that right, Barnabas?"

"Yes it is. Then I departed for Tarsus looking for Paul. When I found him, we returned to Antioch. For a whole year we 'assembled with the church and taught many people. And the disciples were first called Christians in Antioch.'[17]"

"Around this time," Paul continued, "there was a famine throughout the world. This was about eleven years after I saw the Lord on the road. 'Then the disciples, each according to his ability, determined to send relief to the brethren dwelling in Judea.'[18] This they also did, and Barnabas and I were dispatched by the elders.

"'About this time also Herod the king stretched out his hand to harass some of the church. And he killed James the brother of John with the sword.'[19] And we returned from Jerusalem when we had fulfilled our ministry, and brought with us also John Mark, Barnabas' cousin.

"As we continued to minister to the Lord at Antioch, the Holy Spirit said, 'Separate to Me Barnabas and Saul for the work to which I have called them.'[20] And we continued fasting and praying, and the elders laid on us their hands, and sent us away. So, being sent out by the Holy Spirit, we departed and came to Seleucia, and from there we sailed to Cyprus. We also had John Mark as our assistant.

"From there we traveled to Pamphylia, but John Mark returned to Jerusalem. Finally, we came to Antioch in Pisidia. After teaching there for a time, as many as had been appointed to eternal life believed. But the Jews stirred up the chief men and some women against us, and we were expelled from their region. We left Antioch and came to Iconium. Staying there a long time also, the unbelieving Jews again stirred up trouble and caused us to leave. We then came to Lystra, and now also to Derbe."

Having fully recovered from his wounds and fit for travel, Paul, together with Barnabas, went back to Lystra. Upon their return to Lystra, they became much better acquainted with the household of Philemon. When the time came for them to move on, Philemon told them that they would always be welcome in his house.

After Paul and Barnabas had been gone for a time, Gaius also came to Lystra, desirous to reclaim Apphia and Onesimus according to their agreement.

When Gaius arrived, Philemon knew at once the purpose of this visit. He did not hesitate to tell Gaius that he dreaded the moment Apphia would leave. She had become indispensable in her job as governess. Philemon pleaded with Gaius to permit Apphia to stay a while longer.

Finally, Gaius said that if Apphia wanted to stay, he would agree, but he must talk to Apphia privately first.

Apphia and Gaius spent an afternoon alone in the countryside. "I have made final arrangements to move to Ephesus," he told her. "The move has been delayed for too long. My business interests in Ephesus and Cenchrea demand that I devote all of my energy in running them. Through hard work progress has been made in turning a losing situation around."

"I am really happy for you, Gaius. Philemon told me that you wish for us to return to you. I want to do the right thing. On the one hand, I would dearly love to move to Ephesus with you; however, Philemon has said that he would be lost without me. He has treated me decently. It is Onesimus that I am worried about. Philemon has kept his promise to give him a good education. Time and again it was necessary for me to remind him of his status as a slave, but at times he is restless and uneasy."

"Do you think he would settle down if he came to Ephesus? I am afraid that I would not be much of a father image. Perhaps Philemon might be more helpful in that regard than I."

"A change in surroundings might upset him more than if he went to Ephesus is true. He has become friendly with Archippus. It does seem as though the best thing would be to let matters remain as they are, and hope for the best."

"I respect your decision, Apphia," said Gaius. "Please be assured that my feelings for you have not changed."

Paul, meanwhile, retraced his steps to Antioch in Pisidia. Among the Greeks at Antioch who believed was Marcellus, to whom Gaius had given a copy of Matthew's Gospel. Marcellus was elated when Paul returned to visit. His entire household was converts, and his eldest son, Titus, became devoutly interested in Christianity.

"I have read Matthew's Gospel and studied it intently," said Titus. "He writes in such a way that no matter if the reader is a Jew or a Greek, the message is easily understandable. Because of this, I am eager to become more actively involved in proclaiming it."

"That may be easier said than done," replied Paul. "Preparing one's self for the proclamation of the Gospel requires much diligent study and dedication. It would mean separation from family and friends, and enduring potential hardships."

"I am ready," declared Titus, "to do whatever is necessary. My father desires to have the Gospel preached in Crete, his ancestral home. He is hopeful that I could do this."

"That is highly commendable," said Paul. "Under the circumstances, we can have you return to Antioch with us. Do you have means of support? What about a place to stay?"

"My aunt and uncle live in Antioch. I can stay with them. They recently became Christians. Their son has been a follower of Christ for some time. He was a young physician at Damascus when he first heard about Jesus."

"Is his name by chance Luke?" asked Paul.

"Yes, it is."

"I know him," said Paul. "We met immediately after I met the Lord on the road. What is he doing now?"

"He recently accepted a position in the territory of Mysia, and now lives in Troas."

Tutoring and private instruction inaugurated a new phase in the ministry of Paul. He set about this task with the same devotion and enthusiasm he started all other phases of his Christian ministry. Titus returned with Paul and Barnabas to Antioch and was a diligent student. He was never far removed from Paul's presence.

Spring 49

As they stayed with the disciples in Antioch, certain men came from Judea and also taught among the brethren. They espoused the doctrine that 'unless you are circumcised according to the custom of Moses, you cannot be saved.'[21] There was dissension between these men from Judea and Paul and Barnabas. Their dispute was not resolved, so the church sent Paul and Barnabas to see the apostles and elders. Titus went along.

Paul and Barnabas described their work among the Gentiles as they passed through Phoenicia and Samaria, and they caused great joy to all the brethren. In Jerusalem, they were received by the church, the apostles, and the elders; and they reported all things God had done with them.

But some of the Pharisees who were believers backed the claim of the men of Judea, insisting on circumcision. They all came together to dispute the matter. The decision reached after much debate was that 'we should not trouble those from the Gentiles who are turning to God.'[22] Titus was not compelled to be circumcised.

A letter was prepared by the apostles and elders in Jerusalem stating the outcome of the dispute, but included an admonition for the faithful to 'abstain from things offered to idols, from blood, from things strangled, and from sexual immorality.'[23] It pleased the apostles and the elders, with the whole church to send chosen men of their own company to Antioch with Paul and Barnabas, namely, Judas who was also named Barsabbas, and Silas. They were to also deliver the letter.

Some days after returning to Antioch, Paul suggested to Barnabas that they revisit the places where they had preached the Gospel in Galatia. Barnabas wanted to take John Mark with them, but Paul objected because John Mark had left them on their first trip. The contention between them was so sharp that they parted company. Paul chose Silas to accompany him. Mark and Barnabas went to Cyprus.

Paul and Silas did not leave immediately. Instead, Paul wanted to spend a little more time with Titus. After all, Titus had not been with him long. Was he ready to go off on his own? Paul was not sure, and wanted to find someone to go with him. Judas Barsabbas volunteered.

After three more weeks of intensive study, Titus assured Paul that he was ready to proclaim the Gospel of Christ. Paul was anxious to leave for Galatia. The church in Antioch commissioned Titus to go to Crete.

Before leaving, however, Paul spoke to Titus about how he might find Luke in Troas. Paul said that after they visited the Galatian Christians, they would try to go to Bithynia or some place in that area. Titus could not give Paul much information, but said that his cousin became associated with a man named Carpus.

Chapter 7
Fall 49

Paul and Silas arrived in Lystra when Philemon was just about ready to move to Colossae. Philemon explained that business conditions had changed considerably, and this is what necessitated the move. Paul renewed friendships throughout the region and introduced Silas as his new partner.

Timothy, son of Nestor and Eunice of Iconium, was also at Lystra at this time. He had grown to be a dedicated Christian, and was well spoken of in the community. Eunice and Lois had provided a firm foundation in the faith for him.

Paul was impressed with Timothy, and suggested to him that he join Silas as his helper. Timothy welcomed the idea. Paul told his friends that he wished to preach the Gospel in territories where it had not yet been preached. When the churches in Galatia were strengthened in the faith, Paul and Silas and Timothy departed.

Paul would have preached the Gospel in Asia and Bithynia, but he was forbidden by the Holy Spirit to do so. Instead, he and his helpers journeyed to the region of Mysia and finally arrived in Troas.

Upon arrival in Troas, Paul immediately tried to locate Luke. Since Titus' instructions were rather sketchy, it took several days for Paul to find Luke. They warmly greeted each other.

"I am delighted to see you again, Paul," said Luke.

"The feeling is mutual," replied Paul. "Your cousin, Titus, told me you were here."

"I came here several years ago, and like it very much."

"My helpers and I are on a missionary journey," explained Paul. "We came to this area when we were directed by the Holy Spirit."

Luke related how he had had limited success in spreading the Gospel. "Carpus, the man whom I became associated with, is the only one who listened to me. He and his family became Christians."

The next day, Luke took Paul and his partners to meet them. Carpus' son, Tychicus, was also introduced.

As Paul continued to stay with Luke, one night a vision came to him. In it, "A man of Macedonia stood and pleaded with him, saying, 'Come over to Macedonia and help us.'[1]" Paul told Luke that he and his partners would leave as soon as practicable. Luke then asked Paul if he might accompany them in order to do more in the way of promoting the Gospel. By going with them, he said, he could gain valuable on-the-job training. Paul agreed.

Sailing from Troas, they ran a straight course to Samothrace, and the next day came to Neapolis, and from there to Philippi. As they preached the Gospel by the riverside outside the city, Paul and Silas ran into trouble with the authorities when someone complained. They ended up being cast into prison.

At the time of this imprisonment, Timothy and Luke stayed in the house of Lydia, a woman who had been baptized. Lydia was from the city of Thyatira in Asia. She and her household became believers.

After their release from prison, Paul and Silas left for Thessalonica. As they preached the Gospel, certain Jews caused more trouble for them, and they were sent away to Berea. Their preaching in Berea was also disturbed by the unbelieving Jews from Thessalonica, so Paul was directed to Athens. Luke, meanwhile, had returned to Troas, but Silas and Timothy stayed in Berea to await instructions from Paul.

Luke eventually learned that Paul had gone to Athens while leaving Silas and Timothy behind. Not wanting Paul to be alone, he left right away to try to find him. While in Athens, however, he met and became friends with several persons with whom Paul had talked. They were Dionysius, and a woman named Damaris. He was also introduced to a civic official named Theophilus. They told Luke that Paul had left for Corinth and that his helpers would soon join him there.

Theophilus especially was interested in the Gospel that Paul preached, and indicated to Luke that he would like to receive further instruction. Theophilus convinced Luke to write an orderly account of those things which are believed among the disciples of Jesus, and which Luke had known from the beginning. After several weeks in Athens, Luke returned to Troas.

Luke was working diligently with his writing when two unexpected visitors showed up. They were Peter, who had likewise heard of Luke's residency in Troas, and John Mark. Peter had been kind to Luke in Perea and Judea, and Luke felt he knew Peter better than the other disciples. Peter told of his travels with Mark throughout Pontus, Galatia, Asia, and Bithynia. Luke, in turn, related stories about Paul and his helpers.

Mark had become an off-and-on companion of Peter ever since he left Paul and Barnabas at Paphos. Mark explained that he had realized that if he continued on with them, he would be gone for too long a time. He had promised to meet Peter in Jerusalem to help him finish writing a book about the story of Jesus. And that is what he did.

Peter said the book they had written was very helpful to them as they traveled about. They also told Luke about the book that Matthew had written. They showed their copies of each of these books to Luke. Luke was delighted at what he saw, and told Peter and Mark that he, too, was attempting to write a book on the life of Jesus at the request of Theophilus of Athens.

Luke considered ending his efforts to write his story of Jesus and just send a copy of what Matthew and Mark had already written to Theophilus. Peter persuaded him not to, promising to help by relating to Luke events both prior to and subsequent to Christ's crucifixion.

Luke was grateful, but felt he must make a trip to Jerusalem to garner further information to put into his book.

Peter and Mark's stay in Troas lasted not much longer than a month. Peter's wife, Zelina, was not feeling well, and she wanted to return to Galilee. Mark planned to journey to Egypt.

In the meantime, Paul established himself in Corinth. He became well acquainted with many people as he reasoned in the synagogue. Among them were Aquila and Priscilla, Jews from Pontus, who were expelled from Rome by Emperor Claudius, as were most Jews. Aquila and Priscilla were skilled as tentmakers, the same as Paul, and they labored together. As they did, Aquila related their story of meeting a certain Gaius of Derbe in Rome. He had given them a copy of the story of the life of Jesus Christ written by the apostle Matthew. Aquila and Priscilla treasured this gift, and were greatly surprised when Paul told them of his association with Gaius. Knowing this, Aquila sent word to Gaius in Ephesus that Paul was in Corinth.

About this time, Silas and Timothy also arrived in Corinth, and reported to Paul what was happening in the churches at Philippi and Thessalonica. Paul told Silas and Timothy that he was determined to make a trip to Crete to check in on Titus, his young co-worker there. He decided that Timothy should return to Macedonia for a time and then rejoin him in Corinth. Silas was to stay in Corinth while he was away.

Gaius came to Corinth a week before Paul was ready to leave for Crete, and offered to assist and accompany him, since he was already familiar with the country. They left soon afterward.

It had been over a year since Paul and Titus parted, and Paul was anxious about how Titus was faring. Paul's visit to Crete was very welcome by Titus. He had run into a few difficulties in his ministry to these people, and was not altogether sure if he wanted to continue. He needed strengthening in his work. Paul sensed this and offered his help. The rewards of a fruitful ministry are not always easily attained and readily apparent, Paul said. 'In due season we shall reap if we do not lose heart,'[2] Paul told Titus.

Upon their return to Corinth, Gaius told Paul that he was going back to Ephesus, and invited him to visit. Paul, however, decided to stay in Corinth, and sent Silas to Ephesus, instead. Silas was to return to Corinth after a short stay, which would coincide with Timothy's return.

As Paul continued working with Aquila and Priscilla, he also continued teaching in the synagogue every Sabbath, making converts of both Jews and Greeks. Some of the Jews opposed him, however, and blasphemed. Paul said to them, "Your blood be upon your own heads; I am clean. From now on I will go to the Gentiles."[3]

When Silas and Timothy returned to Corinth as Paul directed, he told them of the latest developments. "I have written a letter to the church at Thessalonica, assuring them that I prayerfully remembered them especially since I could not come to visit them at this time. I have exhorted them to live lives pleasing to God. Timothy will accompany me when I leave for Ephesus, while Silas remains here in Corinth. When I continue on to Syria, Timothy can return to Corinth, and then Silas can depart for Thessalonica to deliver my letter."

Luke finished writing his Gospel about this same time. Not knowing how long Paul would remain in Corinth, he traveled there as quickly as possible in the hope of showing it to him before he delivered it to Theophilus in Athens. He arrived just in time. Paul liked what Luke had written. Luke then went to Athens to deliver his Gospel, and Theophilus was very appreciative. He encouraged Luke to continue recording the events in the life of Paul and the church. Luke stayed in Athens a short while visiting also with Dionysius and Damaris and then returned home.

Paul then took leave of the brethren and sailed for Syria, and Aquila and Priscilla were with him as far as Ephesus, along with Timothy. When the Ephesians, Gaius included, tried to prevail upon Paul to stay a bit longer, he did not consent, 'but took leave of them, saying, "I must by all means keep this coming feast in Jerusalem; but I will return again to you, God willing."'[4]

For several years, Gaius had thrown all of his efforts into the operation of his several enterprises in Achaia. His overseers had done a satisfactory job in holding the business together while he was making the transition from Derbe to Ephesus. Now all of Gaius' hard work was beginning to bear fruit. Both his shipping business and his ship-building business were prospering.

Chapter 8
Summer 52

After celebrating the feast in Jerusalem, Paul again headed north to Antioch. From there 'he went over all the region of Galatia and Phrygia in order, strengthening the disciples.'[1] He came also to Colossae where he was a guest in the house of Philemon. Archippus and Celeste were growing rapidly. Apphia and her son, Onesimus, were still in the service of Philemon. They all were happy to see Paul once again, and to hear of his work. Word from Ephesus was spotty, so Paul informed them of the latest news about Gaius.

In the three years Philemon had been in Colossae, he became well acquainted with other Christians in the city. One was a man by the name of Epaphras. He had, likewise, just recently come to Colossae to spread the Gospel. Originally being from Antioch in Pisidia, he was a friend of Marcellus and his son Titus. Epaphras was one of those in Antioch who accepted Paul's preaching when he first came there. Paul was happy to know that Epaphras was an active and faithful minister of Christ.

At Colossae, Paul learned that Peter and John Mark had been there recently. Philemon told Paul the story they had told him, "After Peter and his wife were in Galilee for some time, she still did not feel well and had wearied of traveling. They mutually agreed that she should remain at their home there while Peter would continue to travel on his own.

"Peter had gone to Corinth with the hope of seeing you," Philemon told Paul. "Apparently, he arrived just after you left, so he stayed to assist Timothy. Mark had gone to Alexandria to meet with Matthias and Nathaniel. On the ship returning to Ephesus, Mark met a learned Alexandrian Jew by the name of Apollos. Years before,

Apollos became friends with Gaius of Derbe, and he was now coming to Ephesus at Gaius' invitation.

"When Peter found out that Mark was in Ephesus, he also went there and took Timothy with him. The congregation in Corinth was having troubles, and Timothy felt he was not doing a good job handling the problem. From there, Peter and Mark visited the churches in Asia, coming also to Colossae."

"How long did they stay?" asked Paul.

"Their visit was quite short," said Philemon. "They intended to go to Troas to visit Luke again. From there, Mark would go to Macedonia to see Silas, and Peter planned to go to Bithynia. After a time, Mark would rejoin him and together they intended to go to Cappadocia."

"Then Mark might still be in Macedonia?" Paul wondered.

"It is possible," replied Philemon.

Three years had passed since Paul and Barnabas had split up over the disagreement about Mark. Paul had known that Mark had been associating himself with Peter, and he thought that now would be a good time to reconcile himself to Mark.

This would mean, however, that his trip to Ephesus would be delayed. Paul was in a quandary, for he desperately also wanted to learn more about the harassment given to Timothy by Hymenaeus and Alexander while he was in Corinth. Paul finally decided to go to Macedonia to try to be reconciled with Mark.

He arranged with Philemon to have Archippus and Onesimus go to Ephesus with a brief note for Timothy. Paul instructed Timothy to remain in Ephesus and promised to write more to him in a letter from Troas.

In addition to delivering Paul's note to Timothy, Onesimus had a chance to visit with Gaius. Gaius was always interested in receiving news about Apphia.

Archippus and Onesimus did not waste time getting back to Colossae. Onesimus was responsible for that. Seeing Paul again and this trip put an idea into his head. He intended to run away from Philemon. Philemon was being too harsh with him, he thought. He wanted to do it immediately and try to catch up to Paul, but that did not work out.

On the journey to Troas, Paul stayed a few days at the home of Lydia in Thyatira. At Troas, while staying with Luke, Paul wrote the letter to Timothy. By this time, Peter had gone into Bithynia, but Mark was still with Silas. Tychicus, the son of Carpus, delivered his letter to Timothy in Ephesus, and Paul left for Philippi.

The meeting between Paul and Mark at Philippi was at first rather cool. As Paul carefully explained his actions, however, Mark responded more favorably. After everything about the entire episode had been thoroughly reviewed, Paul apologized. Mark accepted the apology, but added that he was not completely innocent, himself, as he could have given Paul more explicit reasons for his leaving than he did.

The reconciliation strengthened both men. Paul then headed for Ephesus. Apollos, who came to Ephesus at the same time as Mark and was a friend of Gaius, had been in Ephesus for some months now. Gaius was delighted to have him as a guest. "This man had been instructed in the way of the Lord; and being fervent in his spirit, he spoke and taught accurately in the things of the Lord, though he knew only the baptism of John. He began to speak boldly in the synagogue. Aquila and Priscilla heard him and explained to him the way of God more accurately."[2]

Apollos was also introduced to Timothy. When Timothy told Apollos more about himself and his experiences in Corinth, Apollos expressed a desire to visit Corinth also. He was given a letter of recommendation by Gaius and Timothy and Aquila and Priscilla.

In the meantime, Paul, having 'passed through the upper

region,'³ arrived in Ephesus. He learned firsthand from Timothy about the strife in the Corinthian congregation. While Apollos was still in Corinth, Paul sent Timothy to Athens. He, himself, ministered to the church in Ephesus and also to those in Asia. He did this by reasoning daily in the school of Tyrannus and also by making short trips to the surrounding territory. Tychicus stayed on in Ephesus after delivering Paul's letter to Timothy, and eventually became a valued assistant of Paul.

Paul came into contact with people from Laodicea, Philadelphia, Smyrna, Thyatira, Pergamum, Sardis, and other cities. It was while Paul taught in the school of Tyrannus that he became acquainted with the people of Dalmatia. They urged Paul to come to their land.

Apollos encountered the same thing in Corinth that faced Timothy. And contentions had become sharper. Hymenaeus and Alexander were still causing trouble, and they also defamed Paul's name. Despite all the difficulty, Apollos remained in Corinth for some time, achieving some success. Eventually, he had had enough, so he returned to Ephesus. Members of Chloe's family, of the church in Corinth, came with him.

Chloe's family and Apollos corroborated Timothy's reports of what was happening in Corinth. This distressed Paul.

Sosthenes, a ruler of the synagogue in Corinth who was beaten by the Greeks before the judgment seat at the time of Paul's visit to Corinth, also came to Ephesus. He had listened to Apollos and had accepted the teaching that Jesus was the Christ. He wanted to meet again with Paul. A little later, three other men, Stephanas, Fortunatus, and Achaicus, also came to see Paul. They, too, wanted to assure Paul of their support, and attempted to have Apollos return to Corinth.

After much soul searching, Paul decided to communicate with the Corinthian church through a letter. In the letter he covered all the things that seemed to be troubling the congregation, and he promised to visit them again. Paul told them that while Apollos was not willing to return to them for the present, he might do so at a more convenient time. Paul also wrote about his plans.

First he would send Timothy to them again from Athens. Timothy was to stay with them for a short while and then continue on to Ephesus to meet with him there. Paul wanted to spend Pentecost at Ephesus, and then leave for Corinth by way of Macedonia. His time of arrival was unsure.

Apollos eventually expressed to Paul his wish to go to Rome, and hoped that Paul would help him find someone to accompany him. Paul thought of Aquila and Priscilla, but they were not interested in returning to Rome. Instead, they wanted to go to Philippi, and then return to Pontus from there. The man Paul then found to travel with Apollos was Zenas, the lawyer. In return, Apollos consented to Paul's request that he stop off in Crete. Paul had written a letter to Titus to reassure him in his ministry, and he wanted Apollos to deliver it.

As Paul continued in the school of Tyrannus, he began formulating plans to go to Dalmatia. He wanted to take advantage of an 'open door' that was afforded him. He would first revisit the Corinthian church, going there by way of Macedonia. From Corinth, he would travel to Nicopolis in Epirus by the sea. From there he would sail to Dalmatia. Returning by the same route, he planned to spend the winter in Nicopolis as he had written to Titus, and then again come to Corinth.

These plans were upset, however, when his friends from Dalmatia told him that the best way to go to Dalmatia was by way of Macedonia. The Roman government had made many improvements in the roads in the area, and besides, the sea route was not always reliable and safe. Paul, therefore, changed his plans. As Paul was not quite ready to leave when his friends from Dalmatia were, they said they would wait for him in Neapolis.

When Paul finally was ready to leave for Macedonia, his

departure was delayed even longer. Demetrius, a silversmith whose trade depended very much on the silver shrines of Artemis, caused a great disturbance in the city. Paul's preaching was so effective that this trade was diminishing. Demetrius became irate and stirred up the people against Paul.

Paul then sent Timothy and Erastus ahead into Macedonia while he was detained in Ephesus. Only after the rioting stopped was Paul able to make plans to leave. He would take Tychicus with him.

Just prior to the time that Paul was to leave, however, Philemon arrived unexpectedly in Ephesus with his son, Archippus, and Onesimus. Onesimus discovered Paul's plans for the trip to Neapolis quite by accident as Philemon was visiting Gaius. Now would be the time, he thought, to run away from Philemon. He managed to slip away from Philemon and Archippus on the evening before Paul's ship was to sail. Onesimus took a few of their possessions with him, and then stowed away on the ship.

"What are you doing here?" Paul asked Onesimus when he first saw him on the ship.

"I just cannot stay cooped up in Colossae all my life. I had to get away," Onesimus insisted.

"You know, of course, that runaway slaves become fugitives and are hunted down, don't you?" Paul reminded Onesimus.

"I am aware of the consequences," Onesimus replied. "Philemon may appear to be a nice man to you when you come to visit him, but for me, he was becoming unbearable. I could not satisfy him, no matter how hard I tried. The older he gets, the more unreasonable he becomes."

"You should return when we get to Neapolis," Paul said sternly.

"I can't. I want to go with you. I can be your helper."

The pleading affected Paul so that he finally allowed Onesimus his wish, and Paul was obliged to pay Onesimus' fare.

Following instructions Paul had given them, Timothy and Erastus located the men from Dalmatia in Neapolis. These men had been there for a week already when Timothy told them that Paul would be delayed. They were ready to give up on Paul, but Timothy pleaded with them to be patient. Paul arrived in Neapolis six days later, and none too soon.

Since the journey to Dalmatia would involve traveling in unfamiliar territory, Paul decided to take Erastus with him, together with Demas, a man from Thessalonica, and also Onesimus. Timothy was to remain in Philippi with Artemas. Tychicus went home to Troas.

Despite poor traveling conditions, the small group made good time. The people of Dalmatia received their countrymen warmly, and made Paul and his friends welcome. Paul preached the Gospel and the people heard it with great interest. Explaining to them at the outset that he would not be able to stay very long, Paul told them that he arranged to have one of his co-workers, Titus, come to them and stay for a longer time. "I hope that you receive him as warmly as I was received. If everything goes according to plan, Titus should arrive by next spring."

After three months Paul returned to Philippi. He left almost immediately for Corinth, going by way of Thessalonica, Berea, and Athens, taking along Erastus, Artemas, and Onesimus. Timothy and Luke, who also happened to be in Philippi, also went with him, but only as far as Athens.

The conditions at Corinth were still unsettled, for the Jews still plotted against Paul. He was thus prevented from ministering much to the church there. Stopping at the home of Gaius, Paul found that many of the Gentiles were also angry over the letter he had written to them. Paul associated only with Erastus, the city treasurer, Quartus, Jason, who lived next to the synagogue, and Sosipater, in addition to Stephanus, Fortunatus, and Achaicus. After only two weeks in Corinth, Paul returned to Athens to be with Luke and Timothy.

While at Athens, Paul sent Artemas to Crete. The time had come for Titus to work in a new location. Artemas was to tell Titus of the change in Paul's plan.

When a month passed and Paul saw that he was still being harassed, he decided to return to Macedonia to spend the winter there. He was hoping now to meet Titus eventually in Philippi. But Titus did not show up as soon as Paul had expected.

After a couple of months, Titus finally arrived. He told Paul that he and Artemas first stopped in Corinth. He learned of the troubles in the church, and was persuaded by the leaders to remain with them for a time. This he did before continuing on to Philippi.

Paul was happy that Titus' work in Corinth had been effective. He was, in fact, so delighted that he told Titus to return to Corinth for a short time. He sent another letter he had written to the Corinthians along with him. He promised to come to them again a third time, and planned to leave for Syria from there, taking the gifts to the saints in Jerusalem with him. Paul wrote, "But I determined this within myself, that I would not come again to you in sorrow."[4]

Titus returned to Macedonia after a short stay in Corinth and soon preparations were made for him to go to Dalmatia. Paul provided him with the necessary instructions and a letter of recommendation. Demas and Onesimus were to guide him, and Artemas was to be his helper.

Early Spring 56

Paul once again embarked for Corinth. When he arrived, his high hopes for an improved relationship with the congregation there was short-lived. Not only the Jews again plotted against him, but Alexander also caused trouble for him. After two weeks in Corinth, Paul hastily retreated to Cenchrea. He left Erastus, in Corinth, but Quartus and Jason came with him.

Paul began to think about a trip to Spain with a stop in Rome. He enlisted the aid of Tertius to help him write a letter to the church in Rome.

Since he was still being bothered in Cenchrea, Paul left for Athens. He had thought much about going to Rome ever since Apollos went there. He had, in fact, told Apollos that he wished he could have gone with him when he went.

Although he knew the church in Rome only through information supplied by Aquila and Priscilla, Paul wrote to them in a friendly manner as though he knew the Roman Christians personally. He said that when he made his trip to Spain, he would stop to visit them, and added that he no longer had a 'place in these parts,'[5] meaning Achaia. Phoebe, a woman from Cenchrea, who was also with him, was, as bearer of this letter, commended to them by Paul.

Gaius, who now also came to be with Paul, accompanied him as he departed for Macedonia. Luke and Timothy went along.

This trip from Athens to Macedonia was the first good opportunity for Gaius to become acquainted with Luke.

"I have wanted to meet you," said Gaius. "Everything I have heard about you has been positive. What was your introduction in becoming a disciple of Jesus Christ?"

"I have heard many good things about you, too," said Luke. "I was a young physician in Damascus when I heard reports of the wonderful deeds of a man from Galilee. I took a few of my patients to Jesus for healing. And Jesus healed them. A little later, I did the same thing. The miraculous healing that Jesus did amazed everyone. Some time later, when a man came to me with his son who was severely afflicted with epilepsy," Luke said, "I decided to take this boy to Jesus.

"We started out for Galilee, and on the road in the vicinity of Caesarea Philippi, we met pilgrims who told us that Jesus and his disciples were there. We joined them, but when we arrived in this city, we were told that Jesus had gone with three of the disciples on a retreat on a high mountain. The remaining disciples tried to accommodate our request to help this boy, but they could not. After a few days, Jesus returned with Peter, James, and John. Jesus then healed the boy.

"Right then and there," said Luke, "I decided that Jesus was not an ordinary man but that he must be a prophet. I told the father of the boy to go back to Damascus and tell my friends that I was going to follow Jesus to learn everything I could about him.

"And so that is what I did, continuing until the time when Jesus was crucified, rose from the dead, and ascended into heaven. As I joined the crowd as Jesus 'steadfastly set face to go to Jerusalem,'[6] I began to make notes of things that occurred. I also learned many other things about Jesus from his disciples.

"In talking to several of the apostles of the Lord – Peter, in particular, but also Matthew and John – I gradually became proselytized."

"That is quite an inspiring story," said Gaius. "The church is truly blessed to have the story of the life of Jesus Christ written from more than one perspective. You and Matthew and Mark have done a good job. Is there anything more you may wish to add?"

"I also became acquainted with a man named Cleopas from the village of Emmaus. When I was close to Jerusalem, I stayed at this man's house. Finding some place to stay in Jerusalem was not always easy. And so it happened on the Sunday evening of the resurrection of the Lord as we were walking along the road out of Jerusalem, Jesus came walking along with us. We did not recognize him. But later as we dined at Cleopas' home, Jesus opened our eyes and made himself known to us."

Quite an assembly of followers gathered at Philippi to accompany Paul to Jerusalem – Sopater of Berea, Aristarchus and Secundus of Thessalonica, and Gaius of Derbe, and Timothy and Tychicus, and Trophimus of Asia. Others were Luke, Demas, and Onesimus. Only Silas and his helpers were left in Macedonia. Paul sent Onesimus with a parting message for Silas. While Onesimus was doing so, Luke and Demas stayed in Philippi to wait for him, and the others left for Troas.

On the way to Troas, Paul told Gaius about his tentative plans for his trip to Spain.

"Instead of taking my books, the parchments and my cloak along to Jerusalem, I want to leave them with Carpus in Troas. If all goes well, I will return to Troas by way of Galatia, Pisidia, and Colossae. After that, I plan to return to Dalmatia to visit and check in with Titus to see how he is faring. From there, I plan to travel by land to Italy."

Gaius agreed that the plans were well thought through.

After a brief stay at Troas, the entire assembly, except for Paul, boarded the ship for the journey to Syria, stopping at Assos, where Paul had gone on foot. Stopping at several places on the way, the ship also stopped at Miletus. Paul called for the elders at Ephesus to come to Miletus so that he could converse with them one last time. Having finished his meeting with them, Paul concluded, "I have shown you in every way, by laboring like this, that you must support the weak. And remember the words of the Lord Jesus, how he said, 'It is more blessed to give than to receive.' And when he had said these things, he knelt down and prayed with them all. And they all wept greatly, and fell on Paul's neck and kissed him, sorrowing most of all for the words which he spoke, that they would see his face no more."[7] Trophimus fell ill and left the ship.

Running a straight course, they came to Cos, the following day to Rhodes, and from there to Patara. Changing ships at Patara in Lycia, they then sailed for Phoenicia. They landed at Tyre, and Paul, wanting to be in Jerusalem for the day of Pentecost, finally came to Caesarea.

Paul's friends there knew that the Jews at Jerusalem seethed with resentment toward him. The Jews from Asia had stirred up the people. Paul's friends tried to dissuade him from going to Jerusalem, but he felt compelled to go. He had made a vow.

Arriving in Jerusalem, Paul met with the brethren. Later, when he was in the temple, the Jews had Paul arrested.

Gaius took charge of distributing the gifts that were brought from Macedonia and Achaia. The needs of the Jerusalem brethren had almost reached the point of desperation. James and Jude, the Lord's brothers, and John assisted Gaius.

John, who had taken care of Mary, the mother of Jesus, had stayed relatively close to Jerusalem since the crucifixion. Mary had died a year before, and now John desired to leave Jerusalem. When Gaius learned of this, he invited John to come to Ephesus. John accepted the invitation. They left for Ephesus after the needs of the people were taken care of.

Chapter 9
Summer 56

The Jews would have killed Paul had it not been for his sister's son. They had taken an oath that they would not eat anything until they had killed him. Paul's nephew learned of an ambush planned by the Jews, and the Roman officials were alerted. They secretly escorted Paul out of the city by night and took him to Caesarea.

A large contingent of Paul's followers later traveled to Caesarea to be near him to offer him support. Mark, who had come to Jerusalem for the day of Pentecost, also went with them. News of Paul's imprisonment soon spread far and wide. The Philippian congregation even sent Epaproditus to Paul to minister to him.

As Paul remained in prison, the commander of the prison, Lysias, heard his story. He then summoned the chief priests of the Sanhedrin to appear, and brought Paul before them.

Paul defended himself before the Sanhedrin, saying, "Men and brethren, I have lived in all good conscience before God until this day."[1] Paul learned that part of the council was Pharisees and part was Sadducees. He managed to play one side against the other, knowing that they were at odds with each other. A great dissension erupted so that the commander returned Paul to prison.

The following night the Lord stood by him and said, "Be of good cheer, Paul, for as you have testified for Me in Jerusalem, so you must bear witness also in Rome."[2]

Felix, the governor at Caesarea, next summoned Ananias, the high priest. He came with the elders and an orator named Tertuilus, who did most of the speaking as they gave evidence to the governor against Paul. After hearing all the testimony, Felix said, "When Lysias, the commander, comes down, I will make a decision on your case."[3]

Felix commanded a centurion to keep Paul and to let him have liberty, and to allow Paul's friends to visit and provide for him. From time to time, however, Felix and his wife, Drusilla, conversed with Paul about his faith in Christ. Felix was also hoping to receive bribery money.

Paul, meanwhile, was increasingly concerned about Onesimus, the slave who had run away from Philemon. Gaius had told Paul the circumstances surrounding himself, Apphia, and Onesimus, and Philemon. They agreed that Onesimus should return to Philemon in Colossae. At last, Paul wrote a letter to Philemon about Onesimus. He concluded the letter by saying that he should "also prepare a guest room for me, for I trust that through your prayers, I shall be granted to you."[4] Paul allowed Onesimus to read the letter before it was sealed.

Paul also wrote a letter to the church at Colossae. And Onesimus consented to return to Colossae. Tychicus would accompany him, and also deliver the letters. Tychicus and Onesimus had developed a close relationship.

Epaphroditus, the messenger from Philippi, became ill after he was in Caesarea a while. Knowing that Epaphroditus wished to return home, Paul then also wrote a letter to the church at Philippi to send along with him. Paul commended Timothy to the church, saying that Timothy might also be sent to them shortly. He added that, trusting in the Lord, he also would be able to come to them shortly.

About that time, Mark told Paul he wanted to return to Galatia. Upon his arrival there, he was astonished at what was going on. The Galatians were turning away from the true Gospel to a different gospel, a gospel taught by men who wanted to pervert the Gospel of Christ. They were being led astray. These men were not rightly dividing the Law and the Gospel.

Mark immediately returned to Caesarea and reported to Paul.

Paul wasted no time in writing a letter to these Galatians. He told them, "But even if we, or an angel from heaven, preach any other gospel to you than what we have preached to you, let him be accursed. Stand fast, therefore, in the liberty with which Christ has made us free, and do not be entangled again with a yoke of bondage."[5] To show his true concern for the church in Galatia, Paul closed the letter with a prayer, "Brethren, the grace of our Lord Jesus Christ be with your spirit. Amen."[6] Crescens delivered the letter, and Mark went into Asia.

After two years, Porcius Festus succeeded Felix. Felix had left Paul bound and Festus wanted to clear the case. He asked if Paul were willing to go to Jerusalem to be judged there.

Paul answered, "I stand at Caesar's judgment seat, where I ought to be judged. To the Jews I have done no wrong, as you very well know.[7] I appeal to Caesar."[8]

Festus replied, "You have appealed to Caesar? To Caesar you shall go!"[9]

Soon afterward, Festus received important visitors: King Agrippa and his wife Bernice. Festus explained everything about Paul to the king. Agrippa was intrigued, and wanted to meet this man. It was arranged, and the king and Paul had a long conversation.

Agrippa admitted to Paul, "You almost persuade me to become a Christian."[10] Then the king agreed with Festus, saying, "This man is doing nothing worthy of death or chains,"[11] and added, "This man might have been set free if he had not appealed to Caesar."[12]

Paul was placed in the custody of Julius, a centurion of the Augustan Regiment, for the journey to Rome. Aristarchus, a Thessalonian, and Luke would go to Rome with Paul. Demas, who had been a faithful follower of Paul for a number of years, however, became disenchanted with the misfortunes of Paul, forsook him, and went home to Thessalonica.

Autumn 56

As Tychicus and Onesimus traveled to Colossae to deliver Paul's letter to Philemon, they discussed how they should handle it. After the delivery of the letter to the elders of the church at Colossae, Tychicus would approach Philemon alone while Onesimus waited not far away.

Tychicus gave the letter to Philemon, and waited as he read it.

"Where is that bum?" he burst forth.

"He's right outside," Tychicus said, "but before you see him, I think you should reread Paul's letter. I think you need time to calm down."

"Who does Paul think he is, telling everyone what to do?" Philemon threw the crumpled letter on the floor.

"Calm yourself, Philemon," Tychicus exclaimed. "You are forgetting something."

"What?" asked Philemon.

"About the time your wife died, and when Gaius helped you by allowing Apphia to come into your house."

"How did you know about that?"

"Onesimus told me."

Philemon then picked up Paul's letter and reread it. Having had time to reflect, Philemon admitted, "You are right. I guess I am making a fool of myself."

Tychicus moved back and motioned to Onesimus. As Onesimus entered, he and Philemon barely looked at each other. Apphia, who had heard the commotion, also came to the inner door.

Onesimus stepped over to embrace her. Sensing what must be on his mother's mind, Onesimus whispered, "It's all right, Mom. Gaius told me everything about the two of you. He has not forgotten you."

Apphia burst into tears. Philemon went over to them and put his hand on Apphia's shoulder. He then handed Paul's letter to her, saying, "It seems that I have become overly selfish about this matter of keeping you in my household. Will you forgive me?"

Apphia nodded.

"And I do, too," added Onesimus.

Philemon then shook hands with Onesimus. Apphia explained everything to Philemon about her relationship to Gaius while Onesimus and Tychicus listened.

"I hardly know what to say," sighed Philemon. "I wish I had known sooner."

As Tychicus and Onesimus rested from their travels, Apphia prepared the evening meal.

As they ate, Philemon asked, "What are your plans, Onesimus?"

"Tychicus and I thought that we would go to Ephesus. We want to tell Gaius what has happened."

"And you can tell him something else, too," Philemon said. "It has been about fourteen years since my wife died, and Apphia has been a wonderful help to me all this time. Tell Gaius to come here, and Apphia will be ready to return to Ephesus with him."

Apphia looked at Philemon, but did not say anything.

"I am sure Gaius will be happy to do that," Onesimus remarked.

Tychicus kept the conversation going. "Did any of you know that Paul wants to visit Rome?"

No one had.

"Yes, and he would also like to go to Spain. But I can well imagine that all of his plans are up in the air now, however, since his troubles with the Jews at Jerusalem and his confinement at Caesarea. I have no doubt, that eventually he will get to go to Rome."

"If you really think he will, Tychicus, why don't we start thinking of going there, too?" Onesimus suggested.

"That sounds like a good idea to me," Tychicus replied.

The next day, Tychicus and Onesimus headed for Ephesus.

John had stayed in Ephesus ever since he and Gaius had come from Jerusalem. He ministered to the church there. On the voyage from Jerusalem, Gaius and John came to know each other well.

"I am intrigued at your thorough knowledge of the life of Christ," said John. "How did you obtain this information?"

"Almost all of it came from what Matthew has written in his Gospel. I met Matthew at Jerusalem, and he later came to Derbe. He stayed in my home as he was finishing writing it." Gaius told John the whole story surrounding the writing of Matthew's Gospel.

"I have read it, and it made a favorable impression on me," John said.

"I have also obtained a copy of Luke's Gospel account which was written for Theopilus of Athens, and Mark has promised that he would send a copy of the Gospel that he has written in collaboration with Peter.

"I have seen Mark's Gospel, but know nothing of the one by Luke," said John.

Upon arrival in Ephesus, John eagerly reviewed Luke's Gospel. He was impressed and pleased. "Has Paul every written the story?" wondered John.

"Paul," said Gaius, "prefers to rely on preaching. He has a copy of all three Gospels, and has approved them, but he still prefers oral communication over the written word. His copies and his books are now at Troas at the home of Carpus, a friend of Luke.

"Paul has, at certain times, written letters. One of them was addressed to the church at Corinth."

"Is it available for review?"

"I am sure the elders would still have it," said Gaius. "I could go to Corinth to inquire about it if you like."

Gaius was happy when the elders at Corinth produced not only one letter, but also a second letter. After some urging, they gave them to Gaius, and he returned to Ephesus.

"I have an idea," John said as he finished reading the letters. "We should begin to collect all the letters of Paul. Don't you agree?"

"Most assuredly," replied Gaius. "We can use my library as a repository."

Onesimus and Tychicus arrived in Ephesus after a fast journey from Colossae. "I have good news," Onesimus said to Gaius. "We went to Colossae to see Philemon at Paul's suggestion. After reading Paul's letter to him about me, Philemon agreed to release me from service as his slave. He, likewise, said that you should come to Colossae so that you can bring Apphia back to Ephesus with you. He was upset when he learned the full story behind our joining his household, and was very apologetic."

John, who was with Gaius, listened in bewilderment. Now Gaius related the whole story to him. For the first time, Gaius publicly acknowledged that Onesimus was his son.

Gaius would leave for Colossae as soon as possible to claim Apphia, already formulating plans for a grand wedding. John would marry them; Philemon would be best man; Onesimus would give the bride away; and the entire church at Ephesus would be invited. Gaius figured that within two months he and Apphia would be husband and wife.

Philemon had been apprehensive about how Gaius would feel when he arrived in Colossae to claim Apphia, but Gaius, however, dispelled any thought of fear when he got to Colossae. He was too happy to be acrimonious. In fact, Philemon was quite astounded at the affection Gaius displayed toward Apphia. Gaius embraced Apphia tenderly for a long while upon his arrival, as he had thought on this moment fondly for some time. Pressing business affairs always seemed to prevent Gaius from confronting Philemon to have Apphia returned to him.

When Gaius detailed his plans for their wedding, Apphia happily consented. Philemon offered a toast and his sincerest congratulations. Caught up in the joy of the hour, he was surprised to find himself kissing the bride-to-be. When Gaius informed Philemon that he wanted him to be best man, Philemon gladly consented. Gaius invited everyone in Philemon's family to attend the wedding. Archippus was happy for Gaius and Apphia. Celeste, Philemon's teenage daughter, however, was inconsolable at the thought of losing the woman she had come to regard as her mother.

While Gaius was at Colossae, Onesimus and Tychicus took advantage of the time and became better acquainted with John. John was enthused with the zeal instilled in them by Paul. They all agreed that Paul's zeal for the Gospel was contagious.

Tychicus and Onesimus planned to go to Rome after the wedding. They were positive that Paul would ultimately come to Rome, too. The mention of Rome brought to John's mind the letter that Paul had written to these people.

He told the two of them that he and Gaius believed the letters Paul had written should be collected. So far, he said, they were in possession of two letters Paul had written to the church in Corinth. Tychicus said that he had delivered a letter from Paul to Timothy. In addition, he and Onesimus had delivered one to Philemon and another to the church at Colossae. Onesimus also added that Titus had received a letter from Paul.

John requested that if the opportunity arose, they should try to obtain or get copies of these letters and bring them or send them to Gaius in Ephesus. John also mentioned to them that they should not necessarily tell Paul what they were doing concerning his letters. Paul, he said, might not particularly relish the idea of someone collecting his letters.

When Tychicus and Onesimus pressed John for further insights into the life of Christ, John related interesting events not contained in the Gospels of either Matthew or Luke. John, it seemed to Tychicus and Onesimus, told the story of Christ in an altogether different style than what the other Gospel writers did. They pointed this out to John. He agreed with them, and added that it would be next to impossible for any two men to present a story of the same occurrence identically. There would always be variations of emphases in one degree or another.

Onesimus insisted that if such were the case, future generations would be greatly benefited if they could have at their disposal John's story of the life of Christ. Tychicus firmly supported Onesimus' idea. John agreed to think about it.

Plans for the marriage of Gaius and Apphia proceeded. On the great day itself, the whole church at Ephesus celebrated with Gaius. Friends from other places in Asia also came.

Those attending were Andronicus and Junia, Amplias, Urbanus, Apelles, Narcissus and his household, and Mary. So were Herodion, Tryphena and Tryphosa, Rufus and his mother, Philologus, and Julia, Olympas, Persis, Aristobulus, and many others. Aristobulus was accompanied by his son, Diotrephes, whom Gaius considered to be too conceited and overbearing.

The festivities lasted for several days, and then the newlyweds set out on their honeymoon. Their destination was Corinth. Gaius proudly introduced his bride to the congregation there. None of the people of Corinth suspected Apphia to be a former slave. Gaius treated her every bit like a non-slave.

While in Achaia, they also visited Athens and the surrounding countryside, showing her the extent of his business interests. While in Athens, Gaius told Apphia of his wedding gift for her, a travel package. She would have first choice of traveling to any place of her desire, and then he would choose a second place.

Apphia immediately decided on a trip to what she called the 'Holy Land.' She wanted to see the places where the Messiah lived, taught, performed miracles, and traveled. She particularly wanted to visit Bethlehem, the place where her grandfather worshipped the newborn King.

Gaius said he would reveal his choice after the visit to the 'Holy Land.' He had in mind a journey to Arachosia, Apphia's homeland. Wanderlust was still with him.

The next stop on their honeymoon was Nicopolis in Epirus. They stayed in this place by the sea for two months. From there it was on to Berea, Thessalonica, Philippi, and Troas. Over the years, Gaius became acquainted with many people from these places, and, of course, they had a pleasant visit with Silas and his wife.

While in Thessalonica, Gaius inquired about the letter written to them by Paul. The church readily gave it to Gaius when he explained the purpose in requesting it. At Philippi, Gaius learned that this church had recently received a letter from Paul written at Caesarea and delivered by Epaphroditus. They, likewise, gave this letter to Gaius when he told them of the project of collecting Paul's letters. They also visited with Timothy who had just recently come from Caesarea. He told them the latest news of Paul.

Gaius and Apphia then headed back to Ephesus. Their journey through Asia would take them to Pergamum, Thyatira, Smyrna, Sardis, Philadelphia, Laodicea, and Colossae. Philemon was delighted when Gaius and Apphia showed up in Colossae.

While there, Philemon's son, Archippus, voiced an interest in becoming better acquainted with John. This was prompted by his continuing study of the Gospel at the urging of Paul. Gaius, therefore, invited Archippus to come to Ephesus and said he would ask John about tutoring him.

Once again Gaius related to Philemon his and John's project of collecting Paul's letters. Philemon still had Paul's letter to him although it was slightly crumpled, and also secured for them Paul's letter to the elders of the church.

As Onesimus and Tychicus were formulating their plans, word was received in Ephesus that Paul had appealed to Caesar. That meant that Paul would be taken to Rome by the government. This news was excitedly discussed by everyone in Ephesus. Eventually, Onesiphorus, a man from Philippi who had befriended Paul when he was in trouble in Ephesus, and Epaenetus, a beloved friend of Paul, became aware of the plans of Onesimus and Tychicus.

"I would very much like to go to Rome, myself," said Epaenetus.

"I have thought of it, too," replied Onesiphorus, "but having no one to go with deterred me."

"Perhaps if we talked with Onesimus and Tychicus, they might be persuaded to allow us to join them," said Epaenetus.

"I'll be seeing them tomorrow," replied Onesiphorus.

He talked with them about going along with them, and eagerly accepted their invitation to join them.

After an absence of about six months, Gaius and Apphia returned to Ephesus. While his father and mother were preparing to head east on their trip to the 'Holy Land,' Onesimus prepared to head west with Tychicus and Onesiphorus and Epaenetus. After a touching farewell, the two parties were ready to go their separate ways. They all realized that it would perhaps be many years before they would next see each other.

And so, the foursome was off to Rome.

Chapter 10
Spring 58

Gaius and Apphia did not leave immediately on their trip to the Holy Land. They wanted to rest a while after the honeymoon, and Gaius had business to attend to.

When John learned that Gaius and Apphia were making plans for an extended trip to the Holy Land, he offered whatever assistance that might be of value to them. Gaius thankfully accepted John's help, and together they worked on an itinerary. Gaius made notes of all the places of interest, and things to watch for.

Apphia suggested to Gaius that, perhaps, John might be interested in accompanying them as a guide. Gaius presented the idea to him, but John replied that he preferred to remain in Ephesus. He enjoyed tutoring Archippus and several other young men Gaius invited to Ephesus to study with him. In addition, John told Gaius, he had done much contemplating over the suggestion of Onesimus and Tychicus that he also should write the Gospel, and had recently started writing it. Gaius insisted then, in that case, that John stay on in their house while they were away. He was to feel free to use any of the facilities at his discretion.

Three months later, Gaius received another visitor, Simon Peter. He had come from Colossae, where he had gone to look for Mark. Mark was supposed to have returned to Bithynia and he was long overdue. Philemon had guided him to Ephesus. Gaius told Peter that as far as he knew, Mark was still with Paul at Caesarea, but that this information was rather old. Peter was somewhat undecided about what to do.

Again at the suggestion of Apphia, Gaius asked Peter if he would like to accompany them on their upcoming trip to the Holy

Land, and he decided to go with them. Peter had not seen his wife for some time. While waiting for the time of departure, Peter spent many hours renewing his friendship with John, and in becoming better acquainted with the church at Ephesus.

The journey by sea took the three of them – Gaius, Apphia, and Peter – to Tyre. It was appropriate that the first stop on their itinerary was Peter's hometown of Bethsaida. The road from Tyre to Bethsaida took them through mountainous country.

Along the way, Peter pointed to the mountain where the transfiguration of Jesus took place. Peter described that experience as both exhilarating and frightening. "To suddenly see Jesus in majesty talking with Moses and Elijah, great prophets of God, made a lasting impression on us. We weren't sure what it all meant.

"When Jesus told us as we came down from the mountain not to talk about it to anyone until the Son of Man had risen from the dead, we were all the more puzzled. We were with Jesus for more than two years then, and we still did not fully comprehend what was going on.

"Not until Jesus' death, resurrection, ascension, and the coming of the Holy Spirit on Pentecost did we more fully understand and realize what the life and ministry of Jesus was all for. As the Messiah, he came to atone for the sins of the whole world. Likewise, he came to establish His church on earth. The Holy Spirit filled each of our hearts on that day."

As Peter paused, Gaius spoke, "I was also in Jerusalem on the day of Pentecost. I heard the rushing wind and went to see what was happening. I heard you speak on that day, Peter, and I truly believe that the Holy Spirit also entered my heart at that time. My life has taken on an entirely new and different meaning since then."

"The Holy Spirit is indeed a powerful and mighty source of good," Peter said. "He is sent from the Father at our Lord's behest, and leads us into all truth. He, it is, who inspires us as we preach. And 'we have not followed cunningly devised fables when we made known to you the power and coming of our Lord Jesus Christ, but were eyewitnesses of His majesty. For He received from God the Father honor and glory when such a voice came to Him from Excellent Glory: "this is My beloved Son, in whom I am well-pleased." And we heard this voice which came from heaven when we were with Him on the holy mountain. We also have the prophetic word made more sure, which you do well to heed as a light that shines in a dark place, until the day dawns and the morning star rises in your hearts.'[1]"

One the rest of the way to Bethsaida they warmly discussed various events in their lives, and how God had been with them and blessed them despite all the troubles they had encountered.

As they entered the city, Peter remarked that the place hadn't changed much. He told Gaius and Apphia that by mutual consent, his wife would retain residency here in Bethsaida, while he was away fulfilling his commission to preach the Gospel. She no longer wished to travel because of her health.

Zelina was busy with household chores when Peter entered their modest home. As this visit was unexpected, she was stunned. Gaius and Apphia stood silently by as Peter and Zelina greeted each other warmly with kisses.

"Oh, Peter," she exclaimed, "you came at just the right time. Nate came home from Cyrene a month ago and our friends are arranging to celebrate his wedding anniversary a month from now. We have been trying to contact as many of the Lord's disciples as possible."

Peter interrupted, "Before we go further, I think I should introduce my friends. I would like you to meet Gaius and Apphia. They are from Ephesus, and are also friends of John. John is in Ephesus right now."

After the introductory conversation, Peter explained to Gaius and Apphia that Nate was Nathaniel Bar-Tholomew, one of the twelve.

He was the bridegroom at the wedding of Cana where Jesus performed his first miracle by changing water into wine.

Zelina went on to explain, "Matthias also came from Egypt with Nathaniel. Jude and Simon both had been home from Persia for some time. Philip had been contacted at Gaza, but no word had been received whether or not he could make it. James is at Joppa, and promised to come, Brother Andrew is still at Sychem, and, of course, will be here. The last we heard about Thomas was that he and Timon left Parthia and went to India about four years ago. As far as Matthew was concerned, he seemed to have dropped out of sight."

Apphia spoke up, saying that Matthew, whom they knew from Galatia, had gone to Arachosia, her homeland.

"Well, that accounts for the twelve," Zelina said. "It should be a gala reunion."

As the wedding anniversary was some weeks away, Gaius and Apphia made use of this time by exploring the Sea of Galilee and its environment. Peter usually accompanied them. He pointed out various places of interest, such as the grassy field where Jesus fed the multitude. Peter also took them fishing and explained the details of his former life's work.

A boat trip up the River Jordan was also enjoyed by Gaius and Apphia. The highlight of the trip was visiting the area where Jesus was baptized by John the Baptist. When Gaius asked Peter about the desert where John lived, Peter said that they would see plenty of desert when they went south of Jerusalem. It was all pretty much the same.

Andrew, Peter's brother, soon came to Bethsaida. They had not seen each other since before the time Zelina came home sick. Peter had tried to convince Andrew to leave Samaria and come to Asia with him. Andrew hesitated in going such a distance from home with his wife and family. Now Andrew came alone, for his wife, who was a bit older than himself, had passed away, and their children were now on their own. Peter again talked to him about returning to Asia with him. Now Andrew had nothing to prevent him from doing that.

A visit to his home territory would not be complete for Peter if he did not stop in Magdala to see Mary. She was a warm and outgoing person, and it did not take long for Gaius and Apphia to be friends. Her vivid retelling of the events of Easter morning made a lasting impression on her visitors.

"Several women in our company came to the tomb early in the morning on the third day with spices to anoint the Lord's body. We failed to give any thought about the huge stone at its entrance, however. But when we got there, we saw that it was rolled away. We entered the tomb but the body of Jesus was not there. Hurriedly, we ran to tell Peter and the rest. They also raced to the tomb, and when they found only the grave cloths lying there, they went again to their homes, not knowing what to make of it all. I stayed at the tomb crying. Then a man whom I did not recognize approached. As we talked, he spoke my name, and I knew this man was Jesus. I then returned to the disciples to spread the good news that Jesus was alive. He was risen from the dead."

The date of the wedding anniversary was now at hand. Peter, Andrew, and Zelina, decided that after the reunion, they, along with Gaius and Apphia, should continue on together to Nazareth, and then on to Sychem. They were the first to arrive in Cana for the reunion. Inasmuch as so many out-of-town guests were coming to the reunion, Gaius convinced Nathaniel that they could stay at an inn, so that the other guests could make use of the other accommodations provided.

Matthias was next to arrive. His visit to his hometown of Bethel was the first time home since his original departure for Cyrene. Simon and Jude traveled together from Jerusalem. The house was rapidly filling when Jesus' brothers and sisters came. As the festivities began, the only two missing seemed to be James the Less and Philip.

But on the second day of the gathering, they finally arrived. James had waited for Philip at Joppa, and they then came by way of Caesarea, hoping to visit Paul in prison. When they got there, they were told that Paul had recently been taken under guard to Rome. Luke and Aristarchus went with Paul.

They learned that after some delay, Festus heard Paul's case. Paul, not willing to return to Jerusalem as desired by the Jews, finally said to Festus, "I stand at Caesar's judgment seat, where I ought to be judged. To the Jews I have done no wrong, as you very well know. For if I am an offender, or have committed anything worthy of death, I do not refuse to die; but if there is nothing in these things of which these men accuse me, no one can deliver me to them. I appeal to Caesar."[2]

Then Festus, when he had conferred with the council, answered, "You have appealed to Caesar? To Caesar you shall go!"[3]

When the assembly heard these things, everyone was stunned. They surmised that Paul had sealed his own fate.

Peter, realizing the gravity of Paul's situation, spoke up, "Paul is in need of our prayers." And he began to pray, "Most Gracious Heavenly Father of your humble servants, hear our prayer in behalf of our fellow servant, and your chosen vessel, Paul. Send your holy angels to guard and protect him withersoever his paths may lead. He is in peril especially at this time. Send your Holy Spirit to instill in him wisdom and joy and peace. We ask all this in the name and for the sake of your only Son, Jesus, our Savior. Amen."

When he was finished praying, the room buzzed with talk over the recent hostility toward the preaching of the Gospel. This seemed to be happening almost everywhere. It was not only caused by the activity of the Jews, but it was also being directed at the apostles by the Roman government. They all affirmed, however, that although preaching the Gospel seemed to be more imperiled, their commission to preach must be continued.

Meanwhile, Peter inquired if anyone had word about Mark. Someone said he had gone back to Bithynia after leaving Caesarea and then returned after going as far as Galatia.

Over the next few days, Gaius and Apphia were able to talk to each of the apostles, and to Jesus' brothers and sisters. Listening to their tales and experiences was both enlightening and encouraging for them. Gaius reckoned that his path and those of Nathaniel and Matthias must have come quite close on his trip to North Africa. When Matthias and Philip told of their journey and stay in Ethiopia, Gaius conjured up visions of himself also going there, although he knew that the prospect of such a trip was remote.

James described the life he shared with Thomas in Arabia. Jude and Simon the Zealot spoke of the lands of Mesopotamia and Persia. Nathaniel and Matthias intended to go to Armenia and Cappadocia in the near future, while Jude was planning to return to Persia.

As he talked with the apostles, Gaius never missed an opportunity to ask any of them whether they had written letters or epistles. Only Jude and James, the Lord's brothers, replied affirmatively. James had written to the disciples in dispersion after the persecution in Jerusalem following the death of Stephen. Jude had written his letter at the time of the controversy on circumcision. Jude said these letters were now at Jerusalem, and that Gaius could have them if he wanted to pick them up and add them to his collection.

All in all, Gaius and Apphia loved being present at this reunion and wedding anniversary celebration.

When the party was over, Andrew, Peter and Zelina, and Gaius and Apphia set out for Nazareth according to plan. Jesus' brothers and sisters had gone ahead of them and were already home to welcome them as they arrived. After a stay of two days, they went to Sychem. This place, so rich in the history of the Israelites, was where Jesus talked to the woman at the well of Jacob. Andrew later married a woman from this town. She was, in fact, the very woman with whom Jesus had talked. She had put her past life behind her.

As Peter was making ready to leave for Jerusalem with Gaius and Apphia, he and Andrew agreed to meet again back in Bethsaida. Meanwhile, Jerusalem was to be their headquarters for three months. Many side trips were anticipated, and Gaius wanted to study more of the history of the children of Israel.

As they approached the city, Gaius recognized many of the sights from his previous visits. He went directly to the inn where he always stayed, and made arrangements for their protracted stay. Peter would also lodge there.

The first trip in their plans was the one to Bethlehem. Although Peter could not point with certainty the exact location of the stable where Christ was born, they visited nearly every one in town. Apphia felt an overwhelming sense of awe at the one nearest the inn. While she could not say that she was at the same house where her grandfather worshipped the newborn King and brought Him gifts, she was delighted beyond measure with this visit.

That evening Gaius and Apphia left the inn and headed for the countryside. Together they walked hand in hand toward the hillsides where the shepherds grazed their sheep. They envisioned for themselves the sky being filled and lit up by a choir of angels singing "Glory to God in the Highest, and on Earth Peace, Good Will Toward Men."[4]

In the next few days, Peter guided Gaius and Apphia on a tour of the city, including the Garden of Gethsemane and the area surrounding the temple. The entire events of the week of the crucifixion of Jesus were reviewed by Peter as they went from place to place. This included the route of the triumphal entry of Jesus into the city, the Upper Room where Jesus ate his last meal with the disciples and instituted the sacrament of the Lord's Supper, and other places. Peter also pointed out the courtyard of the palace of the high priest. He did not refrain from telling them of the bitter memories he had of that spot.

Nearby was Pilate's palace, and Peter showed them the porch on which Pilate faced the crowd of angry Jews calling for Jesus' death. They then walked the road to Golgotha. They stood in silence on Calvary's holy mount.

Peter broke the silence by asserting, "By death Christ has overcome death. Our salvation for eternity has been assured. Satan and the powers of evil and darkness have been conquered." He went on to explain that Christ also went into hell "and preached to the spirits in prison,"[5] proclaiming His triumphant victory over sin and Satan.

Not far from Calvary was the tomb of Joseph of Arimathea. "Of all the places in Jerusalem," said Peter, "this is the place that has the most significance for me. Were it not for this open tomb, everything Jesus did or said would be meaningless."

Revisiting the house where the disciples stayed while awaiting the coming of the Holy Spirit was a wonderful experience for Gaius and Peter. Here Gaius first heard from Peter's lips the Gospel of Jesus Christ. Here Peter received the gift of the Spirit from God appearing as a tongue of fire on each of the disciples. Gaius received the gift of the Spirit through Peter's words spoken on behalf of God.

Gaius and Apphia would have liked to enter the Holy Temple, but not being Jews, they were prohibited. Peter explained as much of it as he could while they walked around it.

Gaius expressed interest also in the other historical places around Jerusalem. Among them was Jericho, the spot where the children of Israel entered Palestine after Joshua had surrounded the city, had the trumpets blown, and the walls fell down; the Dead Sea, where Lot's wife was turned into a pillar of salt as she looked back as the cities of Sodom and Gomorrah were being destroyed; and also again the River Jordan.

Peter took Gaius and Apphia to Bethany to visit Martha and

Mary. While they were glad to see Peter once again, their infirmities kept them from being the gracious hosts they once were. Gaius and Apphia were also taken to the place where Jesus ascended into heaven. Jesus told the disciples He was going to prepare a place for the believers, and then would come again in judgment of all men. He said, "Go into all the world and preach the gospel to every creature. He who believes and is baptized will be saved; but he who does not believe will be condemned."[6] 'He lifted up His hands and blessed them. And it came to pass, while He blessed them, that He was parted from them and carried up into heaven.'[7]

During their last days in Jerusalem, Peter met with church officials. Their economic circumstances had improved in the past few years. They were no longer following the communal arrangements prevalent in the early years of the church. They were particularly thankful for the assistance received from the brethren in Macedonia, Asia, and Achaia several years previously.

Simon the Zealot again discussed with Peter the increased opposition faced by the church. Peter reminded Simon how Jesus told them when he talked about the signs of the times at the end of the age, "You will be hated by all men for My name's sake."[8] Attempting then to strengthen Simon and the rest, Peter added, "But he who endures to the end will be saved."[9]

Gaius meanwhile met with Jude, who gave him his letter and the letter written by James. Gaius arranged with Peter to deliver them back in Ephesus.

Soon the travelers found themselves once again on the road, heading south to Bethlehem. From there, they continued on to Hebron and the desert country of Beersheba. They did not tarry long in any one spot. Now they traveled to Gaza, where Philip was located. This was in the territories of Philistines at the time of David, and they recounted many of the events from the times of the Prophets.

After a short time at Gaza, they continued north along the coast to Joppa, visiting again with James the Less. From there they went along the Plain of Sharon to Caesarea. As they traveled in this area, Peter told them the story of Dorcas of Joppa. He also renewed his acquaintance with Simon, the tanner. As they neared Caesarea, Peter told them the story of the conversion of Cornelius, a centurion, and his household. This was his initiation, he said, in preaching the Gospel to Gentiles. Cornelius, by this time, had been transferred, but Peter visited with other friends in this city. Gaius marveled at the fine port facilities of this city and the wonderful buildings of the Roman government, and sought to make connections to expand his business.

Before leaving Caesarea, Peter related his ongoing association with Cornelius.

"After the conversion of Cornelius and his family," Peter said, "I made it a point to come to Caesarea regularly to minister to these new followers of Jesus. They were interested in increasing their knowledge of the Messiah. Since they knew practically nothing of the ancient history of the Jews, I spent many hours telling them of the writings of the prophets, and gradually introduced them to their holy writings. They eagerly engrossed themselves in these writings.

"Inasmuch as I could not stay permanently in Caesarea, they eventually inquired whether anyone had written anything about the recent history in the life of Jesus Christ. At that time, I had only lately heard that Matthew had started such a project."

"Were you aware of how Matthew came to start writing?" asked Gaius.

"No," said Peter. "I learned the whole story later."

"I was greatly pleased that Matthew wrote as he did," commented Gaius.

"As it turned out," continued Peter, "I became closely associated with John Mark, a young man in our community of believers. I mentioned to him one day that Cornelius expressed his wish to have something of the life of Christ put into writing. He consented to work with me to produce a book. We started slowly, mostly because it seemed as though we were never able to get together to work on it. And so the progress dragged on. When a copy of Matthew's Gospel was brought to Jerusalem, John Mark and I were separated, and the project stalled.

"A year later we started again. My imprisonment interrupted our work, but when I was miraculously rescued, Mark and I went to Antioch to stay with his cousin, Barnabas. After my confrontation with Paul, we returned to Jerusalem. However, Mark returned to Antioch, and went to Cyprus with his cousin and Paul. Upon realizing that he still needed to finish the Gospel, he left them and returned to Jerusalem.

"In the meantime, I learned that the entire Italian Regiment and Cornelius was ordered to return to Rome so that they might be reassigned to a frontier outpost. I then gave a copy of the not-quite-completed Gospel to Cornelius."

"This must have been some time just before Paul first came to Galatia," said Gaius. "I am sure Cornelius was well pleased."

"He was indeed," Peter said, and then added, "Cornelius was influential in spreading the Gospel in the entire regiment."

From Caesarea it was homeward bound. Andrew was waiting in Bethsaida when they arrived. Their journey from one end of the Holy Land to the other was as delightful as Gaius and Apphia expected it to be, and they were thankful to Peter for accompanying them. Their next destination was Damascus. Peter once again bade good-bye to Zelina, and with Andrew departed for Tyre en route to Ephesus and Asia.

On the road to Damascus, Gaius remembered the story Matthew told in his Gospel about what happened at the city of Caesarea Philippi. He decided to go there.

Matthew told it this way: "When Jesus came into the region of Caesarea Philippi, He asked His disciples, saying, 'Who do men say that I, the Son of Man, am?' And they said, 'Some say John the Baptist, some Elijah, and others Jeremiah or one of the prophets.' He said to them, 'But who do you say that I am?' And Simon Peter answered and said, 'You are the Christ, the Son of the Living God.' And Jesus answered and said to him, "Blessed are you, Simon Bar-Jonah, for flesh and blood has not revealed this to you, but My Father who is in heaven.

"'And I also say to you that you are Peter, and on this rock I will build My church, and the gates of Hades shall not prevail against it. And I will give you the keys of the kingdom of heaven, and whatever you bind on earth will be bound in heaven, and whatever you loose on earth will be loosed in heaven.' Then He commanded His disciples that they should tell no one that He was Jesus the Christ."[10]

This portion of the Gospel of Matthew posed a few questions for Gaius. The next part of the Gospel was equally perplexing for Gaius. "From that time on, Jesus began to show to His disciples that He must go to Jerusalem, and suffer many things from the elders and chief priests and scribes, and be killed, and be raised again on the third day. Then Peter took Him aside and began to rebuke Him, saying, 'Far be it from You, Lord; this shall not happen to You!' But he turned and said to Peter, 'Get behind Me, Satan! You are an offense to Me, for you are not mindful of the things of God, but the things of men!"[11]

Gaius was astonished that Jesus could make such a 180-degree turnabout – one minute blessing Peter, and then saying that he was an offense to him.

Gaius said to Apphia, "I am sorry I didn't think of this while we were with Peter so I could have asked him about it."

Apphia replied by saying that when they returned to Ephesus, he could ask John, and promised that she would remind him.

Chapter 11
Fall 59

As Gaius and Apphia were leaving Damascus for Antioch, Apphia asked if they would sail for Ephesus from there.

Sooner or later, Gaius thought to himself, he would have to reveal his plans for this surprise trip to Arachosia – no better time than the present.

When he finished telling her, Apphia exclaimed, "I'm dumbfounded. I had given up ever seeing my homeland again. I think I am going to cry."

Cradling her in his arms, Gaius said, "Go ahead, dear, you have every right to."

Antioch had developed into an important city in the east and west trade. Her nearby port facilities were increasingly used by the caravan traders rather than the overland routes.

When they arrived in Antioch, Gaius learned that a large caravan for the east had just left. There would not be another one for some time. Gaius took advantage of this delay to run up to Derbe. But, there, Gaius had a difficult time finding anyone he knew. Barak was dead, and most of his friends had moved away. Derbe had changed and for the worse.

However, visiting his native city was not the only reason for coming to Derbe. Gaius had made the trip to inquire about the letter Paul had written to the Galatian Christians while he was still in Caesarea. Gaius learned of this letter as he conversed with Philip and James at Nate's anniversary celebration. A few people had heard of the letter, but they could not give Gaius any details.

Back in Antioch, Gaius and Apphia soon departed with a caravan to Apphia's homeland. Caravans did not travel as fast as smaller groups of people, but this was the safest way to go. Apphia had been on a camel several times as a youngster, but riding one was a new experience for Gaius.

They passed through Babylon, crossing over the Euphrates and the Tigris rivers, and then going on to Persepolis by way of Susa. The people here were quite different from any Gaius had known. Thus far on the trip, Apphia did not recognize any landmarks.

From there, the caravan headed for Pura in Gedrosia. Since the caravan's ultimate destination was Pattala on the Indus River in India, Gaius and Apphia left it there and made arrangements to go to Arachosia from Pura.

At Pura, they learned that few people traveled to Arachosia any more. The reason for this was because the native people of Arachosia had been constantly harassed by marauders from the northern hill country. The community's leaders had decided to look for a different place where they might live in more peaceful surroundings. After years of searching, they determined to relocate their entire society to the east. The marauders had retained control of the land, and travelers and strangers were looked upon suspiciously.

At this point, Gaius and Apphia almost lost heart, but since they had come such a long way, they decided to carry on. Upon arrival at their destination of Arachososiorum, they discovered what they had been told was true. Everything was strange to Apphia. The people at this place were all strangers.

Through an interpreter from the group of fellow travelers, Apphia was told that a remnant of former inhabitants of the area lived in a small village nearby. It comprised mostly of elderly persons who did not wish to leave with the others. Gaius and Apphia left immediately for this village. When inquiring about her home village, Apphia was told that the entire village was abandoned. None of the people she talked with knew her family directly. As Apphia continued telling her personal experience, they were amazed. Her abduction and the killing of her family, they told her, was just the beginning of the troubles experienced by their people. These marauders were vicious people with no regard for the dignity of human life. Apphia would dearly have loved to probe deeper into the history of her people, but she felt that since the territory was held by an alien people, she would not take the risk.

Apphia did, however, inquire if anyone knew of a man named Matthew. She breathed a sigh of relief as they told her about him and the message of peace that he brought with him. They said that the entire community had become Christians, and Matthew and his wife left for the new settlement with the rest. A sense of gratification fell on Apphia as she recalled the many hours she spent translating Matthew's Gospel and teaching Matthew her native tongue.

These people described this place of resettlement as a place beyond the two great rivers and the very high mountains. It was a place in a verdant secluded valley far to the east. They also said it was in a region from which much fine silk came. It was called Asim.

Gaius and Apphia then recalled how when Matthew left Derbe for Pontus that he joked slightly about going to the end of the earth. "For Matthew to go to this new settlement," Apphia said to Gaius, "was in reality going to the end of the earth."

Gaius and Apphia began to make plans for their homeward journey. They returned to Pura and waited to join another caravan. A feeling of contentment overtook them as once they were on the way.

The first days of the journey were uneventful. But when the caravan stopped for camp one evening, something totally unexpected happened.

Gaius and Apphia noticed a number of people gathering around one of their fellow travelers. They drew close and discovered to their astonishment that this man was talking to the gathering about Jesus of Nazareth. As the group broke up, Gaius approached this man and was surprised to find that it was Timon, the evangelist. Gaius had heard of Timon when Paul spoke of the life of Stephen, also an evangelist.

Timon explained that he was returning to Palestine. He had been in India with the Apostle Thomas, and they eventually ran into an uprising against them. Thomas was caught by the mob and was slain. Timon said that through the assistance of a faithful native friend, he managed to escape. This meant that he was left alone in India. He was going back to Jerusalem to see if he could get a companion so that the work in India could be resumed. Timon was not deterred by the difficulty he encountered and wanted the evangelizing of India to go on. As this journey continued, the three of them enjoyed fellowship and shared many of their experiences with each other.

When Gaius and Apphia reached Antioch on their homeward journey, Apphia supposed that they would travel directly to Ephesus by ship. Instead, they headed toward Galatia once again. Gaius told her that he wanted to, if at all possible, acquire the letter Paul had written to the churches there for their collection of Paul's letters. He had tried before unsuccessfully.

Stops at Derbe and Lystra did not produce the letter, but he was informed that the letter had been sent around to all the churches. At Iconium they called on Eunice and Nestor. Since Apphia was known to them as a slave, it took a little while for Eunice and Nestor to get used to the idea that she was now Gaius' wife.

As they talked about Paul's letter, Gaius realized that the Galatian Christians were more than a little put out at being called foolish by Paul. This was the reaction of the people wherever the letter was sent. But, Eunice admitted, the stinging tone of the letter was effective. As far as she knew, it was still in the North Country. While Apphia remained in Iconium, Gaius continued his search.

The people at Ancyra told him that they had it over a year before, and then sent it to Germanicopolis. From there Gaius went to Amasea, and finally to Tavium, his last hope. At Tavium, the people marveled that anyone would come that far just to obtain a letter. They told him that it would have been discarded long ago had it not been for the efforts of one elderly man who wanted to keep it. Gaius talked this man into letting him have it.

Returning to Iconium, Gaius and Apphia again discussed the letter with Eunice. It seems the people were having difficulty in understanding all of what Paul had to say. This was especially true of Paul's remarks about the relationship between the promise of God and the Law.

Eunice, herself, did not understand what Paul meant when he wrote, "There is neither Jew nor Greek, there is neither slave nor free, there is neither male nor female; for you are all one in Christ Jesus."[1] Gaius said that he thought in order to understand this verse, one must look forward to the next and the thoughts must not be taken out of context, "and if you are Christ's, then you are Abraham's seed, and heirs according to the promise."[2]

As they were now anxious to return to Ephesus, Gaius and Apphia did not tarry in Iconium. They did not even plan to take time to go to Colossae to visit Philemon.

Chapter 12
Spring 60

Having been gone for such a lengthy time, much news awaited Gaius and Apphia. John still lived in their home teaching Archippus and the other young men who had come to study under him.

Mark kept his promise to bring a copy of his Gospel. John told Mark about Peter going to Palestine with Gaius and Apphia, so Mark stayed close to Ephesus, working in Asia. When Peter finally returned to Ephesus with his brother Andrew, he was reunited with Mark. After a while they went into Cappadocia. Andrew, who had never really shown much interest in studying the Greek language, began studying it in earnest in anticipation of going to Achaia and Macedonia.

Tychicus had come to Ephesus some nine months ago or so, bringing a letter that Paul had written to the church at Ephesus from Rome. Aristarchus, who had come to Rome with Paul and Luke from Caesarea, accompanied Tychicus as far as Crete, and then went on to Thessalonica, his home, from there.

In addition, Tychicus obtained a copy of Paul's letter to the Roman Church written from Athens. He had tried to get the original letter, but Linus, a leader in church, refused to give it up. Linus insisted the letter was intended for them, and they were going to keep it. What's more, Linus told Tychicus that since Rome was the headquarters for the whole empire, he felt that Rome should also be the headquarters for the whole church. He stated flatly that the collection of Paul's letters in Ephesus now in Gaius' library should be turned over to the church in Rome.

After a short stay in Ephesus, Tychicus returned to Rome because he thought that Paul, who was still under house arrest, might need his further assistance, since Luke was the only one permanently with him.

"Tychicus also told me," John said, "that Linus told him that he privately hoped Peter would eventually come to Rome. Linus had read in Matthew's Gospel that Christ said, 'And I also say to you that you are Peter, and on this rock I will build My church.'[1]"

Together Gaius and John looked up the passage in Matthew's sixteenth chapter. Apphia joined them as they did.

"On our journey to Antioch from Galilee," Gaius mentioned to John, "I was reminded of this passage as we passed through Caesarea Philippi. The passage had puzzled me for some time, and I neglected to ask Peter about it while he was with us in the Holy Land."

"At no time," commented John, "did Jesus ever make arrangements for an earthly administration of His church. He repeatedly reiterated that His Kingdom was not of this world.

"When Jesus said, 'On this rock I will build My church,' He was not referring to Peter's person. He was referring to the confident and positive confession that Peter had just made. Jesus wants His church on earth to make a strong confession of His being True God and True Man. It must be recognized that Jesus and His Father are One!

"And, of course, Peter, in what he had said, was pointing to Jesus. Jesus Christ is the Everlasting Rock. Verily, He is the Rock of our salvation, whom the Father has sent into the world."

"That is what I was inclined to believe," Gaius replied, "and I am happy that you have given me reassurance."

"And as I now recall," Apphia inserted, "Matthew wrote in his Gospel about witnessing for Christ, 'Whoever confesses Me before men, him I will also confess before My Father who is in heaven. But whoever denies Me before men, him I will also deny before My Father who is in heaven.'[2]"

"Yes," John said, "and when persecutions come to professing

Christians, they are to remember not to 'fear those who kill the body but cannot kill the soul. But rather fear Him who is able to destroy both soul and body in hell.'[3]"

"I think Peter would be appalled," Gaius continued, "to learn that there are some who are looking upon him as some sort of hierarchical person. All the time Apphia and I were with him in the Holy Land, he never once gave us that impression."

Then John said, "One day the disciples were walking along the road talking among ourselves and disputing which of us would be the greatest. Jesus perceived our thoughts, took a little child and set him by Himself, and said, 'Whoever receives this little child in My name receives Me; and whoever receives Me receives Him who sent Me. For he who is least among you all will be great.'[4]

"I want to share another thought with you," John continued. "I have read Paul's letter from Rome to the church here in Ephesus a number of times, and I find it truly impressive. The first three chapters describe the person of Christ and His redeeming work. The fourth chapter deals with man's relationship to God; and the other two chapters deal with man's relationship to his fellow man. It is actually an explanation of what God's law is all about, when it is stated that the sum of the commandments is that we should first love God with our heart, mind, and soul; and then we should love our neighbor as our self.

"We should recognize that when we are endeavoring to 'keep the unity of the Spirit in the bond of peace,'[5] as Paul mentions in the fourth chapter, that we as humans fall far short of doing just that. So long as we are in the body, we are to look solely to God for true unity. To that end, He sends His Holy Spirit, and gives us 'one hope of your calling, one Lord, one faith, one baptism; one God and Father of all, who is above all, and through all, and in you all.'[6] These are nothing less than His gifts and blessings to us, but imperfect as we are, we should, nevertheless, strive for oneness with each other under our oneness with Him.

"Paul touches on this topic also in his first letter to the church at Corinth when he writes, 'Now I plead with you, brethren, by the name of our Lord Jesus Christ, that you all speak the same thing, and that there be no divisions among you, but that you be perfectly joined together in the same mind and in the same judgment.'[7] It is a matter of being objective, rather than being subjective."

"There is another item we would like you to explain," said Apphia. "How is it that Matthew writes that Jesus blesses Peter as he makes his confession, and then soon afterward says that Peter is an offense to Him when Peter wanted to deter Jesus from going to Jerusalem to die?"

"Before we can understand everything Jesus meant by doing that," John answered, "we must realize that Jesus added, 'You are not mindful of the things of God, but the things of men.'[8] Our thoughts are not God's thoughts.

"There are other times when Jesus speaks in this manner. Jesus once said, 'Do not think that I have come to bring peace on earth. I did not come to bring peace but a sword.'[9] What He says seems contradictory to us. Jesus clarifies somewhat when he adds, 'He who loves father or mother more than Me is not worthy of Me. And he who loves son or daughter more than Me is not worthy of Me. And who does not take his cross and follow after Me is not worthy of Me. He who finds his life will lose it, and he who loses his life for My sake will find it.'[10] Jesus wants our total commitment.

"Luke approaches the topic from the opposite direction. He writes, 'If anyone comes to Me and does not hate his father and mother, wife and children, brothers and sisters, yes, and his own life also, he cannot be My disciple.'[11]"

"But," John concluded, "'how are we to understand the word

hate? That Love Himself should be commanding what we ordinarily mean by hatred – commanding us to cherish resentment, to gloat over another's misery, to delight in injuring him – is almost a contradiction in terms. I think Our Lord, in the sense here intended, "hated" Saint Peter when he said, "Get thee behind me.'[12]"

"What you are saying then, John," said Gaius, "is that we should 'fear, love, and trust God above all things.'[13]"

"Exactly," said John. "'So, in the last resort, we must turn down or disqualify our nearest and dearest when they come between us and our obedience to God.'[14]"

"It is comforting to me to know all you have just explained," Gaius said. "Quite frankly, when I sit and read the Gospels and the things Paul writes, I am overpowered by not only a sense of awe, but also a feeling of inadequacy on my part. Despite an honest effort to understand what is written, there is so much that just seems to pass over my head. I value very highly every explanation of the Word of God that you give."

"I was going to mention one more facet of Paul's letter to the Ephesians," John replied. "But it is a rather intriguing and deep subject."

"We are willing to listen, as always," Gaius and Apphia assured him.

"It is about what Paul says at the end of his letter," John began, "about putting on the whole armor of God. Paul has on occasion mentioned the enemies of the Gospel that he has encountered."

"These have primarily been the Jews?" asked Gaius.

"Yes," John continued, "but this refers to something altogether different. I have not read anything in his letters that has been as strong as this. Of course, the devil is behind all this opposition. He does not stop at anything.

"We need to look very carefully at what Paul writes, 'For we do not wrestle against flesh and blood, but against principalities, against powers, against the rulers of the darkness of this age, against spiritual wickedness in heavenly places.'[15]

"The devil will incite evil against God's church and His apostles and teachers. This evil will come from every strata of society. What is even more insidious is that it even will come from within the church itself.

"From what Tychicus told us of his experience at Rome with Linus, this ugliness has already appeared. There is much more about this development that, at present, lies beneath the surface; and I am sure we will learn more of it as time passes."

"It surely sounds mysterious," Gaius commented.

A week later, John called Gaius to his room to show him the scrolls that comprised his Gospel. "As you know, Onesimus and Tychicus suggested to me that I also write the Gospel; to complement those of Matthew, Mark, and Luke. I worked on it while you were away and have recently finished it. I would like to have you read it to see what you think of it. You will be the first to do so."

"I am honored," Gaius replied. "I shall be happy to comply with your request, not that I am a great critic. Apphia excels at that sort of thing."

"If you wish, have her join you in reading it."

That very evening Gaius and Apphia began reading John's Gospel. About a week later, they sat down with John to discuss his Gospel.

"At the outset," Gaius began, "Apphia and I want to say that we thoroughly enjoyed reading what you have written. Both of us have read it several times. For myself, I was very impressed with the way you stressed Christ's relationship to His Father. I wonder if you mind telling us the reason for this strong accent."

"I am pleased," John replied, "that you mentioned this as your first comment. This emphasis was done purposefully. Whenever I visited the churches in Asia and elsewhere, there were always these reports of Jews steadfastly harassing the churches. In addition, as I talked with Paul and others, they reminded me that they continuously encountered opposition from the Jews. In fact, the Jews had become so obstinate toward Paul's preaching in Corinth that Paul even vowed that, henceforth, he would preach only to the Gentiles. And you are personally aware of the resentment toward Christ displayed by them in Galatia.

"No doubt you notice from my story that Jesus met with the same reaction by the Jews. Jesus tried to break down their resistance by pointing out His relationship to His Father. The Jews had a long history of experiences with God the Father. After all, the Nation of Israel was God's chosen people. By convincing them of His Oneness with the Father, Jesus hoped to win them; but they closed their ears.

"By reviewing all that Jesus had said to the Jews of His time, I, too, hoped one more time to convince at least some of them that Jesus is truly the Christ. Then, too, this fact must also be emphasized among the new believers."

"It seems to me," Gaius said, "that you have expanded on my knowledge of the dimension of God. God is spoken of as The Father, The Son – Jesus, and The Holy Spirit. But this all seems so complex. Perhaps you would like to enlighten us further on this subject."

"Gladly. God is indeed comprised of three distinct persons as you say – Father, Son, and Spirit. They may rightly be called 'The Holy Trinity.' This does not mean there are three Gods. There is One God. God is One.

"Paul alludes to the Trinity in his letter to the Ephesians in chapter four, verses 4-6, and Matthew states at the end of his Gospel that baptism is to be performed in the name of the Father, Son, and Holy Spirit.

"The Father is the Creator of all things. Without Him there is not anything made that was made. The Son was begotten of the Father from eternity. The Father sent Him to earth to redeem sinful men who had rebelled against God by following the devil, and had become a lost and condemned people. The Holy Spirit proceeds from the Father and the Son. He strengthens, quickens, and sanctifies all those who are members of the Body of Christ; that is, all those who by faith have come to know Jesus as their Savior from sin. The Holy Spirit, Himself, creates faith in the hearts of men.

"When Jesus is quoted as saying, 'I and the Father are One,'[16] He is saying that they each have the same substance. Since the Holy Spirit proceeds from them, He also is the same substance. Paul states it nicely when in his letter to the congregation at Colossae he writes, 'For in Him (Christ) dwells all the fullness of the Godhead bodily.'[17] As this is all above our reasoning ability, we must accept it in faith. We will understand more fully when we enter into eternal bliss."

Apphia remarked, "I cannot help saying, John, that the language you use vividly brings out the message you are giving. This is especially true in the dialogues you write. I made a list of the various ways Jesus describes Himself. They are all lovely. True Vine, Good Shepherd, Door of the Sheep, Light of the World, Bread from Heaven, Living Water, and Resurrection of the Life, all paint an endearing picture of Jesus."

"And don't forget 'The Way, the Truth, and the Life,'[18]" John added. "This sums up, I believe, the entire ministry of Jesus. It can also be used as an allegorical description of the Holy Trinity. The Father is the Way – He has the entire world in His hand; The Son is the Lord of Life – He assures us eternal life; and the Holy Spirit is Truth – He leads us into all truth as He creates faith in our heart. God's Word is Truth."

"John," Apphia then added, "my favorite story is the one about Nicodemus. Jesus makes quick work of his apparent naiveté in regard to being born again. Whereas Nicodemus related being born again to things physical, Jesus makes it plain that being born again is solely the operation of the Holy Spirit. I like that. We cannot by our own reason or strength come to faith; we cannot on our own make a determined decision to be a dedicated follower of Jesus.

"It is the Holy Spirit who came to Gaius on Pentecost day so long ago as he listened to Peter preach the Word. And the Holy Spirit entered my heart as I read God's Word, which Matthew had written.

"Before I am finished, I want to add that the passage in this story that most impressed me was 'For God so loved the world that He gave His only begotten Son, that whoever believes in Him should not perish but have everlasting life!'[19] This, it seems to me, is the Gospel in a nutshell."

"An astute observation, Apphia," John replied. "And may I say, we must never tire of doing everything within our means to proclaim this very Gospel."

"John," Gaius said, "I believe your Gospel is excellent in supplementing the Gospels of Matthew, Mark, and Luke. What you write truly evokes one to think. And that is good. Studying God's Word should be a regular part of one's life.

"I've been thinking about one particular chapter in your Gospel, the one where Jesus prays to His Father in Heaven. He not only prays for Himself, but also for those whom the Father has given to Him, you and the other apostles, and then his disciples and all believers.

"You write, 'That they may be one as We are,'[20] and again, 'That they all may be one, as You, Father, are in Me, and I in You; that they also may be one in Us, that the world may believe that You have sent Me.'[21] and again, 'That they may be one just as We are one.'[22]

"I know that Christ's kingdom is not an earthly kingdom, but rather a heavenly one. Yet, as you write, while we still live, we are in the world. We have human relationships – to those of the faith as well as to those not of the faith. How does what you write affect those relationships?"

"As I reminded Apphia, while we are in the world, we have the task of taking the Gospel to the entire world. One way is by preaching. Another way is by fulfilling the new commandment given to us by Christ, which I mention in another part of my Gospel – 'A new commandment I give to you, that you love one another; as I have loved you, that you also love one another. By this all will know that you are My disciples, if you have love for one another.'[23] And, of course, love embraces obeying Jesus in what He has taught us. Living a sanctified life is another way. We are to let our light shine among men that they may see our good works and glorify the Heavenly Father.

"A fourth way is the way mentioned in the portion quoted by you. When Jesus prayed that all believers be one, as He and the Father are one, He was praying for a spiritual oneness among the believers. The Father and the Son are One in Spirit. All believers should be spiritual one by faith. They are to be of one mind in Christ.

"As I wrote in another portion, 'God is Spirit, and those who worship Him must worship Him in spirit and truth.'[24] Anyone who does not worship God in this manner is not 'One' with God; and it follows that he is not 'one' with the true believers.

"When I say that the believers should be of one mind in Christ, I mean that in their walk together as Christians, they should all agree. Amos, the Old Testament prophet, puts it this way, 'Can two walk together except they be agreed?'[25]

"Some may attempt to relate this spiritual oneness in Christ to things that pertain to earthly matters, but that is not what is meant in Jesus' prayer. Verse 21 of the 17th chapter of my Gospel should not be interpreted to read, 'that they all may be one <u>with each other</u>,[26] as you, Father, are in Me, and I in You,' but rather, 'that they all may be one 'in me,' as You, Father, are in Me, and I in You.'"

"This is all very enlightening," Gaius replied. "Apphia and I thank you for your explanations."

A few days later, Apphia came to John privately. She told him that as she listened to him discuss the confident and positive confession of Peter, the thought struck her that the church should have such a confession of faith as they gathered for worship. Consequently, she said, she had composed just such a confession.

She handed John a slip of paper. On it were the words:
> "I believe in God the Father Almighty, Maker of heaven and earth.
>
> "And in Jesus Christ, His only Son; who was conceived by the Holy Ghost, Born of the Virgin Mary; Suffered under Pontius Pilate, was crucified, dead, and buried; He descended into hell; The third day He arose again from the dead; He ascended into heaven and sitteth on the right hand of God the Father Almighty; From thence He shall come to judge the quick and the dead.
>
> "I believe in the Holy Ghost; The holy Christian Church; The forgiveness of sins; The resurrection of the body; and the life everlasting. Amen."

Having finished reading what Apphia had written, John thoughtfully commented, "Apphia, this is splendid. You have said everything that needs to be said in a statement of our Christian faith. I would make only one small addition. The phrase, 'The holy Christian Church,' I believe, needs amplification. The insertion of the clause 'the communion of saints' should do it."

Gaius was in the yard, and John called to him to come in. As he did, John said, "Look what your wife has written. At the next church council meeting we can present it for consideration."

When Gaius finished reading it, Apphia spoke up, "But won't it make a difference to them that it was written by a woman?"

"Not in the least," chided John. "This is a sincere confession of faith. If anyone wishes to try to do better, let them. When we present it, we will not state who wrote it. But if anyone questions the authorship, we will tell them."

In the weeks following, Gaius again focused his attention to matters of operating his businesses.

Chapter 13
Fall 59

By the time Tychicus returned to Rome, Onesimus was no longer there. Paul had written another letter to Timothy, which Onesimus was delivering.

Paul had had a preliminary hearing (he called it his first defense), and no one stood with him. Now, inasmuch as he was unsure when he would be heard by Caesar, he wanted another opportunity to reassure Timothy in his ministry.

The uncertainty surrounding his presence in Rome also brought disparaging thoughts to Paul. The loss of the support of many friends around him gave him a forsaken feeling. Only Luke remained with him. Therefore, Paul desired Timothy to come to Rome as quickly as possible.

Paul also wanted Timothy to bring Mark. He instructed Timothy to go to Troas to pick up the cloak that he left with Carpus, as winter soon would be coming and Paul wanted to be prepared. Likewise, some of those in Rome suggested to him that perhaps as possible punishment, he may be banished to a place called Britain, a place said to be cold and damp. Timothy was also to bring the books, especially the parchments. These were things Paul would have taken care of himself, had he made the trip to Philippi, as he had hoped when he was in prison at Caesarea.

Onesimus noted the sense of urgency in Paul's letter. As far as was known, Timothy was at Philippi, so Onesimus planned to sail to Crete. From there he could go directly to Philippi, bypassing Ephesus or Athens altogether. He made good connections, and arrived in Philippi without undue delay.

Timothy was in Philippi as presumed, but Mark was nowhere

in the vicinity. As Timothy felt it necessary that he should bring someone with him, he thought first of Silas. He directed Onesimus to go to Troas to pick up Paul's possessions. In the meantime, he would journey to Thessalonica to get Silas. After receiving an explanation from Timothy, Silas, who was in Berea and not Thessalonica, agreed to return with him. His wife came with him.

Before they left, Onesimus asked Timothy if he still had the first letter Paul had written to him. He was thinking of the collection of Paul's letters being made by Gaius. Timothy said he had it, so they changed their return trip plans so they could drop Paul's letters to Timothy off at Ephesus. In three weeks the four of them were on their way to Rome.

Meanwhile, there was no progress in the hearing with Caesar. Paul's accusers were not showing up. Apparently, it was going to take as long to get a hearing in Rome as it did in Caesarea.

Since his arrival in Rome, Paul had met with the leaders of the Jews. He explained everything about his troubles with those Jews in Jerusalem, and said that he was compelled to appeal to Caesar. Paul had his own house, guarded only by one soldier. The Jews came there to listen to Paul expound the teaching of Jesus. Having told them that the Gospel was also for the Gentiles, the Jews disputed among themselves. Some believed what Paul had said, but most did not.

But Paul continued preaching with all confidence the kingdom of God and teaching the things which concern the Lord Jesus Christ. And he received all who came to him.

One of those who sought and found Paul in Rome was Onesiphorus, a man from Philippi who had aided him in Ephesus, and came with Onesimus and Tychicus. Apollos also came from the Cisalpine Gaul provinces. He had gone there after spending only a short time in Rome. The Jews in Rome were similar to those in Corinth, and would not listen to him. Then, too, the loose living of the

Roman citizens did not appeal to him. So he set out to do mission work in Genua and Luca. He eventually helped to spread the Gospel by lecturing throughout the provinces.

The main purpose of his coming to Rome to see Paul was to show him a treatise he had written. The constant harassment of the believing Jews by the unbelieving Jews worried him. He was thinking primarily of those Jews in Corinth and Ephesus, and now also in Rome. He wanted to do something to help these Christians.

Paul read the treatise with great care, and complimented Apollos on his work. They discussed it openly and frankly at great length. "Jesus," Apollos said the Jews told him, "did not come to start a religion. It was, they said, Paul who was perpetrating a new religion. 'For Jesus only unwittingly laid the foundation for a new religion by an excessive emphasis upon certain radical Jewish ideas – and no more; only by his unnatural death as a suffering Messiah did he become the authoritative source upon which depended a new religion.'[1]"

Apollos told him, "They say that you, Paul, used this event as a springboard to launch a new religion and brought it about by compromise. 'For compromise between Judaism and Hellenism, between Israel and paganism, is the foundation and basis of all Christianity – not the compromise of Jesus, but that of Paul . . . If it had not been for this compromise, the Gentiles would not have accepted a purely Jewish doctrine at all.'[2]

"The foundation of your compromising teaching arises from four sources of Hellenistic thought. These sources of Hellenistic thought come from the writings of Philo Judeaus of Alexandria, mainly the 'Sibylline Oracles' and 'The Wisdom of Solomon.' Through you, Paul, 'Christianity borrowed much from Philo.'[3] Among the ideas borrowed by you, they say, is his idea of 'Logos,' and, they say, you introduced the idea of Son of god (Logos-Messiah) and later as God-man, who is one of the three members of the half-pagan trinity.

Another thing borrowed from Philo is biblical allegory. Finally, Philo was also the source of your idea of grace.

"The fourth book of Maccabees, they say, also provided you with one of the foundations of your teaching. 'The Jews interpret Isaiah 53 ... as applying to the nation of Israel which was persecuted by the other peoples. In that way he 'bore their pains and carried their sorrows' and 'they were healed by his stripes'; and thus he, Israel, 'bore the sins of many.'[4] The nation of Israel, by the way, is claimed by them to be masculine. Propitiary suffering of the individual is not strong in ancient Judaism; but Christianity through you, they say, applies Isaiah 53 to Jesus as a ransom."

Apollos continued, "'In spite of this Judaistic world view of Philo, Judaism does not accept him, but Christianity does accept him – this Christianity which sets aside the ceremonial laws makes the Messiah a deity, and removes from its teaching Jewish national separateness and all the territorial and nationalistic aspirations contained in the Jewish Messianic conception.'[5]

"They say," Apollos added, "'In other words, the views of Paul are stamped with the religious syncretism which prevailed at that time, when a flood of Oriental religions came into the West, and a mixture of Occidental – Greek and Roman – religions penetrated into the East.'[6] You took advantage of this religious upheaval by producing a Christianity which in 'no very long time became a half-Jewish, half-pagan faith.'[7]

"You must remember, they said, that 'Judaism also knows redemption from death – but only by The Torah.'[8] And you 'must understand that, for a Jew, The Torah always and in all times is inseparable from the ceremonial laws.'[9]

"And also the leaders in Jerusalem," Apollos said, "are aware of the disciples questioning Jesus about Jewish nationalism when they asked, 'Lord, will You at this time restore the kingdom of Israel?'[10]

Jesus, they said, shrugged off this question, so 'there is here a clear indication that shortly after the crucifixion the disciples of Jesus decided to give up the politico-national Messianic conception of the Jews, which involved a certain danger in the Roman Empire on account of its revolutionary implications, and to devote themselves solely to the propagation of the primitive Christian Messianic idea, which was abstract, mystical, and entirely spiritual.'[11]"

Paul explained to Apollos that he had heard most of those arguments and had vigorously defended himself. "The Jews," Paul said, "are letting imagination get the better of them. Philo Judaeus played no part whatsoever in the formulation of the message I preach.

"I realize," said Paul, "that you did not have any way of knowing what I wrote to the churches of Galatia, so I will repeat what was written to them. 'But I make known to you, brethren, that the Gospel, which was preached by me, is not according to man. For I neither received it from man, nor was I taught it, but it came by the revelation of Jesus Christ. For you have heard of my former conduct in Judaism, how I persecuted the church of God beyond measure and tried to destroy it. And I advanced in Judaism beyond many of my contemporaries in my own nation, being more exceedingly zealous for the traditions of my fathers. But when it pleased God, who had separated me from my mother's womb and called me by His grace, to reveal His Son in me that I might preach Him among the Gentiles, I did not immediately confer with flesh and blood.'[12]

"And apparently," Paul continued, "the Jews are not aware of how Peter was told by Jesus that he was a Rock and that upon this Rock, He would build His church. Jesus was pleased with the strong confession of his faith in Him which Peter had just made.

"As far as Isaiah's 53rd chapter is concerned," Paul said, "Luke relates it quite clearly in his chronicle of The Acts of the Apostles which he is currently writing. As told by Peter, Philip the evangelist

'Preached Jesus' to the eunuch of Ethiopia when explaining to him about this chapter. This all took place about the same time as my conversion on the Damascus road."

Paul told Apollos that the Jews were being pig-headedly stubborn. They went over the entire document point by point, and Apollos carefully noted everything that Paul said.

Paul questioned Apollos about his strong emphasis on the 'Once for all' sacrifice of Jesus, saying that this occurs five times in chapters seven, nine, and ten. Paul quoted Apollos, "For such a High Priest was fitting for us, who is holy, harmless, undefiled, separate from sinners, and has become higher than the heavens; who does not need daily, as those high priests, to offer sacrifices, first for His own sins and then for the people's, for this He did once for all when He offered up Himself."[13]

Apollos replied that in his discussions with the Christians in Rome, some were of the opinion that the sacrament of the Lord's Supper instituted by Christ on the night of His betrayal was to be thought of as a continuing sacrifice. Paul answered that if this were so, his treatment of the subject was quite sufficient to dispel any doubt. And, Paul added, he would keep alert to see if he could detect the source of this erroneous concept.

Paul then suggested to Apollos that he should include in his treatise a portion pertaining to faith. The Scriptures were full of examples of the faith of many people – Abel, Enoch, Abraham, Sarah, Isaac, Jacob, Joseph, Moses, and, yes, by faith even the harlot Rahab, who received the spies with peace at the time of the fall of Jericho, did not perish with those who did not believe.

Apollos asked Paul if he would give a concise definition of the word 'faith.'

Paul replied, "Faith is the substance of things hoped for, the evidence of things not seen."[14]

Apollos then returned to Luca to rework his treatise, and to bid farewell to his friends in the area. He planned to return to his native Alexandria after first visiting the churches in Corinth and Ephesus.

The coming of Timothy and Silas greatly renewed Paul's spirit. But when Silas told him of the conditions of the congregation at Thessalonica, Paul was troubled. Silas told Paul that some were walking in a disorderly manner, not working at all, but were busybodies.

Paul would write them another letter calling them to task. Furthermore, he would write to them about something that had begun to weigh more heavily upon his mind as he stayed on in Rome, something he had spoken to them about in his last visit with them.

He wrote, "Now we ask you, brethren, by the coming of our Lord Jesus Christ and our gathering together to Him, that you not be soon shaken in mind or be troubled, neither by spirit, nor by word, nor by letter, as if from us, as though the day of Christ had come. Let no one deceive you by any means; for that Day will not come unless the falling away comes first; and the man of sin is revealed, the son of perdition, who opposes and exalts himself above all that is called God or that is worshipped, so that he sits as God in the temple of God, showing himself that he is God.

"Do you not remember that when I was still with you, I told you these things? And now you know what is restraining, that he may be revealed in his own time. For the mystery of lawlessness is already at work; only He who now restrains will do so until He is taken out of the way. And then the lawless one will be revealed, whom the Lord will consume with the breath of his mouth and destroy with the brightness of His coming.

"The coming of the lawless one is according to the working of Satan with all power, signs, and lying wonders, and with all deception of unrighteousness in those who perish, because they did not receive the love of the truth, that they might be saved. And for this reason, God will send them strong delusion, that they should believe the lie, that they all might be condemned who did not believe the truth but had pleasure in unrighteousness."[15]

The salutation of Paul was written with his own hand, a sign in every epistle. The letter was kept in Rome until someone could be spared to deliver it.

There was still no indication from Roman officials when a hearing might take place. Paul continued to stay in his house. Silas was sent by Paul to Puteoli to preach the Word and to minister to the brethren there. Timothy and Onesimus made a trip to Luca to look in on Apollos. They stayed two months and became acquainted with many of the friends of Apollos.

While they were in Luca, Apollos decided to return to Rome with them. His treatise was again complete, and Apollos wanted to have Paul reread it. Paul did and gave his approval of it. Apollos continued on in Rome, wanting to offer his support to Paul.

Meanwhile, Luke also remained in Rome close to Paul. He worked at putting the finishing touches on the journal he had kept of The Acts of the Apostles. This he had been doing at the request of Theophilus of Athens.

As Paul was more or less confined to his house, he relied on Tychicus and Onesimus to do his errands. They became well acquainted with the city of Rome in this way. Apollos and Timothy also spent much time in the city.

One day as Timothy and Apollos made their way along a crowded street, they were jostled by a few playful boys. Timothy lost his balance and bumped into another man. This man happened to be a Roman Senator. The Senator lost no time in having Timothy arrested for having insulted his dignity.

Timothy, being a Greek, was treated with respect. An ordinary citizen would have been treated more harshly. As his interrogation continued, however, it revealed that Timothy was a member of this new obnoxious sect in the city, and Timothy was given a short jail sentence. And he was ordered to leave the country within one month after his release.

While Timothy was still in prison, Paul received word that his hearing with Caesar would be held in two weeks. It was now almost two years since Paul first arrived in Rome.

Paul and his friends, including Eubulus, Pudens, Linus, and Claudia of Rome, met to talk about the possibilities for their future. His own future, he admitted, truly appeared to be foreboding. He expressed the desire that they all remain strong in the faith regardless of the outcome of the hearing.

Luke and Onesimus told Paul they would stand by him at his hearing. Arrangements were made to have Tychicus leave immediately for Puteoli and take along Paul's letter to the church at Thessalonica. He was also to carry with him Luke's 'The Acts of the Apostles' for delivery to Theophilus at Athens. Apollos, who was not yet ready to leave Rome, asked Tychicus to also take with him his treatise to the Hebrews. He wanted it to be delivered to the believing Jews at Corinth, and told Tychicus that it was also intended for the Jews at Ephesus. Silas, who was still in Puteoli, was to be given the latest news of what was happening in regard to Paul's hearing before Caesar.

Apollos was staying in Rome to await Timothy's release from prison, so they could leave together. Timothy was freed in a week, but when he told Apollos that he wanted to stay in Rome long enough to learn the results of the hearing, Apollos left without him, saying that he would wait for him in Puteoli.

When Apollos arrived in Puteoli, Tychicus was still there. His ship would sail the next day. Apollos hastily added a few more closing remarks to his treatise. He told of the latest news of Timothy and extended greetings of those Jews in Italy.

In the morning of the appointed day, Paul's guard escorted Paul and Luke and Onesimus to the building where the hearing was to take place. They waited – and waited. Noon came and went, but there was still no sign of Nero. At three o'clock Nero arrived. The case ahead of Paul's took only fifteen minutes.

Paul, Luke, and Onesimus were then ushered in. Nero was sitting on the dais. To his left were the court officials. At his right side was his woman companion with her retinue behind her.

The court clerk read the charges. This was done because the accusing Jews from Jerusalem did not put in an appearance, and Nero wanted to clear the docket. When he finished, Paul was told to present his defense. Just as he had done before Felix, Festus, and King Agrippa, Paul told his side of the story of his struggle with the Jews at Jerusalem. Everyone was quiet when Paul finished, and he remained where he was standing. Finally, the clerk approached Paul and asked him if he had completed his testimony. When Paul indicated that he had, the clerk told him to take a few steps backward.

Nero spoke, "If my ears do not deceive me, you claim to be a Jew and also a Roman citizen. I have never heard of such a ridiculous thing. It is impossible for a Jew to be a Roman citizen. By doing so, you have displayed unbelievable arrogance, and are an enemy of the state. You are hereby stripped of the citizenship."

Paul attempted to object, but Nero shouted, "SILENCE!" He continued, "The beloved Claudius some years back banished all Jews from Rome, but now they persist in returning to our fair city. We shall put an end to that. Paul, you are guilty as charged, and I, Nero, sentence you to die."

By his irrational decision, it was apparent to everyone that Nero wanted to make an example of Paul.

Gasping with shock, Luke jumped forward so that the sergeant-at-arms had to restrain him. Luke demanded to be heard as a witness, even though he knew well that it probably would be of no avail. The clerk insisted that he return to his place, but Nero intervened.

"No, no," said Nero. "If he wants to speak, let him."

"My name is Luke; I am from Asia; I have known the condemned man, Paul, for many years; he is not deserving of the sentence you have meted out. But, if you cannot be persuaded to reverse your decision, I offer myself for punishment in his stead so that he may continue to live.

"If it is your wish to grant this humble request, our friend with us here will be needed to be a companion to Paul, to be with him wherever you may send him, because of Paul's infirmities." In saying this, Luke was thinking more of Paul's circumstances rather than of Onesimus, hoping that Onesimus would not be disagreeable.

Nero leaned toward his lady friend and whispered, "Did you hear what this fool said? This idiot has lost his head and gone mad. When he answers after I ask him to repeat what he said, I want you and your ladies to let go with a sustained guffaw. Stop when I signal."

Nero waited a short time for the ladies to pass the word, and then asked Luke to repeat himself. Luke did and the ladies all laughed hilariously.

Having signaled them to stop, Nero gleefully announced, "You shall have your wish; any fool who loses his head and goes mad by making such an offer as you did deserves to literally lose his head. Let the guards take him out and obey my decree."

As they led Luke away to be executed, Nero instructed the court clerk to see to it that Paul and his friend be placed on the next ship leaving Ostia bound for Britain and exile.

Onesimus was allowed to go under guard to Paul's house to gather his belongings. During this time, he also reported to Timothy what had happened.

Once Timothy knew the results of the hearing, he also sorrowfully

left for Puteoli. Wanting to leave as quickly as possible, Timothy did not even tell Eubulus or the rest of Paul's friends the outcome of the hearing.
    Timothy and Apollos then sailed from Puteoli for Achaia and Asia.

Chapter 14
Spring 61

As Peter and Mark had been in Cappadocia and Pontus for some time, they were contemplating spending more time in Galatia and Bithynia. To their surprise Nathaniel and Matthias appeared in Cappadocia. Both of these apostles had spent much of their ministry in Africa, so laboring in this area was a great change for them. Peter arranged introductions throughout the territory for these fellow workers in the kingdom. Soon Peter and Mark left for Bithynia.

Not long after their arrival, news of the tragic events occurring in Rome reached them. Peter's first reaction to the news was that the church had suffered a great setback. Mark agreed with Peter that the consequence of these events would be far reaching, and that the preaching of the Gospel would be done in ever-greater peril.

The report they received did not contain full details, so Peter and Mark decided to go to Troas to find out more. There Carpus told them everything he knew, adding that if they still wanted more information, they would have to go to Philippi. Timothy, he said, had returned to Philippi from Rome after having gone there to be with Paul. However, he got into trouble with the government, and he was told to leave the country.

When Peter and Mark met with Timothy in Philippi, he related everything to them. It was considerably more than Peter expected. Timothy, it seemed, had been reluctant to tell the whole story. Carpus did not even know that Luke had lost his life.

Peter at once asked, "But who is left in Rome and Italy to serve the brethren?"

Timothy answered that as far as he knew, Silas was the only one still in Italy, and that he was at Puteoli. Peter considered it a shame no one was in Rome, and indicated that perhaps he should go there.

Timothy cautioned Peter to weigh everything carefully before making a commitment. "The Roman government has taken an opposing attitude toward the preaching of the Gospel. They looked upon the Christians as an obnoxious sect determined to undermine their society. At his hearing, Paul was called an enemy of the state by Nero. This was not only because Paul was preaching the Gospel, but because he was a Jew. The emperor has let it be known that he will be intolerant toward Jews in Rome."

"Nevertheless," Peter said, "the Christians in Rome need our support."

When Timothy saw that he was not dissuading Peter in his thoughts of going to Rome, he asked that Peter consult John at Ephesus.

"That would be the sensible thing to do," said Mark.

"Perhaps you're right," Peter replied. "But before we do, I want to visit Andrew and see how he is doing."

Peter and Mark were soon on their way to visit the churches in Asia. At Philadelphia, Peter found his brother. Andrew was preaching in Asia for a time prior to leaving for Macedonia. Now, however, he decided to go to Ephesus with Peter and Mark.

They arrived in Ephesus in due course and were warmly received by Gaius and John. Peter remarked how good it was to return to this place where he felt so welcome.

Timothy had talked to Peter and Mark about Gaius making a collection of Paul's letters, and they mentioned this to Gaius. Gaius showed them his entire collection of the four Gospels, the letters of Jude and James, Paul's twelve letters, Apollos' treatise, and Luke's account of the 'The Acts of the Apostles.'

Gaius explained that when Tychicus returned from Italy, he came first to Ephesus with Paul's second letter to the church at Thessalonica, and the works of Apollos and Luke. They made copies of them before Tychicus continued on his way to deliver them. Peter, Andrew, and Mark then read the latest additions to Gaius' collection. These writings made a favorable impression on them. But when Peter finished reading Paul's letter to the churches of Galatia, he regretted that he had not spent more time there. He added that since Crescens was alone in Galatia, someone might suggest to Timothy that he return to his native province.

Peter and Andrew and Mark were also shown the confession of faith that Apphia had drawn up. John told them that the congregation at Ephesus had adopted it as their confession. Peter commented on its fine quality and stated that it could well serve as a confession of all the apostles and the whole church. It could well be called 'The Apostolic Creed.'

In time, Peter brought up the main reason for his coming to Ephesus. Gaius and John agreed with Timothy when Peter told them what he had said.

"You would just be heading into a hornet's nest were you to go to Rome," said John.

Gaius added, "Nero sounds like a very irrational person. The kind of person his own mother could not trust."

As Gaius and John presented further evidence that Peter should not go to Rome, it seemed as if Peter became more and more determined to ignore their warning. Finally, Peter told them he wanted to give it more thought. But as he and Mark talked it over between themselves, they made up their minds. They would go to Rome.

What convinced Peter more than anything else was what Paul had written in his second letter to the congregation at Thessalonica. Paul, he thought, must have found out something about this 'man of sin'[1] while he was in Rome. And his statement, 'The mystery of lawlessness is already at work'[2] really intrigued him.

"What was your impression of Paul's letters as you read them?" Peter asked Mark.

"Paul certainly does not hesitate to say what's on his mind, does he?"

"You're right about that," answered Peter.

"It seems to me," added Mark, "that Paul has the knack of putting his finger on what needs to be said."

"You're also right about that, and do not hesitate to say that I, too, could write in such a fine fashion. His work is top-notch."

"Style is not always everything," Mark replied. "What is being said is of greater importance; not that the contents of Paul's letters are unimportant."

"Well," concluded Peter, "I would certainly like to write a letter to the congregations where I served."

Gaius learned of Peter's wish and provided him with materials. Once they were on the ship bound for Italy and Rome, Peter, with the help and encouragement of Mark, began to write a letter to his churches.

Peter's letter was nearly complete when they arrived in Puteoli. Once ashore, Peter and Mark sought out Silas. Silas was surprised and delighted to once again see Peter and Mark. He could not believe that they actually wanted to go to Rome, where the Roman government was increasingly opposed to the preaching done by the Christian sect. Silas related tales of church meetings and worship services being watched in Puteoli.

When Peter would not be persuaded to refrain from going to Rome, Silas reluctantly agreed to be their guide.

He took Peter and Mark to the home of Eubulus, a leader in the church at Rome. Silas felt uneasy, and stayed only long enough for Peter to finish his letter. Silas left and took Peter's letter with him. He wanted to leave Italy as soon as possible, so he and his wife left for Asia almost immediately.

As Peter and Mark continued to stay in Rome, Eubulus told them of a visit of the leaders in the churches in the Cisalpine Gaul provinces. They had no one to preach to them since Apollos left. Eubulus told Peter he had to send them back empty handed, which he hated to do. When Peter asked Eubulus about the conditions for preaching in the north, he assured Peter that the government harassment there was almost unknown. Upon learning this, Peter and Mark conferred, and soon Mark left for the north in the company of Cletus, a young man provided by Eubulus.

The Roman military knew immediately of Peter's arrival in Rome. Eubulus' home was under surveillance. Any sign of a meeting or preaching activity would be a cause for a raid. Had they known that Peter was Jewish, they would have arrested him on the spot.

After Mark left, Eubulus abandoned his residence for security reasons. Peter moved with Eubulus, and after being in Rome for a while, he wondered if he would ever get a chance to preach and meet with the other members of the church. At last Eubulus arranged a meeting with Pudens, Linus, and Claudia. They, too, were being watched by soldiers, and even a meeting with them was risky.

The meeting took place in secret late at night. Peter expressed his anguish about meeting this way, but conceded that doing otherwise would mean an end to their activity. The group decided that some way had to be found to keep the Christian community alive and functioning.

After a lengthy discussion, they decided that, to begin with, Eubulus would escort Peter to the various homes of the Christians in Rome. Care would have to be taken to insure security from the eyes of Roman soldiers. This system of visiting soon began to be tiresome upon both Eubulus and Peter. There seemed to be so much duplication of effort.

The next method of communication and preaching tried was meeting in relatively obscure places, often at some distance from the city. This was successful for some time, but also here the risk of being discovered gradually increased. On several occasions the group had to disperse hurriedly.

For the sake of convenience, the congregation then decided to break into smaller groups. The meetings would be held secretly – and mostly late in the evening. As a sign of recognition, each member was furnished with an emblem with the image of a fish on it. This was suggested by Peter both remembering his former occupation, and the time when Jesus told his disciples, "Come after Me, and I will make you become fishers of men."[3]

This system worked well for a while. However, one evening Peter was detained, and as he approached the home of Claudia, where the meeting was scheduled to take place, he saw a platoon of soldiers in front of the house. As he watched from a distance, Peter saw that the whole group was being taken into custody. None of them was heard from again.

The congregation was at a loss to explain how the soldiers knew of the meeting at Claudia's house. Everyone felt someone had alerted the authorities. Was it possible that someone in their midst betrayed them? They all became edgy and decided to discontinue meeting for a while.

Peter, who was still staying with Eubulus, became upset over this inactivity. He wanted to be doing something, even if it meant placing his life in jeopardy. Eubulus tried to think of something for Peter to do to occupy the time. Inasmuch as Silas had left the congregation at Puteoli, he thought, there was no one there to minister to them. Therefore, he suggested to Peter that they journey to Puteoli to do that. They stayed several months.

Upon returning to Rome, Eubulus, knowing that Peter had written one letter to the churches he had once served, suggested that he write another letter. Peter thought that the idea was inappropriate in a way. "Who would deliver it?" he wondered.

Eubulus insisted that the Lord would provide a messenger. "Even if the letter was not delivered to his former churches," Eubulus said, "some benefit would be derived by those who did read it."

"If that were true," Peter replied, "the letter might better be addressed to the church at large."

Then, with Eubulus helping him, Peter wrote another letter.

Peter had now been in Italy for nearly two years. Ever in his mind was what Paul had written in his second letter to the church at Thessalonica concerning 'the man of sin,' and 'the son of perdition,'[4] and 'the mystery of lawlessness.'[5] In his first letter, Peter likened the city of Rome to Babylon, but these other terms which Paul used seemed so abstract. Peter was not able to comprehend just what Paul was saying. And he finished his second letter with these words:

> "But the day of the Lord will come as a thief in the night in which the heavens will pass away with a great noise, and the elements will melt with fervent heat; both the earth and the worlds that are in it will be burned up. Seeing then that all these things will be dissolved, what manner of persons ought you to be in holy conduct and godliness, looking for and hastening the coming of the day of God, because of which the heavens, being on fire, will be dissolved, and the elements will melt with fervent heat? Nevertheless, we, according to His promise, look for a new Heavens and a new earth in which righteousness dwells. "Therefore, beloved, seeing that you look for such things, be diligent that you may be found by Him in peace, without spot, and blameless; and account that the longsuffering of our Lord is salvation – as also our beloved brother Paul, according to the wisdom given to him, has written to you, as also in all his epistles,

speaking in them of these things, in which are some things hard to understand, which those who are untaught and unstable twist to their own destruction, as they do also the rest of the Scripture. You, therefore, beloved, seeing you know these things beforehand, beware lest you also, being led away with the error of the wicked, fall from your own steadfastness; but grow in the grace and knowledge of our Lord and Savior Jesus Christ. To Him be the glory both now and forever. Amen."[6]

As Peter finished writing his letter, Eubulus asked him about what he had written concerning Paul's letters, namely, that untaught and unstable people twist his writings to their own destruction, as they do also the <u>rest</u> of the Scripture. He said that it sounded as if he, Peter, looked upon Paul's writings as being on an equal footing with the ancient prophets and writers. Peter did not hesitate to tell Eubulus that he indeed regarded the writings of Paul and also the Gospels written by Matthew, Mark, Luke, and John as sacred writings. The Holy Spirit inspired each of the apostles on the day of Pentecost, and all of them spoke with His authority. So also, the Holy Spirit inspired men to write the written Word.

"They absolutely are," Peter asserted. "They are God's New Testament written by the inspiration of the Holy Spirit."

"Perhaps you should include some such statement in your letter," Eubulus suggested.

"Paul covers this topic adequately in his second letter to Timothy," said Peter.

"He writes, 'All Scripture is given by inspiration of God, and is profitable for doctrine, for reproof, for correction, for instruction in righteousness, that the man of God may be complete, thoroughly equipped for every good work.'"[7]

Chapter 15
Spring 63

On a fresh and sunny early spring morning, three teenage girls frolicked on the beach. This day was especially stimulating because it was their first time on the beach since winter, and also because the day came just after a particularly violent spring storm.

Seventeen-year-old Marci was leading her younger sister Jacqui, and her close friend, Sheri, as they raced along the shore. Sheri was sixteen while Jacqui was thirteen. Suddenly Marci stopped short.

"There's something in the water," she shouted. "I'm going to wade out to see what it is."

She was over her knees in the cold water when she reached the object, and excitedly called out, "It's a man on a large piece of wood. He's lying on his stomach! He's not moving!"

Hurriedly Sheri and Jacqui joined her. "Is he dead? Is he dead?" cried Jacqui. "I don't want to look! Do I have to?"

"Calm down," Marci answered.

"C'mon, Sheri, let's tow it ashore."

Sheri maneuvered herself to assist Marci. She impulsively felt the man's hand. "Just feel how cold he is," she said. "Surely he isn't alive!"

As they neared the shore, Marci directed Jacqui to run home to fetch some blankets. Jacqui started for their home, about a mile from the shore.

"While we're waiting," Marci said to Sheri, "I think we should try to make him a little warmer ourselves. Our bodies are warm, and I think if we lie close to him, we can warm him up a bit."

"I don't know. He seemed awfully cold to me."

"We've got to help him. If this were your father in a similar fix, wouldn't you like to have someone try to help save him?"

"Well…"

"I tell you what," Marci pleaded, "I'm going to take off my outer clothing and lie next to him. You can do the same thing."

"But," said Sheri, "I don't have much of anything on underneath."

"Neither do I!"

"But…"

"There's not a soul around to notice. C'mon!"

Having said this, Marci removed her blouse. She rolled the man on his side and lay down so they faced each other. Sheri obligingly followed, lying on the other side. Together they nestled as closely as possible.

"His wet clothing is enough to make you shiver," Sheri commented.

"We'll be shivering soon enough without thinking about it," Marci answered.

After lying quietly for a time, Marci mused, "I wonder where he's from?"

"Hard to say," was the chilly reply.

The thought going through Marci's mind was that this man was going to be hers if he survived. She found him and she was going to claim him for her own. Men available for marriage in the countryside were few and far between. All eligible men just seemed to be grabbed by the squires and barons to be used in their fighting and feuding. If not that, they went to sea to fish with their fathers and did not come back.

"I was just thinking," Marci said along an altogether different line, "instead of lying here so still, maybe we should attempt to stimulate him with a massage."

"It's worth a try," said Sheri, who was tired of doing what she was doing.

They got up and placed the man on his stomach and began to rub his back and legs. Several moments passed and suddenly Onesimus groaned.

"Did you hear that?" Marci excitedly exclaimed. "He's alive!" Sheri stopped rubbing, but Marci cried out, "What are you doing?"

"I'm tired, and I think we've done enough."

"We can't quit now just because he groaned. We've got to continue. He is still a long way from recovering."

Sheri resumed massaging, and they kept working on Onesimus until they heard sounds that Jacqui was returning and then put their outer clothing back on.

They were happy when they learned that Jacqui had not only brought the blankets but also her mother. When Marci told her mother what they had done, she commended Marci, and wasted no time in removing his wet clothing and wrapping the man in the blankets.

Now that they knew the man was still alive, another problem confronted them. It was the question of moving him. Certainly they could not leave him on the beach. They knew they would have a very difficult time dragging the large piece of wood with him on it back to the house. They tried it, but was impractical. They were not strong enough.

Finally, Lili, Marci and Jacqui's mother, suggested that they take one of the blankets and use it to carry the man. There were four of them, and they each could take one corner. They tried that, and it worked, even though it was cumbersome. And after some trying efforts they reached home.

Lili used her medical skill and know-how to care for the stranger. She was a widow whose fisherman husband was lost at sea several years previously. Her eldest son, a few years older than Marci, was also lost in that disaster. Besides Marci and Jacqui, there were two other younger children.

Among other things, Lili used hot pads and massaging. She also tried using pungent herbs and spices held to the man's nose. In addition to this, she kept talking to him. Marci questioned her about it, and she explained that she believed that sound would somehow register in a semi-conscious mind just as much as in a conscious mind. She figured that her talking would have the same effect as that of singing or humming to small babies. It was a method of stimulation.

After several days, there was no apparent change in the man's condition. Marci was beginning to lose heart. Her mother, however, told her to be a little more patient.

And then, the day after, as Lili was busy working, she heard a faint sneeze. She wheeled about and went to the man's side. Holding his hand, she could see that his eyes were open.

Onesimus knew at that moment he was in a warm bed and no longer on the storm raging sea. He rested.

Lili prepared warm broth. All the time she continued to talk. Onesimus could not understand a word. But that did not matter to him; he was rescued. He was satisfied with the broth and continued to rest and sleep.

The next morning when Onesimus awoke, Lili was up and around continuing her intermittent chattering. In a moment of silence, Onesimus asked, "Where am I?"

Lili answered, "You are in Gaul."

Marci spoke up, "Mama, why do you keep on talking to him as if you understand each other? We don't know what he said, and he doesn't know what we are saying."

The only answer she could give was that if she were rescued and in a strange place, the first thing to come to her mind was to wonder where she was. That is why she said what she did. And she did, indeed, say the only word that was common to both of them. Onesimus now felt considerable more at ease and continued to rest.

In a few more days, Onesimus sat up. And in another few days he stood up, and as Marci helped him, walked around a bit. Gradually as he became stronger, Lili provided Onesimus with some of her husband's old clothes, and he moved about on his own. He tried to show in any way possible his gratitude for the hospitality given to him. But there was practically no oral communication between them. They did, however, learn each other's names.

Marci stammered as Onesimus pronounced his name. "O-ne-si-mus?" What do they call you for short? was her unspoken question. She decided to give Onesimus a nickname of her own. She would call him Pinky.

As Lili and Marci pondered the problem of the language barrier, Lili came to the conclusion that a trip to Lutetia would be necessary. She had been there only once herself, but she knew that scholars in the school there might be able to act as interpreters. Marci volunteered to be Onesimus' guide.

Behind Marci's willingness to go was her longing desire to become Onesimus' woman. She did not tell her mother about her plans until shortly before they left. Lili accepted Marci's decision, and did not try to prevent her from carrying them out.

They explained the plan of going to Lutetia to Onesimus by means of drawing a diagram on the ground showing two spots and indicating traveling from one to the other. Onesimus seemed to understand. Lili provided a few provisions for them.

The trip to Lutetia would take about a week, so Marci tried to warm up to Onesimus every chance she got. All of her efforts to hold hands with him, and otherwise snuggle with him produced no results whatsoever. With only a few more nights before arriving in Lutetia, Marci had reached a point of desperation.

As Onesimus rested near the bank of the river under a tree, Marci indicated to him that she wished to bathe in the river. Having finished bathing, Marci left the water, ignored her clothing, and went directly to where Onesimus was resting. He was already half dozing. Marci threw herself on top of him, and began kissing him passionately.

Onesimus was aghast, unaccustomed to this sort of behavior by a woman. As he attempted to resist, Marci increased her efforts to have Onesimus make love to her. They wrestled. Marci was the victor. The driving force for Marci's action was her compelling desire to become pregnant.

Following her mother's directions, Marci did not have much trouble in locating the school in Lutetia. Marci talked with the scholars and explained everything to them.

They began their inquiry using the Latin tongue because it was the most widely understood language in the world. Onesimus responded most heartily. An expression of joy came to his face, and he talked freely.

He told these men that he was from Asia, and that he also knew Greek. He had gone from Rome to Britain, was on the return trip to Rome when he became shipwrecked. He did not say anything about the circumstances of his trip to Britain, certainly not that he was under guard.

The scholars translated what Onesimus told them to Marci.

"Where is Asia?" she wanted to know.

"It is at the eastern end of the Great Sea."

"Where is the Great Sea?"

"It is to the south of us."

All of this information meant almost nothing to Marci. She had no comprehension of geography at all. She was left with the thought that it must be very far away. Knowing all this, however, did not deter her from her wish to claim Pinky for her man. She let the scholars know of her intention, and found out from them how to say, 'I am pregnant,' 'I must go with you,' 'I can help you,' and 'I am your woman' in Latin.

The men in Lutetia understood Marci's wish, and as they gave instructions on how to reach the river that flows to the south, they did so in both Marci's language and in Latin.

It was only when it came time to leave that Onesimus discovered that Marci intended to go with him. Onesimus wanted to have no part of it. And through the scholars they argued. Marci shouted out the phrases she learned. Onesimus reasoned that he could make it on his own. But the scholars sided with Marci.

Finally, Marci requested them to ask Onesimus if he was thankful that she had helped save him. Pinky had to admit that he was, and his resistance began wearing down. As Marci kept appealing to his sympathy, he became irritated. In the next moment, however, the thought of his standing before Paul on the ship pleading as he was running away from Philemon flashed through his mind. And so he finally agreed to allow Marci to come with him. "I am doing this only because you helped save me!" he asserted.

Before they left Lutetia, Onesimus insisted that as their provisions ran out along the way, he would seek work in order to provide for themselves, and not as Marci suggested that they scrounge and pilfer.

Since she was leaving her former life behind, Marci tried to have Pinky teach her Latin as they went along. Onesimus was not cooperative. He only accepted the fact that she was with him, and was in no way affectionate. In contrast to his somber attitude, Marci displayed continued vivaciousness.

At the first village they came to, no one knew Latin. Marci handled the communication with the natives. It was the same story in the next several towns. She was, indeed, being helpful to Pinky. From then on, though, Latin was spoken in all the towns.

Five weeks had now passed, and now Marci had some exciting news to tell Pinky. Through the people native to the area, her message was, "Back in Lutetia I lied when I told you that I was pregnant, but now I know for sure, I am going to have a baby."

Before, Onesimus was aware that Marci was being untruthful about being pregnant; but now this news caused him to reflect, and his attitude began to change. He started to show a little more awareness to Marci. There was more communication. The thing that did not change, though, was the lack of any display of affection on Onesimus' part.

Chapter 16
Fall 63

Onesimus' goal was to reach Genua before winter. In late fall, he and Marci arrived. Onesimus was hopeful of contacting the people he and Timothy had met when they visited there with Apollos.

One couple in particular stood out in Onesimus' mind, and he and Marci called at their home. They barely remembered Onesimus. As they renewed their acquaintance, however, he and Marci were given shelter. From the time Apollos left, they said, they had lost contact with the Gospel of Jesus Christ. Mainly because there was no one to teach and preach to them. There were not many Christians in Genua anyway.

Onesimus told them he and Marci were very appreciative for what they had done for them, and promised that, if at all possible, he would have someone visit them. Onesimus and Marci then left for Luca.

In Luca they were more fortunate. They called upon a farmer who lived near the city. After having their memories refreshed from his previous visit, Dominic and Theresa told Onesimus all that had transpired in the past several years. Onesimus learned that John Mark was in the territory, taking over what Apollos had been doing. Mark was in the city at that very time. A trip into town the next day was arranged to meet him.

Meanwhile, Theresa, a motherly person by nature, looked at Marci and took her under her care. She replaced Marci's shabby and ill-fitting clothes. Since Marci's Latin vocabulary was still limited, Theresa did most of the talking. They were friends immediately. Marci was not accustomed to having so much warmth showered upon her, especially after being with Pinky ever since leaving Lutetia. She was overwhelmed by the kindness shown to her.

Dominic and Onesimus went into the city the next day to find Mark, who was astonished when Dominic showed up at his house with Onesimus. Mark and Onesimus had not seen each other since being with Paul at Caesarea. And there they had spent only a short time together.

Of course, Mark knew that Onesimus had gone with Paul to Britain, but what, he asked him, was he doing in Luca.

"It is my sad duty to tell you that Paul is dead," Onesimus said slowly. "We arrived in Britain and immediately Paul found the weather very disagreeable. It was wet and foggy constantly. Paul survived the first winter, but doubted that he could stand another. And he was right. He took sick and died.

"The journey to Britain, nevertheless, was not without its benefits. Already on the ship, Paul preached the Gospel to the captain and his crew, and the military personnel. They were surprisingly eager to hear what Paul had to say.

"Upon arrival in Britain, Paul was given permission to move about freely. Soon he made contact with the people who lived in the vicinity. He also continued to minister to the members of the Roman garrison at Verulamium. Paul very forcefully preached the good news of salvation in Jesus Christ. By the time he died, there was a goodly number of believers, both among the military and the civilians."

"But what about yourself?" inquired Mark.

"It's a long story," Onesimus said. "After Paul died and was buried, I talked to the officer in charge about my status. You know I was only Paul's companion. He said that since I was not technically a prisoner that I should be taken back to Rome, but still under guard. That would happen when the first ship sailed in the spring. They even allowed me to take Paul's books and possessions with me, including also copies of the letters Paul had written.

"We set sail but before we had gone far, our ship was overtaken by a sudden squall. It soon became a fierce storm, and the ship was battered to pieces. I managed to grab on to a large piece of wood after I was tossed into the water, and it seemed that just as I had done so, the storm abated. I was able to climb on to this piece of wood, and spent I don't know how many hours floating about. It was terribly cold, and eventually I became unconscious.

"The next thing I remember was being in a warm bed. It turned out that I was in Gaul. This girl who is with me, and is now with Theresa, helped rescue me. She keeps insisting that she is my woman. At her persistent wishes, we have traveled together from her home by the sea to Lutetia and on to the Great Sea and to Genua and now to Luca. And I am the father of the child she is carrying."

"Astounding, absolutely astounding."

Mark was quick to reassure Onesimus that they would be well taken care of. "These people here in this country are as hospitable as you would want to find," he said. He then explained to Onesimus how he came to be here. "And Peter," he added, "is still in Rome. However, Nero is persecuting the Christians there, and I fear for Peter's safety."

"I must go there, too, to tell them about Paul," Onesimus replied.

"Winter is not the best time to do that," said Mark.

"Yes, I know."

"Well, then, it will be in spring?"

"Yes, and maybe the baby will be born by then."

Just then an obviously pregnant woman entered the room. "Onesimus, I want you to meet my wife, Cecilia," Mark said.

"So happy to meet you," Onesimus replied, and I want to congratulate you on your marriage."

"When these people here found out that I was still single," Mark said, "they insisted on finding a mate for me. I resisted for a while but they prevailed. By the way, please tell us about your wife."

"Oh, Marci and I are not married," Onesimus replied. "She just insisted on coming with me."

"I don't understand," Mark stated.

"And how do you explain her condition?" Dominic wanted to know.

"It was her idea."

"You mean she is with child, too?" asked Cecilia.

"Yes, but I never intended to ever marry. I had my heart set on emulating Paul, and remaining single, to better serve the Lord Christ."

"I also had the same idea, but you know that Paul himself said that marriage is honorable among all. It was just that some persons were not suited for marriage. Jesus said so Himself. Presumably, Paul included himself in that group. Under the circumstances, Onesimus, I think you will have to alter your thinking."

"Yes," added Dominic. "The people here will not tolerate the situation the way that it is."

"It is really the best for everyone if you marry this woman," concluded Cecilia.

"Do you think so, too, Mark?"

"Yes."

"I hardly know how to ask her. She doesn't speak much Latin."

"That will be taken care of," said Dominic. "My wife will see to it."

Marci and Onesimus were married within two weeks. In the ensuing months, Dominic kept Onesimus busy on the farm. Theresa relished the opportunity of mothering Marci. Aside from knitting clothes for the baby, she taught Marci more Latin. They continued becoming more closely attached to each other.

After the wedding Onesimus talked with Mark about his plans for the future. In the spring, as he indicated, he would go to Rome while Marci and the baby stayed here. Mark thought that odd, and asked him if it wouldn't be more appropriate to take her with him. They then could travel to Asia together from there.

Onesimus told Mark, "That is out of the question. I never intend to travel by water again."

"Do you want to stay in this country?" Mark asked.

"No, I don't," Onesimus answered. "I plan to return to Asia by way of Dalmatia."

Surprised, Mark asked Onesimus, "Do you know how rugged that country is?"

"I know. I've been there once with Paul," Onesimus said, and added, "but it still would be better than going by sea."

Mark reminded him of his family, but Onesimus did not change his mind. Having exhausted all avenues of persuasion, Mark promised to help him in In midwinter Cecelia gave birth to a boy. Mark couldn't have been prouder. Onesimus hoped he would be similarly blessed.

As Marci was nearing the time to give birth, she began to confide more and more in Theresa. She said she was becoming increasingly apprehensive about her relationship with Pinky. She also told Theresa that he had not been intimate with her since the first time, not even after they were married. She wondered if all men were that way. Theresa assured her otherwise, adding that she thought in Onesimus' case, it was a little different. Theresa attempted to ease her mind by telling her that after the birth, things would change.

A month later, Marci had twin daughters. She named them Lili and Sheri, for her mother and her best friend. Onesimus was dazed. He knew traveling with one infant would be difficult, but now there was two. Nevertheless, he did not change his mind.

When the babies were born, Theresa let Onesimus know in no uncertain terms that he would have to show more affection toward Marci. She told him to go in to Marci and hold her hand, and not to leave her without giving her a kiss.

As Onesimus was sitting next to Marci holding her hand, Theresa brought the babies to Marci for nursing. Onesimus got up to kiss her and leave, but Marci wouldn't let go of his hand. He stayed with her a while longer.

As soon as spring arrived, Onesimus' thoughts were on his trip to Rome. Marci began to worry when he told her of his trip, but Onesimus said it was necessary for him to go. He had an obligation to Paul to fulfill. He promised resolutely to return. Mark also reassured her. Dominic provided an animal for Onesimus to ride, and a month after the twins were born, he was off to Rome.

The obligation Onesimus spoke of was to deliver Paul's second letter to the church at Rome. Inasmuch as he was tossed into the sea when his ship was battered in the storm, he not only lost Paul's possessions, but also Paul's letter to the church at Rome.

As best he could, he would have to rely on his memory and deliver the letter orally. On the trip to Rome, Onesimus tried to reconstruct the letter in his mind. He went over the whole letter repeatedly.

Rome seemed to Onesimus pretty much the same as it was when he left it. He felt confident that his beard would protect him from possible recognition.

His first stop was at Eubulus' home. The house was vacant, and the people next door did not know where he had moved. Onesimus next tried Paul's old residence. Strangers now lived there. He then went to the area of the Ostian Gate. Claudia lived in that neighborhood. Her home was also vacant.

Puzzled, Onesimus tried the home of Linus who also lived in that area. The people answering the door told him that Linus had moved, but they did not know where. The only choice Onesimus now had was to go across town through the slums to the northeast section of the city. Pudens lived by the Tiburtine Way several miles into the country.

It was almost dusk when Onesimus arrived. He had to rap several times before someone came to the door. Onesimus greeted Pudens by name, but Pudens remained wary. It was necessary for Onesimus to tell him who he was. And then Pudens welcomed him. Onesimus and Pudens spent the rest of the evening exchanging information.

After resting a day, Onesimus was taken by Pudens to the home of Eubulus where Peter was staying. It was near the municipal baths, close to the Appian Way. This was the first time Onesimus met Peter.

Peter was dismayed when he learned of the death of Paul. "Truly," he said, "he was a stalwart soldier of the Cross of Christ."

After again relating his story to Peter and Eubulus, Onesimus told them of Paul's letter. Peter thought it appropriate to have at least a few more members of the church present when Onesimus told them of it, so they postponed the telling until several days later. That would give them an opportunity to summon Linus and Cletus.

In the meantime, Peter gave the letter he had written with the help of Eubulus to Onesimus.

"Onesimus," Eubulus said to Peter, "was the messenger whom God would provide to deliver it."

Onesimus returned with Pudens to his home, and kept Peter's letter there.

At the appointed time, they came back to the home of Eubulus. Cletus was already there. Onesimus renewed his acquaintance with the man he had once traveled with to Luca. As time passed and there was no sign of Linus, they debated whether they should proceed without him. Peter said that since Linus did not live too far away, they should seek him out. Cletus and Onesimus volunteered to go.

As they crossed the Appian Way, Onesimus spotted a number of soldiers headed in that direction, coming from the center of the city. He and Cletus waited by the side of a building to see what might happen. The soldiers turned at that very corner in the direction from which they themselves came. Looking closer, they could see that the soldiers were stopping at the home of Eubulus. Peter, Eubulus, and Pudens were being led away bound. The soldiers then took their prisoners along the Appian Way to the outskirts of the city. A wagon loaded with timber followed them.

Onesimus and Cletus also followed at a safe distance. What was going to happen was becoming all too clear. Peter and Eubulus and Pudens were going to die in the same manner Jesus himself had died. Being frightened, Onesimus and Cletus lingered in the area only long enough to see the three of them being crucified. They then went to Cletus' home and remained inside.

The next day, Cletus and Onesimus went to the home of Pudens to notify his widow and pick up Peter's letter. They then visited five other members of the church to tell them what had happened. Each one of them in turn told Cletus and Onesimus identical stories. Linus, the Tuscan, had been there, too, with the news about Peter and the others. He had also proclaimed to each of them that he, Linus, was Peter's successor as the Bishop of Rome.

"Peter," Linus said to them, "had appointed him as his successor before he died, so that," he told the Christians, "'You always may be able to have a reminder of these things (that I preach) after my decease.'[1]"

And then they added that Linus said, "I now possess the keys of the kingdom here on earth and in heaven."

As they were returning to Cletus' home discussing this newest development, Onesimus positively asserted, "That does not at all sound like Peter! The preaching of the Gospel of Jesus Christ is not dependent solely on the preaching of any one particular person, or even on any one particular group of people. This statement of Linus violates the humbleness of Peter. Peter never elevated himself above the message that he was preaching.

"Nor do any of the apostles. Their message points directly to Christ, and Him only as the world's redeemer. The apostles all know that they are but earthen vessels carrying out the Savior's commission to bring the Gospel to the entire world.

"The Holy Spirit is the One who reminds the believers of the Gospel. John reminds us of this in his Gospel, where he writes, 'But the Helper, the Holy Spirit, whom the Father will send in My name, He will teach you all things, and bring to your remembrance all the things that I said to you.'[2]

"The Holy Spirit uses men as befits His purpose, and it is He who chooses those who are to serve. He issues to them a divine calling. No human being can be appointed by others to be above the rest of the believers.

"All of the saints of God have equal access to the throne of grace. All those called to serve must consider themselves servants of the Word. They all have an obligation to follow the lead of their Lord Jesus Christ, who was the Suffering Servant.

"In addition, Christ has freed all men from the bondage of the Law. His followers should not, therefore, be further placed under any bondage of the dictates of other men. Concisely put, it may be stated that:

'A Christian is a perfectly free lord of all, subject to none,' and

'A Christian is a perfectly dutiful servant of all, subject to all.'[3]"

As Onesimus was speaking, he realized that much of what he said was in Paul's letter. He explained this to Cletus. Onesimus also apologized to him for not being able to quote Paul's letter more accurately. Some of these things, Onesimus said, were from what he and Paul had discussed privately.

Cletus, however, asked Onesimus to continue with the remainder of the letter, to the best of his ability. "It has mostly to do with the oneness of the body of Christ," said Onesimus.

"Paul, by the name of our Lord Jesus Christ, pleads that the brethren 'all speak the same thing, and that there be no division among you, but that you be perfectly joined together in the same mind, and in the same judgment.'[4] He had written the same thing to the church at Corinth. We have a oneness in Christ and also His Father in heaven. This oneness begins at the moment the Holy Spirit creates faith in our heart, either at our baptism, or when we hear the Gospel preached.

"This was all made possible by His taking upon Himself our human nature. Christ combines our human nature and His divine nature into one. These then are what may be called 'The Two Natures in Christ.' Graphically explained, a piece of iron, which is placed in fire, is changed and becomes red hot, but its basic form remains the same.

"It can be said then that Christ is 'One, not by conversion of the Godhead into flesh, but by taking manhood into God.'[5] By this action 'both He who sanctifies and those who are being sanctified are all of one, for which reason He is not ashamed to call them brethren.'[6]

"It is under this arrangement that Paul reminds us to endeavor 'to keep the unity of the Spirit in the bond of peace.'[7] We are to 'walk worthy of the calling with which you were called, with all lowliness and gentleness, and longsuffering, bearing with one another in love.'[8]

"Since we know that we are all still sinful beings, we know that such a thing is impossible humanly speaking. We are to control our action according to Christ's love. Jesus said, 'As the Father loved Me, I also have loved you; continue in My love. If you keep My commandments, you will abide in My love, just as I have kept My Father's commandments and abide in His love. These things I have spoken to you that My joy may remain in you, and that your joy may be full. This is My commandment, that you love one another as I have loved you.'⁹

"There may be some who will come and say that yes, Christians can and should be one here on earth, perfectly organized together in one earthly body. This is not what is meant by being 'perfectly joined together in the same mind, and in the same judgment.' We are to be objectively perfectly joined together in Jesus and His love.

"Unless it is so with us, all of our efforts to be one with each other here on earth will be fruitless. Jesus once said, 'Without Me you can do nothing.'¹⁰ Those who do say that men can be perfectly one with each other here in this life without being perfectly one in Christ are denying Christ's oneness with His heavenly Father. We must maintain our spiritual oneness with God in Christ above all else. To do otherwise means to be anti-Christ.

"Something else Paul mentioned in his letter concerned the celebration of the Holy Supper. I did not fully understand all of what he wrote. Maybe you could shed some light on it."

"Of course, if I am able," said Cletus.

"Paul seemed to be saying that he got the impression that here in the church at Rome, whenever the sacrament was celebrated, the people were led to believe that as they received the bread and wine, they were <u>becoming one</u> with Christ, or in other words, they were <u>made one</u> with Him."

"Yes, this is what our leaders teach. They say that through the Eucharist we <u>become</u> members of the body of Christ, and that thus all who partake <u>become</u> one body. The believers' <u>being made</u> one with Christ is both spiritual and bodily."

"Well, then, this explains the message Paul was giving. He wrote, 'We approach the Lord's Table (a) chiefly to receive forgiveness of our sins and thus to be strengthened in our faith in our Lord Jesus Christ; (b) to obtain strength for a holier life; and (c) to bear testimony that we are of one faith with those who commune with us.'¹¹

"In regard to this last statement, our celebration of the Sacrament of the Lord's Supper is not an act of becoming one with Christ. We are one in Christ the moment the Holy Spirit creates faith in our heart. He works faith in our heart though the preaching of God's Holy Word, and through the Sacrament of Holy Baptism. As such, we are members of Christ's Holy Church and are one with Him and His Father, and are heirs of His Kingdom.

"Our celebration of the Sacrament of the Lord's Supper, then, is an act of affirmation on our part that as members of Christ's Holy Church, we have faith in Jesus Christ as our Savior from sin and from eternal damnation through His suffering, death, resurrection, and ascension. This is what is called 'showing His death.' And this 'showing (proclaiming) His death' should not be considered in the same sense as our proclaiming the Gospel message to the whole world as he has commanded us to do.

"Continuously time and again believing that we become one with Christ in the celebration of the sacrament is a subtle form of synergism, and may eventually even lead to Gnosticism. All the blessings the communicant receives in the sacrament come from God's Holy Spirit. Also, there are no degrees in the believers' oneness in Christ. The more frequent celebration of the sacrament does not in any way enhance our individual oneness in Christ. And at the same time, our more frequent celebration should not be considered as some meritorious service, which can so easily be misconstrued by an unwary believer. In other words, there is no such thing as being more one in Christ because of our more frequent celebration of the sacrament.

"Paul closed his letter by repeating what he once wrote to the church at Corinth, 'For by one Spirit we were all baptized into one body ... and have all been made to drink into one Spirit.'[12]" Onesimus then added that much of what Paul had written in this letter was the same as what he had written in letters previously.

Having finished, Onesimus told Cletus that the events of the past week had saddened him immensely. He would be leaving Rome right away, taking Peter's letter with him.

The soldiers who obeyed their orders to crucify Peter, Eubulus, and Pudens reported back to their commanding officer. Upon learning that only three Christians had been put to death, the officer remarked to one of his fellow officers, "Nero isn't going to like what I must tell him."

"Maybe if you tell him that among those who were crucified was the leader of the Christian sect, it will make a difference."

"I don't think so," he replied.

Sure enough, Nero raged at the officer's report. "I told you to go and see to it that some Christians were killed. And you report that you have killed three. THREE! I could have done better myself. There must be hundreds in the city. Get out of my sight, you imbecile. When I say I want some action, that is precisely what I mean. By all the gods! I'll show you what I mean."

In the evening of the day Onesimus left Rome, he was resting by the side of the road leading north to Luca. It was a very windy day and he was tired. As Onesimus turned to look back toward Rome, there was a giant red glow in the sky. He was thankful that he was gone from there, and was not too greatly concerned.

Chapter 17
Summer 64

As Onesimus journeyed to Luca, it seemed as though he became more downcast. As the days passed, he was besieged with gloomy thoughts. He was on another trip to bring sad news. First Paul; now Peter.

As he rode along despairingly, however, he began to compare this trip to his earlier one with Marci in Gaul. They were, indeed, similar, but the trip with her was not that gloomy. Onesimus wondered to himself if her presence was the difference. He had to agree that her carefree disposition did seem to clear the air of all gloom. The more he thought, the more he longed to be in Luca with her near. Time now passed more swiftly and soon he was 'home.'

He went directly to the farm of Dominic and Theresa, saying to himself that the sad news for Mark could wait. He found Marci, and embraced her and showered her with hugs and kisses. Marci was ecstatic. She was delighted to have her man with her again.

Marci was equally happy to show Pinky the girls. As he held them in his arms, Onesimus commented on how chubby they were and said, "They surely look well fed."

"Yes," said Marci. "They have been feeding well."

As they continued to talk, Onesimus marveled how much Marci's Latin had improved.

"Theresa was responsible," said Marci.

After the evening meal, Marci and Pinky retired to their quarters. They talked mostly about themselves. Marci was astonished to learn that Pinky was quite a bit older than she. Had she known back in Gaul, she said, she may not have gone to such lengths to seduce him.

Onesimus told her that he was satisfied that everything turned out as it had.

"I was never much of a ladies' man," Onesimus said. He then went into his family background, explaining that his mother was a slave when he was born and that he also was a former slave. "My mother always told me that as a slave, I shouldn't expect to enjoy many of the pleasures that free men enjoy. She taught me to be content with things that we have. She was especially grateful, herself, to be in the household of Gaius. I guess her life before that time was none too pleasant. She hardly ever mentioned it."

He also went on to say that actually Gaius was his father, and that his mother was now his wife, and that now, too, he was Gaius' legal son. Very shortly they would be leaving Luca for Asia, and she would meet them.

At last, Onesimus asked Marci to tell him where she picked up his nickname of Pinky. Marci was a bit reluctant, but finally said she got it from the time of his rescue on the beach. "As we took your wet clothes off, your bottom appeared to me to be so very pink," she said. They both had a good laugh and went to bed.

The next day, Marci got the twins ready, and they all went to the city to see Mark. Onesimus painfully told him about Peter and the others, and the subsequent events. Mark was clearly upset. Overcome with grief, he found difficulty in expressing himself.

Onesimus also showed him Peter's letter, and recalled what John wrote in his Gospel:

> "If the world hates you, you know that it hated Me before it hated you. If you were of the world, the world would love its own. Yet because you are not of the world, but I have chosen you out of the world, therefore the world hates you. Remember the word that I said to

you, 'A servant is not greater than his master.' If they have persecuted Me, they will also persecute you. If they have kept My word, they will keep yours also. But all these things they will do to you for My name's sake, because they do not know Him who sent Me. If I had not come and spoken to them, they would have no sin, but now they have no excuse for their sin. He who hates Me hates My Father also. If I had not done among them the works which no one else has done, they would have no sin; but now they have seen and also hated both Me and My Father."

These are the words of Jesus.

Mark then commented, "Peter was equally aware of just what you have said. My Gospel reflects this, 'And you will be hated by all men for My name's sake. But he who endures to the end will be saved.'[2]"

Onesimus inquired of Mark about the trip to Aquileia. He was hopeful that they would be able to start soon. Mark agreed that since he wanted to reach Asia before winter, they would have to leave soon. He told Onesimus arrangements could be made so that they could leave in about ten days. Onesimus then requested Mark to baptize Lili and Sheri, which he did.

Marci had heard much about God since she arrived in Luca. The lives of her husband, Mark, Dominic, and Theresa all seemed to be centered around Him. Thus far, she had remained silent about the matter. Now her curiosity made her ask, "What is this thing you call God, and this baptizing? I don't understand anything that you say or do. And what is this praying?"

"I'll have to admit," Onesimus said to Mark, "I have not discussed any of this with Marci. I think we will have to start at the very beginning."

Mark took Onesimus' cue and began by saying that "God is a spirit. He is from everlasting to everlasting, and is all-powerful, all-knowing, and present everywhere. He has many other attributes. We know this from the existence of the world. God made the world and everything that is in it. 'The heavens declare the glory of God, and the firmament shows His handiwork.'[3] All of the animals, birds, fish, and other creatures were made by Him. He also made the trees and flowers and all other growing things; the lakes, rivers, and mountains, too. God also made mankind, the crown of His creation.

"We also know of God from the testimony of our conscience. The work of the Law is written in our hearts. This is what conscience is. It accuses us when we behave in an evil manner. Of course, not everyone's conscience is equally acute. This is all called the natural knowledge of God. In addition to creating everything in the world, God has given us the gift of the birth of children. This is all made possible by Him."

"We aren't going too fast for you are we, Marci?" asked Onesimus. "There is much more."

"No, that's all right," she said. "It is just that I find it difficult to comprehend all of this information. But I will keep listening if you want to continue."

"Make a mental note of anything you think you want clarified," Onesimus suggested. "Then at home we can talk about it further."

Mark continued, "There is also something called the revealed knowledge of God. He did this through His prophets. Some thirteen hundred years ago, a prophet by the name of Moses wrote down the history of humanity since the beginning of time when God created the world. This was about four thousand years ago. The first man and woman, called Adam and Eve, were created in God's image. Adam was made first, and God formed Eve from a rib taken from Adam's side. They were without sin and lived in a garden called Eden. Then the devil, also called Satan, a fallen angel, tempted Eve by means of a snake, to eat of the fruit of a tree in the garden that God had forbidden them to do. Eve succumbed to this temptation, and disobediently ate the fruit. She induced Adam to do likewise.

"They had sinned by disobeying God, and God was displeased. So God expelled them from Eden. As He did so, He made a promise to Adam and Eve that He would crush the head of the serpent, as a symbol of Satan, by sending someone to atone for the sin that was committed. Through the years, God revealed more about His plan of salvation for sinners. A man by the name of Abraham was told by God that through his seed, He would send His only Son, the Seed, to redeem all people. Abraham was to be the father of a great nation; God's very own. These people were called Hebrews. They also came to be known as Jews. By all of this action, all of the nations of the world would be blessed.

"As time went by, the human race became increasingly sinful and wicked. God used the prophet Moses to issue a written law for men. This law is called The Ten Commandments. It is divided into two parts. The first part tells us that we should love the Lord, our God, with all our heart, soul, and mind. The second part tells us that we should love our neighbor as ourselves. We are told to keep these commandments perfectly. Since we're all sinners, we know that this is impossible, because we are at enmity with God. We need someone to do this for us. This Someone is God's very own Son, the One promised by God to Adam and Eve, and also to Abraham.

"God revealed more of His plan of salvation through other prophets as time passed. He also renewed His covenant with His chosen nation, also called Israel. More writings were added to those of Moses. This collection of books is called Holy Scripture. The prophet Isaiah foretold the birth of God's Son. He wrote, 'Behold, a virgin shall conceive, and bear a son, and shall call his name Immanuel.'[4] Immanuel means 'God with us.' Other names for God's Son are Messiah, Jesus, the Christ. The prophet Micah prophesied the place where Jesus was to be born. He wrote, 'But you, Bethlehem Ephratah...out of you shall He come forth unto me that is to be ruler in Israel.'[5]

"Jesus was born in Bethlehem more than sixty years ago to a virgin whose name was Mary. He lived in the city of Nazareth in the country of Palestine for thirty years. And then He taught publicly throughout the land for the last three years of His life; performing many miracles, and healing the sick. Many disciples followed Him. Finally, He was put to death by crucifixion at the hands of His own people, the Jews.

"But Jesus Christ rose from the dead on the third day after His death, just as He had said He would. He had died and rose again for the sins of not only the Jews, but for all people. The Jews, however, refused to accept Him as the Messiah.

"Jesus remained on earth for another forty days, and then ascended bodily into heaven. Just prior to ascending into heaven, Jesus came and spoke to His disciples, saying, 'All authority has been given to Me in heaven and on earth. Go therefore and make disciples of all nations, baptizing them in the name of the Father and of the Son and of the Holy Spirit, teaching them to observe all things whatever I have commanded you; and behold, I am with you always, even to the end of the age.'[6]

"This is what Paul and Peter and the other apostles of Jesus Christ have been doing. And not only they, but I and Onesimus and Apollos and many others."

"Perhaps we should add," remarked Onesimus, "another aspect of God. The only true God is composed of three distinct Persons in One divine being, or essence. It is in His name that we baptize. The

Father has begotten the Son from eternity; the Son is begotten of the Father from eternity; the Holy Spirit from eternity proceeds from the Father and the Son.

"To the Father especially is ascribed the work of Creation; to the Son, the work of Redemption; to the Holy Spirit, the work of Sanctification. God is the Triune God, and may properly be called The Holy Trinity.

"We accept all that God has done for us by faith. 'Faith is the substance of things hoped for; the evidence of things not seen.'[7] The Holy Spirit works faith in our hearts. We confess, 'I believe that I cannot by my own reason or strength believe in Jesus Christ, my Lord, or come to Him: but the Holy Spirit has called me by the Gospel, enlightened me with His gifts, sanctified and kept me in the true faith; even as He calls, gathers, enlightens the whole Christian Church on earth, and keeps it with Jesus Christ in the one true faith.'[8]

"He does so by the preaching of God's Holy Word, and the administration of the sacraments, one of which is Holy Baptism. The other sacrament is that of the Sacrament of the Lord's Supper, or Holy Communion. The two sacraments and the written and spoken Word are what is known as the 'Means of Grace.'"

Onesimus then proceeded to explain to Marci about prayer. "We pray first of all because God commands us to pray. He wants us to call upon Him in the day of trouble. He has given His promise that our petitions will be heard and that He will deliver us from all evil. In our every need, we are to call upon the name of the Lord. We are likewise to call on His name to offer our gratitude for blessings received from Him and thus glorify God.

"When the disciples asked Jesus to teach them to pray, He gave them this prayer: 'Our Father in Heaven. Hallowed be Your name. Your kingdom come. Your will be done on earth as it is in heaven. Give us this day our daily bread. And forgive us our debts, as we forgive our debtors. And do not lead us into temptation, But deliver us from the evil one. For Yours is the kingdom and the power and the glory forever. Amen.'[9]

"We should pray only to the True God, Father, Son, and Holy Spirit since He alone is able and willing to hear and grant our prayer. We should pray with confidence in the name of Jesus, that is, with faith in Him as our redeemer, and with firm trust that for His name's sake our prayer will be answered.

"And finally now," said Onesimus, "Mark will provide information in regard to your inquiry about baptism."

"'Baptize means to apply water by washing, pouring, sprinkling, or immersing,'[10]" Mark began. "'Baptism is not simple water only, but it is the water comprehended in God's command and connected with God's Word.'[11] 'It works forgiveness of sins, delivers from death and the devil, and gives eternal salvation to all who believe this.'[12] That is what I wrote in my Gospel in collaboration with Peter, 'He who believes and is baptized will be saved; but he who does not believe will be condemned.'[13]

"While our sins are forgiven in Holy Baptism, our sinful nature, often referred to as original sin, remains. Our sinful nature is often called 'Our Old Adam.' This 'Old Adam' in us is to be drowned by daily contrition and repentance, by which we resist our evil desires and suppress them. Thus, the Christian is engaged in a never-ending struggle against the devil, the world, and our own flesh. We are to maintain vigilance over against our old evil foe, Satan, lest we fall from the grace given to us by God."

Marci was overwhelmed with all the information supplied by Mark and Onesimus. She promised them that she would keep thinking about what they had all said.

Mark was ready to leave for Aquileia in about the time he had hoped. Another man from Luca was also ready to go with them. They both had animals for the journey. Dominic allowed Onesimus to have the animal that he used for his trip to Rome.

The trip was then made without a hitch, except that travel with two infants slowed them down. During the trip, Onesimus let it be known to Marci that in Asia the spoken language was Greek. She was none too happy to learn that this would necessitate the start of studying all over again. Onesimus began instructing her right away, telling her that by what he had observed, she seemed to be a fast learner.

Once in Aquileia, Mark began inquiry about travel to Dalmatia. From a man in the market place, he learned that occasionally people from there came to Aquileia. This man promised to inform Mark if anyone from there was in the city. Within a week, a meeting was arranged by this man.

Onesimus' and Mark's hopes soared, and at the meeting, Onesimus met a man who looked quite familiar. He turned out to be who he thought he was. It was Artemas. Both of them went with Paul into Dalmatia some years earlier. Both were overjoyed to see each other again.

Soon Marci, Onesimus and the girls were off to Dalmatia with Artemas and his wife and two other couples. Marci was very relieved when the other women offered to assist her in the caring for Lili and Sheri. Artemas told Onesimus that he was living in Narona, and that Titus was living in Scodra, where they each served churches. The long journey was quite tiring, and when they arrived in Narona, Marci told Onesimus that what she suspected was apparently true – she was pregnant again.

After a short stay in Narona, they were again on the road; this time accompanied only by Artemas and his wife. They agreed to go on with them to Scodra; not only as guides, but because it had been some time since they last visited Titus.

Titus was really quite astonished to see Onesimus. News of the events in the church in other places was very meager, and not always that reliable. Titus had gotten the impression that both Paul and Onesimus had died. Onesimus then related to Titus all that had happened in Italy, Britain, and Gaul.

As he showed Peter's letter to Artemas and Titus, he also asked Titus if he still had the letter Paul had written to him while he was still in Crete. Titus could only tell him that it was brought with them to Dalmatia. He put his wife to work looking for it. She finally found it, and Titus gave it to Onesimus.

When Onesimus told Titus about the collection of letters and the Gospels Gaius had in his library, Titus expressed an interest in them. Onesimus then invited Titus to visit Ephesus if the opportunity ever presented itself.

In several weeks, Marci and Onesimus started on the last leg of their journey. A man from Titus' congregation went with them as far as Berea. Here they stayed with Silas for a few days. Silas was not too surprised at the fate of Peter, but he was dismayed. At Thessalonica, Onesimus found out that Timothy was no longer in Macedonia, but had returned to Iconium.

He also learned that Andrew, Simon Peter's brother, had come to Macedonia. They had a sad visit when Onesimus and Marci arrived in Philippi. Andrew recalled, however, that his brother was dedicated to his calling as an apostle, and that Peter was ready to suffer anything, even death, for his Lord. Andrew also told Onesimus that he was exploring the possibility of going to Thrace, and even to the country north of there.

As winter was approaching, Marci and Onesimus then headed directly for Ephesus, stopping only in Troas to see Carpus and Tychicus, and in Thyatira at the home of Lydia. Several copies of Peter's second letter were made, but Onesimus took the original letter with him.

Chapter 18
Winter 64

The arrival of Onesimus and Marci in Ephesus was one of mixed emotion. Much had happened since Onesimus had last seen his parents. Gaius and Apphia were taken by surprise when Onesimus returned home with not only a wife but also grandchildren. It took some time for them to exchange information about their lives over the past few years.

Gaius and Apphia told of their trip to the Holy Land, and also of the trip to Arachosia, Apphia's native land. Onesimus gave a first-hand report of the tragic events surrounding the deaths of Paul and Peter, and told of his marriage to Marci and the birth of the twins.

It took less time for the assimilation of Marci, Lili, and Sheri into the family. Inasmuch as Marci's knowledge of Greek was still limited, Latin was occasionally used. Apphia and Gaius were thrilled to be grandparents, and the prospect of having another grandchild also pleased them. Gaius was intrigued at having a daughter-in-law from such a distant place. He wanted her to tell him as much about Gaul as possible.

"What are Marci's religious beliefs," Apphia and Gaius curiously asked Onesimus.

"Gaul is a primitive place, and as far as I know, there is no religion. Marci had no knowledge of God," answered Onesimus. "Mark and I explained a few basic things about Christianity to her several times, and she listened attentively. She said she would think about what we had said. When I tried to talk further to her about it, she always seemed to be busy with the girls."

Apphia learned that Marci could not read, even in her own language. She knew immediately what would occupy much of her time in the near future: teaching Marci to read, and helping her with the twins. The progress was slow at first, but by the time Marci was due for delivery, Marci showed signs of increasing interest.

The baby born to Marci and Onesimus was a boy. Not comfortable in naming him for either Paul or Peter or even Gaius, Onesimus selected an entirely different name, Eusebius.

In the meantime, Onesimus presented Paul's letter to Titus and Peter's second letter to the churches to Gaius. Gaius stated that Silas had stopped in Ephesus and furnished him with a copy of Peter's first letter.

Gaius now told Onesimus of his latest project. He was sponsoring the production of a dozen copies of all the letters and writings of the apostles and evangelists.

Copies would be distributed initially to the churches at Berea, Philippi, Thessalonica, Smyrna, Philadelphia, Corinth, Nicomedia, Iconium, Antioch, and Jerusalem. A copy would also go to Apollos in Alexandria. Onesimus remembered Titus in Dalmatia, and alerted Gaius of a possible visit from him. Gaius said additional copies could be made available if warranted.

Three copies of the 'New Testament,' as Gaius called the writings of the apostles and evangelists, were already completed. Onesimus volunteered to participate in their delivery, and soon he was leaving for Jerusalem. He stopped on the way at Colossae to see his old boyhood friend Archippus and his father Philemon. Their home and business had suffered extensive damage in a recent earthquake. Philemon was becoming feeble, but he warmly welcomed Onesimus.

Upon learning of the nature of his mission, Archippus indicated that inasmuch as he had never been to Jerusalem, that he would like to take time from his pastoral duties to accompany Onesimus. He quickly made arrangements, and in a week he and Onesimus were on the road to Iconium.

Timothy gladly received his visitors, and was very appreciative of the gift of the New Testament. Once again Onesimus recounted the events surrounding the deaths of Paul and Peter.

Timothy was kept busy not only in Iconium, but also throughout Galatia. Occasionally, he went to Pontus where he visited with Aquila and Priscilla who had returned to their native land following a brief stay in Philippi.

The next stop was Antioch, and after a short stay, Onesimus and Archippus headed south to Palestine. From directions given to him by Gaius, Onesimus called on Peter's widow, Zelina, in Bethsaida to express his condolences. From there they headed toward Jerusalem.

Although Onesimus had been in Jerusalem with Paul, it was while he was still a slave. He did not get to meet many of the brethren at that time. The only ones he came to know were James and Jude, the Lord's brothers. So now Onesimus sought Jude, and after a time found him. Jude told Onesimus and Archippus that the Roman government had been quite oppressive for some time now, and the situation was not improving. Jude made them feel at home, and introduced them to everyone. And receiving a copy of the writings of the apostles and evangelists was for Jude and the rest of the brethren like getting a breath of fresh air.

Onesimus was happy to meet everyone. He felt sure he had known one of them from somewhere. This man was none other than Barnabas. Onesimus had first seen him with Paul as a lad in Lystra. Barnabas explained to Onesimus, "After splitting with Paul so long ago, I spent my entire ministry on the island of Cyprus. I now long to take heed of what Matthew had quoted Jesus saying, 'Make disciples of all nations.'[1]

"I came to Jerusalem to learn from the brethren whether there was some place they might send me. But the officials here are not in a position to send anyone anywhere."

"You might want to consider going to Gaul," Onesimus suggested.

"Gaul? Why Gaul?" Barnabas wondered. "It seems so remote."

"Gaul is where my wife's family lives," was the reply.

Onesimus stated that he did not know how this would all fully be brought about, but that something would have to be worked out. Barnabas explained that he was short of funds.

But after a few days of contemplation, Barnabas decided to accept the challenge. Soon after Barnabas, Onesimus, and Archippus were off to Caesarea to sail for Cyprus to pick up Barnabas' possessions. There was only one problem. Onesimus objected to traveling by water. Barnabas soon convinced Onesimus that he was just being childish. One bad experience, he said, didn't necessarily mean that all traveling by water would be bad. And so they sailed to Cyprus, and from there to Ephesus. Archippus went home to Colossae from there.

When Archippus arrived home, he found his father to be a very sick man. John, who had been in Philadelphia, and also shepherded the church in Colossae while Archippus was away, ministered to Philemon. Archippus was home only a week before his father died. Word was sent to Ephesus and Gaius and his entire family came for the funeral.

John preached the funeral sermon. He used what Paul had written to the Corinthians in his first letter as the basis for his sermon. 'The Risen Christ, Faith's Reality; The Risen Christ, Our Hope."

He quoted directly from Paul's letter, "But now Christ is risen from the dead, and has become the first fruits of those who have fallen asleep. For since by man came death, by Man also came the resurrection of the dead. For as in Adam all die, even so in Christ all will be made alive. But each one in his own order: Christ the first fruits, afterward those who are Christ's at His coming. Then comes the end, when He delivers the kingdom of God, even the Father, when He puts down all rule and all authority and power. For He must reign till He has put all enemies under His feet.

"The last enemy that will be destroyed is death. For 'He has put all things under His feet.' But when He says, 'all things are put under Him,' it is evident that He is excepted who put all things under Him. And when all things are made subject to Him, then the Son Himself will also be subject to Him who put all things under Him, that God may be all in all."[2]

John explained the effects of denying the resurrection and the everlasting condemnation. In Christ, we are to awake to righteousness. The body of this life is sown in corruption, in dishonor, in weakness; it will be raised in incorruption, in glory, in power. It is sown a natural body; it will be raised a spiritual body. Our body will be changed into a glorious body. 'Death is swallowed up in victory'[3] – Christ's victory over death. 'Thanks be to God, who gives us the victory through our Lord Jesus Christ.'[4]

One day on the return trip to Ephesus, when Onesimus and Marci were talking, Marci exclaimed, "I want to be a Christian. I have been thinking about it ever since you and Mark mentioned it in Luca. Then I also listened to Apphia as she was teaching me to read and to write. John's sermon at the funeral helped me to make up my mind."

"I am happy for you, Marci," said Onesimus. "You are sure to find the inner peace in Christ that He Himself wants for His disciples if you abide in Him.

"'If anyone is in Christ, he is a new creation; the old things have passed away; behold, all things have become new. And all things are of God, Who has reconciled us to Himself through Jesus Christ, and has given us the ministry of reconciliation, that is, That God was in Christ reconciling the world to Himself, not imputing their trespasses to them, and has committed to us the word of reconciliation.

"'Therefore we are ambassadors for Christ, as though God were pleading by us: We implore you in Christ's behalf, be reconciled to God. For He has made Him who knew no sin to be sin for us, that we might become the righteousness of God in Him.'[5] Knowing this, we are to 'be steadfast, immovable, always abounding in the work of the Lord, inasmuch as you know that your labor is not in vain in the Lord.'[6]"

Marci was baptized when they reached home.

Onesimus had revealed the purpose of Barnabas' coming to Ephesus as soon as he had arrived. Gaius liked Onesimus' idea of having Barnabas go to Gaul. After Philemon's funeral, he and Onesimus talked to Marci about Barnabas's planned trip to Gaul. They wondered if she would assist him in preparing for it by teaching her native tongue and telling him more about the country of Gaul. She agreed.

Some time later, Titus and his wife showed up in Ephesus. They had been to Crete on a visit, and were now going back to Dalmatia. This visit seemed to be timed just right, because Onesimus was preparing to leave for Macedonia and Bithynia to deliver copies of the New Testament. Onesimus traveled together with them to Philippi. From there Titus went his way to Thessalonica and Berea, while Onesimus headed for Nicomedia by way of Troas. Tychicus went along with him.

This was the first trip to Bithynia for Onesimus. And he wanted to find out as much as possible about the country. Also of interest to him was the sea to the north and its surroundings.

On his return to Ephesus some time later, an unexpected development awaited him. As Marci and Barnabas studied together, Apphia remembered how she and Matthew had studied her native language and had translated Matthew's Gospel at the same time. Apphia suggested to Marci and Barnabas that they do likewise, and they were following her suggestion. Onesimus encouraged them to continue.

Another trip was in store for Onesimus, a journey to Alexandria. Other messengers would be sent to Achaia and Asia with copies of the New Testament.

After spending a few months at home, Onesimus sailed for Egypt. Not knowing where to look for Apollos, it took some time to locate him.

"You have no idea how much this means to me," Apollos told Onesimus as he handed the New Testament to him. "The writings of the apostles and the evangelists are a treasure."

Upon inspecting the document closely, Apollos added, "I am pleased and surprised that my treatise to the Hebrews is included with them."

"I talked with Paul about your work while I was with him, and I am happy to say that he held your treatise in high regard," Onesimus replied.

Apollos prevailed upon Onesimus to stay in Egypt for a little while so that he might show him the sights. Besides a trip up the Nile River and a journey to the Pyramids, Apollos traveled to Libya with him.

Another startling development awaited Onesimus upon his return from Alexandria. Gaius was determined to make the trip to Gaul with Barnabas. It had been in the back of his mind ever since Barnabas came from Jerusalem with Onesimus.

While Onesimus was in Egypt, Gaius suggested to Apphia that the whole family make the trip. Marci could visit her family and have her mother come to know her grandchildren. Gaius would underwrite the entire cost, including Barnabas's expense. One of his ships could be used for their transportation, and he would furnish the crew.

By the time Onesimus learned about this idea, everyone was eagerly anticipating the start of the journey. After Onesimus was home for a while, the plans were finalized, and soon they were all bound for Gaul.

Chapter 19
Spring 67

The itinerary Gaius arranged for the trip to Gaul called for stops at Crete, Sicily, Ostia, and Genua. At Genua, Gaius intended to charter a smaller vessel to take them over to Luca because of the lack of port facilities. Barnabas wanted to visit his cousin, Mark, there. After retracing their way back to Genua, they could then continue on to the mouth of the river coming from the north and center of Gaul.

Marci and Onesimus had assured Gaius that this river was large enough so that they could navigate a fairly good-sized vessel for some distance upstream. Depending upon the circumstances, then, they would go as far as possible. They then could arrange for dockage, and proceed on land from there. Gaius made certain that sufficient funds and materials were brought along to be used for bartering purposes.

The trip as far as Ostia went very smoothly, with no difficulties experienced. From there to Genua, it was a different story. Stormy weather overtook them, and most everyone on the ship was overcome with seasickness. The children were especially irritable. Onesimus was thankful that the storm was not nearly as severe as the one he endured sailing from Britain. By the time they arrived in Genua, the seas were more calm, and they were able to enjoy the voyage.

Genua was a bustling seaport, and the choice of vessels available for charter was substantially larger than Gaius anticipated. He had no trouble in finding a suitable craft.

With the aid of several seamen from his own vessel, Gaius planned to handle the chartered vessel. But he learned that the owners stipulated that some of their own men go along for security reasons. Gaius did not like it. He was aware of the dangers of piracy, but he thought they could handle such an emergency.

They soon became sufficiently acquainted with their newly acquired vessel, and the group of travelers set sail for Luca. They arrived safely in a short time. With Onesimus and Marci leading them, they made their way straight to the home of Mark and Cecilia.

Mark and Cecilia gave them all a warm welcome. Mark had just returned from Genua himself. Their home was not sufficiently large enough to accommodate eight additional persons, however. At Marci's insistence, they immediately arranged to go to visit Dominic and Theresa at their farm with the idea that perhaps she and Onesimus and the children could again stay with them just as they had when they first arrived in Luca four years previously. Dominic and Theresa were delighted to be host to Onesimus and his family once again, and before nightfall, everyone was comfortably situated.

It had been years since Mark had last seen his cousin, and Barnabas was glad for the opportunity to meet Mark's wife and family. They now had three children. Mark was equally pleased to hear that Barnabas was undertaking the responsibility of bringing the Gospel to the people of Gaul.

"How much territory do you cover in your work?" Barnabas asked.

"Most of the Cisalpine provinces," replied Mark, "which extends all the way over to Aquileia. Apollos was the pioneer missionary in this territory. I took over for him when he decided to return to Alexandria. I am planning to take some time off soon so that I can visit him. Since Cecilia does not care to go because of the children, I will be going alone."

When Onesimus learned of this, he told of his visit to Alexandria and gave Mark instructions.

Not wishing to delay their journey to Gaul and overextend the hospitality given to them, the visitors were again on their way in ten days. Mark again warned Gaius of the craftiness of some of the seamen of the area; they were not to be trusted. On their return trip to Genua, Gaius made sure that his crew was to be vigilant. His seamen were to be on separate watches.

As they neared Genua, the three accompanying seamen from Genua struck suddenly during the night, targeting Gaius' seamen. One went after the man on watch; the others attacked the two who were sleeping. Had it not been for the fact that Marci was on deck with Eusebius, who was fussing, their attack may have been successful. Marci was in the shadows when she noticed the stranger creep towards the watchman. Just as he was ready to strike, she cried out so that Gaius' seaman was able to defend himself. Marci immediately put Eusebius down, and, grabbing the first thing she could lay her hands on, came to his help.

Everyone on the ship was roused, and the three men from Genua were quickly repulsed. They jumped into the sea and were picked up by others who were apparent accomplices. One of the other seamen of Gaius was not as fortunate as his fellow seaman. He sustained a severe blow to his head. Gaius registered a complaint to the port official about the incident, but did not receive satisfaction. The injury sustained was not serious enough to slow the voyagers on their journey, however, and they continued on their way to Gaul.

Steady progress was made despite the fact they were without guides. They eventually came to a fairly good-sized port. It was Massillia. There they obtained the needed guidance and entered the Rhone River.

Gaius decided to stay with his ship, for the river was navigable just as he was told. They remained on the ship until they reached Lugdunum. With Marci's help, Gaius found a place to moor the ship. It was not without some dickering, however. Marci convinced Gaius that it would be best to give gratuities to the employees of the owner of the dock. Inasmuch as the length of their stay in Gaul was in doubt, they made sure the owner of the dock understood that the final settlement of accounts would be handled at their departure.

During their stay in this city, Barnabas and Onesimus were astonished to find a number of people who spoke Greek. They talked to them about the Gospel, and several men seemed to be genuinely interested. Barnabas promised to revisit them.

They now changed to traveling by land, covering much of the same territory taken by Onesimus and Marci when they left her home in Dieppe. Soon they arrived in Lutetia.

Since Barnabas planned on using this city as a base of operation, they stayed for a few days. Marci introduced him to the officials at the school where she had first gone with Onesimus. He was now also in a better position to become acquainted with these men. Gaius, too, was interested in getting to know them.

Once again on their way, Marci could scarcely contain herself as they neared her former home. There was no sign of life around the house when they arrived; only a solitary figure working in the field. Marci went out to see him. It was Pepe, her younger brother now well into his teens. They did not recognize each other at first sight, but once they did, they joyfully embraced.

The rest of the family was in the village. When they came home that evening, Lili was flabbergasted. She had never expected to see Marci again, and they both cried for joy. And she was thrilled to see her grandchildren. As things calmed down, Lili began to fret about accommodating all her guests. Makeshift arrangements were necessary.

On the journey to Gaul, Barnabas and Onesimus discussed the possibility of going over to Britain and perhaps visiting the grave of Paul. Barnabas told Onesimus that the one thing in life he regretted most was not apologizing to Paul for what happened between them. He told Onesimus that he said some nasty and uncalled for things to him.

After they had been in Dieppe for a few days, Barnabas and Onesimus suggested a possible trip to Britain to Gaius, saying that perhaps Pepe might be able to help them. Pepe wasn't sure. The people there were not always friendly. But after inquiring around the village, he found a man who had friends there, and was willing to take them. The trip to Verulamium went smoothly and soon Barnabas, Gaius, Onesimus, and Pepe were standing at the place where Onesimus had buried Paul; not far from the river. As they placed additional stone markers at the site, they noticed that a small building was being erected nearby. They were told it was to be a place of worship.

Marci found out from her mother that shortly after she and Onesimus left Dieppe, some men came searching for her. They had already abducted Sheri, and Sheri's mother had not heard from her since. Lili was constantly afraid that the same fate might eventually befall Jacqui.

After their return from Britain, Barnabas and Gaius, and also Apphia returned to Lutetia. Barnabas was eager to begin his work, and Gaius wanted to inquire about seeing more of Gaul. They became good friends with one of the scholars. He was from the city of Trier, in the country to the northeast, and planned to start a school in his hometown.

When Onesimus came from Dieppe shortly afterward, they made plans to go to Trier with this man. Recalling his visit to Caesarea with Peter much earlier, Gaius, in particular, was interested in making this trip. Although he was not sure about the area surrounding Trier, he felt that possibly it was somewhere close to the place where Cornelius and the Italian Regiment were presently stationed.

Everywhere they went Gaius made inquiries, and finally their group made contact with the Roman garrison. Cornelius was not among them. However, Gaius learned that these Roman soldiers had a copy of Mark's Gospel.

After that, Gaius and Apphia visited many other places in the territory surrounding Lutetia.

Gaius and his family were in Gaul for a year, and he was now anxious to return to Ephesus. A recent development, however, posed a question for Gaius. His friend from Trier was contemplating making a trip on the river Danube from its source in the mountains to its outlet in the sea to the east. He would use this trip as a basis for his doctoral dissertation, and was looking for several persons to go with him. One he was considering was Onesimus.

Onesimus was willing to do this, but that would leave Gaius shorthanded for manpower on the trip home. Since her brother was a husky lad with not much of a future for him in this land, Marci proposed that he go with them to Ephesus.

It was finally settled, and Onesimus left for the trip on the Danube River, while Pepe joined the others on their return journey.

Gaius' vessel moored in Lugdunum was ready and waiting for him, and when settlements of accounts were made, they sailed for home. Before they reached the Great Sea, Marci discovered that she was again going to have a child.

Sailing went smoothly and Pepe was a good addition to their crew. Soon they were back in Ostia, and from there they sailed the same route as in their voyage coming over to Gaul.

Chapter 20
Winter 68

The weary travelers, especially Gaius, were happy to be back in Ephesus. He confided with Apphia that this trip had been more tiring to him than any other. Apphia reminded him that he was no longer as young as he once was.

After resting a week or so, Gaius tended to matters of business. It was at this time that Gaius finally explained more of the operation of his business affairs to Apphia. In the past, whenever she displayed interest, Gaius always put her off.

Gaius also looked into the welfare of the Christian Church in Ephesus. He was not pleased with what he found. Diotrephes, son of his good friend, Aristobulus, had inserted himself into a position of prominence in the church. He was causing the church much distress.

Diotrephes had visited Linus in Rome. Upon the death of Peter, Linus consolidated his control in the church as the Bishop of Rome. This happened despite the many hardships in the church brought about by the persecutions of Nero. Linus had made a favorable impression on Diotrephes.

What he liked most of all was that Linus insisted on the celebration of the Sacrament of the Lord's Supper on every Lord's Day, and that all the members were compelled to participate in the sacrament lest they miss out in the blessings bestowed in it. Diotrephes introduced the same practice in the church in Ephesus. These changes brought contention to the church and enmities were formed. People did not like to be told when or how often they were to participate in the sacrament.

Diotrephes also became acquainted with the writings of Simon Magus. He and his followers were Gnostics. They were a group of intellectuals, and proclaimed themselves superior to others in understanding and spiritual knowledge. They were all given to affectation.

John, who was now at Philadelphia, knew what was going on in the church in Ephesus. Shortly after Gaius returned from Gaul, the congregation received a letter from him. This letter was primarily a refutation of Gnosticism. John summed his letter thus:

> "We know that whoever is born of God does not sin; but he who has been born of God keeps himself, and the wicked one does not touch him. We know that we are of God and the whole world lies in the power of the wicked one. And we know that the Son of God has come and has given us an understanding, that we may know Him who is true; and we are in Him who is true, in His Son Jesus Christ. This is the true God and eternal life. Little children, keep yourselves from idols. Amen."[1]

He did not want them to abandon their first love.

Diotrephes treated John's letter with contempt, and did not follow its directive. Gaius, however, kept the letter, adding it to the other writings of the apostles and evangelists.

During this entire time, Onesimus had not yet returned to Ephesus. Marci, although not openly, was becoming concerned. The baby would soon be here.

A month later Onesimus came home. His trip on the Danube River with his friend from Trier took longer than he anticipated. Travel was at a much more leisurely pace, since his friend wanted to find out as much as he could about the entire region. They were also twice detained by the local inhabitants for questioning.

Toward the end of the journey Onesimus tried to inquire of the natives whether they had seen or heard anything of a stranger from the country to the south of them. At this one village, he was told that just such a man who was preaching some nonsense about the forgiveness of sins by faith in a Jesus Christ had recently been chased from the area at the order of the chieftain. Some say that he was later put to death. Farther on, Onesimus found out that this was true. But the seed sown by Andrew had taken root, for Onesimus found a small group of believers at that place.

Onesimus eventually reached the Black Sea. Finding transportation to Byzantium was not easy, and this also delayed him.

Shortly after Onesimus arrived home, Marci gave birth to another boy child. He was named Polycarp, and they vowed to dedicate him to the service of the Lord at his baptism.

Late Winter 69

Word eventually got back to John as to what the reaction to his letter was. John was distressed, and after a while, he wrote another letter to the elders of the church, to offer them hope in their walking in the truth.

Gaius, who was also an elder, keenly felt the disruption of the peace in the congregation. He prayed fervently that peace would be restored. This anxiety, coupled with the weariness from his trip to Gaul, soon took its toll on Gaius and his health began to decline.

The brethren, including Demetrius, went to John in Philadelphia and reported to him about Gaius and his declining health. John promised to come after he first went to Hierapolis. Thereupon, John sent another short letter addressed directly to Gaius. He said he would shortly be able to speak face to face with him. Meanwhile, Gaius' condition became worse. He was now bedridden. John arrived in Ephesus after two weeks had passed.

As John and Gaius discussed the plight of the congregation in Ephesus, Onesimus joined them. Together they agreed that the aberrations introduced by Diotrephes could not be tolerated. Since the church was split down the middle, it was certain that a reconciliation could not be reached. Diotrephes and his followers were set in their thinking, and they would not listen to even John.

"Diotrephes," John said, "was not displaying Christian love. You will recall that I wrote in my Gospel, 'A new commandment I give to you, that you love one another; as I have loved you, that you also love one another. By this all will know that you are My disciples, if you have love for one another.'[2] I was quoting Jesus. Besides this being one of the ways in which we witness the Gospel to the world, our loving one another demonstrates that we are members of the body of Christ. This is what I wrote about in my first letter to the church here in Ephesus.

"'Do not love the world or the things in the world. If anyone loves the world, the love of the Father is not in him.'[3] Those who do not love their brothers are the children of the devil, and they abide in death. They become as murderers because of their hatred. This is the manifest difference between the children of God and the children of the devil. Whoever does not practice righteousness is not of God, nor is he who does not love his brother. The children of God practice righteousness and love their brothers. This means that they are born of Christ. And because of this, the world will hate the children of God.

"'Beloved, let us love one another, for love is of God, and everyone who loves is born of God and knows God. He who does not love does not know God, for God is love.'[5]

"Paul writes of the very thing in his first letter to the church at Corinth. 'Love suffers long and is kind; love does not envy; love does not parade itself, is not puffed up; does not behave rudely, does not seek its own, is not provoked, thinks no evil; does not rejoice in iniquity, but rejoices in the truth; bears all things, believes all things, hopes all things, endures all things. Love never fails.'[6]

"'In this our love has been made perfect, that we may have boldness in the day of Judgment; because as He is, so are we in this world. There is no fear in love; but perfect love casts out fear, because fear involves torment. But he who fears has not been made perfect in love. We love Him because He first loved us.'[7]

"Love is one of the fruits of the Spirit. Paul mentions this in his letter to the Galatians, 'But the fruit of the Spirit is love, joy, peace, longsuffering, kindness, goodness, faithfulness, gentleness, and self-control.'[8]

"Love can easily be misconstrued. It is never to be compared to conjugal love. And neither is it to be thought of in terms of doting. Nor is it to be thought of in permissive terms. Parents do their children no favor when they allow them freedom to do whatever they wish without any restraints; nor when they give in to their every whim without guidance of any kind. It is the same in our relationship with God. He chastens those whom He loves. 'As many as I love I rebuke and chasten. Therefore be zealous and repent.'[9]

Matthew brings his Gospel to a close with the direction to go and make disciples of all nations, and includes this imperative: 'Teaching them to observe all things whatever I have commanded you.'[10] This is vitally important. We are to obey Christ. It is apparent that Diotrephes has not learned this truth."

Following John's advice, Gaius and his followers separated themselves from Diotrephes and his followers. Diotrephes promised them that he would not forget what took place and who was responsible for it. Onesimus was placed in charge of the new group.

As John continued to minister to Gaius, their conversation gradually centered on the celebration of the Lord's Supper, or the Sacrament of Holy Communion, as Gaius was wont to call it. Gaius asked John to give a detailed explanation of it. He recalled that John did not mention the sacrament in his Gospel directly, whereas Matthew, Mark, and Luke did. Even Paul discussed it thoroughly in his first letter to the church in Corinth.

John told Gaius, "The other Gospel writers and Paul described the institution of the sacrament adequately. Instead of repeating what they had written, I concentrated more on the rest of what Jesus said during the same evening. Since much of this pertains to things other than the celebration of the sacrament, I will go over what seems to me to be of primary importance.

"Christ made it plain that He was giving His very own body and blood in, with, and under the bread and wine, for 'us Christians to eat and to drink.'[11] The real presence of Christ's body and blood in the sacrament are given to us in, with, and under the visible elements, namely, the bread and wine.

"Each communicant is to receive both the bread and wine. Whereas, we receive the bread and wine in a natural manner by eating and drinking, we receive Christ's body and blood in a supernatural manner. We are to do this in remembrance of Him. We are to remember everything that Christ has done for us to secure for us the remission of our sins. This is how we 'proclaim his death.'[12] His sacrificial death on the cross obtains for us forgiveness before God and assures for us eternal life in heaven with God. When we partake of the sacrament, we are in communion with Christ as <u>One</u> with Him, and likewise also with the entire body of Christ on earth, namely, all true believers. This is what may truly be called 'the communion of saints.'

"When we say that we 'proclaim' Christ's death until He comes again, we must not confuse this with the preaching of the Gospel that is done in the world. This proclamation is our affirmation to the elders of the church that we possess the gifts of the Holy Spirit, gifts that were given to us by the Spirit.

"It is these gifts that Matthew speaks of when relating how Jesus taught His disciples on the mountain. He wrote, 'Therefore if you bring your gift to the altar, and there remember that your brother has something against you, leave your gift there before the altar, and go your way. First be reconciled to your brother, and then come and offer your gift.'[13] The gift that we bring to the altar is really our sanctified selves; nothing else than the fruit of the Spirit within us.

"As we approach the Lord's Table to receive His body and blood, we must be at peace with God, and also our fellow believers. That is to say, we must be in union with them. We know, however, that as long as we are in this life, that this union remains an imperfect union. Only as we are received into eternal bliss will this union with Christ and other believers be complete and perfect.

"This is what Matthew, Mark, and Luke were writing about when they mention in their story of the institution of the Holy Supper that Christ said, 'But I say to you, I will not drink of this fruit of the vine from now on until that day when I will drink it new with you in My Father's kingdom.'[14] 'Drinking of the fruit of the vine new' means that the glorified saints in heaven will eternally be celebrating the Lamb's victory over death, and singing praises to the Lamb who sits at the right hand of His Father.

"Our celebration of the Sacrament of Holy Communion is something that we should forever do until He comes again. This is one of the great differences between this sacrament and the Sacrament of Holy Baptism. Baptism is administered only once in the Christian's life. We should partake of the Lord's Supper frequently, that is to say, repeatedly and periodically.

"The other great difference in the two sacraments is that in Holy

Baptism, the Holy Spirit bestows His gifts and blessings on all who are baptized. We are One in Christ in that very instant. The sacrament of Holy Communion, however, may or may not be received with a blessing, depending on whether or not the communicant receives the sacrament worthily.

"To receive the sacrament worthily, each communicant must examine himself or herself to see whether he or she truly believes that their sins are forgiven in what Christ has done for us, namely, His vicarious atonement for all of the sins of the whole world. All those who receive the sacrament while not truly believing this, receive the sacrament unworthily. This is not 'child's play!'[15] Everyone must be taught how to diligently examine themselves prior to going to the Lord's Table.

"Paul writes about this in his first letter to the Corinthians, 'Let a man examine himself, and so let him eat of that bread and drink of that cup. For he who eats and drinks in an unworthy manner eats and drinks judgment to himself, not discerning the Lord's body.'[16] We must confess our sins and remember that they are washed white in Christ's blood. By the grace given to us by the Holy Spirit, we are to approach God's altar in true penitence.

"The pastor, as a called and ordained servant of the Word acting in Christ's stead, then announces the grace of God unto us, and in His stead forgives us our sin. The pastor can do this because he has been bestowed with the 'Office of the Keys.' After the resurrection, Christ appeared to the disciples, and said to them, 'Receive the Holy Spirit. If you forgive the sins of any, they are forgiven them; and if you retain the sins of any, they are retained.'[17]

"Let me state once more," John told Gaius, "how we should examine ourselves before partaking of Communion. We should examine ourselves 'to see (a) Whether we truly repent of our sins; (b) Whether we believe in Jesus Christ as our Savior; and (c) Whether we have the good and earnest purpose with the aid of God the Holy Spirit henceforth to amend our sinful lives.'[18]"

As John paused, Gaius asked a question. "How important is it to have so much concern in our daily life for living an upright life?"

John assured him that it is of great importance. "When our Lord and Master Jesus Christ said, 'Repent,' He willed the entire life of believers to be one of repentance."[19]

John continued, "Thus far, I have said little relating to the frequency of partaking of the sacrament other than that it should be often. 'Often' covers a lot of ground. At the time of my departure from Jerusalem for Ephesus with you, this was one aspect of the sacrament in which there was already a small disagreement among Christians. Some of them were of the opinion that since Christ instituted the sacrament at the observance of the Passover, the Lord's Supper was to be likewise observed only once a year. Others, myself included, argued that the observance should take place more often. Still others insisted that bread should be broken every Lord's Day.

"Immediately after the day of Pentecost until persecutions arose, we 'continued steadfastly in the apostles' doctrine and fellowship, in the breaking of bread, and in prayer.'[20] This time was one of special significance for the apostles and the early disciples. As we began our ministry without the Lord physically at our side, we were in need of special blessings bestowed by God from on high.

"As the apostles and evangelists departed from Jerusalem to go into all the world with the Gospel, different practices in regard to the celebration of the sacrament developed. Over the latter years, the question was never fully resolved. It has been my experience that there is in the church today a wide divergence about this in the observation of Holy Communion. In some places it takes place every week, in others once a month, and so on.

"It is interesting that Paul wrote to the congregation at Corinth,

'When you come together in one place, it is not to eat the Lord's Supper.'[21] Paul was talking about their unity of faith, making sure that divisions among them were taken care of, and that those confirmed in the faith and approved of were recognized. Celebration of the sacrament was to be preceded by preaching of the Word in the unity of faith. It is important for us to note that Paul wants us to realize that preparedness in receiving the sacrament is by far more critical for us than is the frequency of our receiving the sacrament.

"Neither Matthew nor Mark nor Luke give us any clue as to the frequency of our celebration. When Paul writes, therefore, "This do, as often as you drink it, in remembrance of Me,'[22] this may be paraphrased thusly: 'do this, whenever you drink it, in remembrance of Me.'[23] I believe that Jesus wants each member of His body to decide for themselves how often they should go to communion; but again, I must reiterate that it must be done repeatedly. He did not want to place upon them some new regulation, thereby burdening their conscience. His members are to be free to make this choice. No one should be placed into the position of having to ask themselves, 'Am I receiving the sacrament often enough?'

"In their freedom, however, they are to realize that partaking of the sacrament is not to be neglected. Our faith is strengthened in our participation. Our worthiness to receive the blessings given in the sacrament does not depend on our own goodness, but rests solely in the grace supplied by the Holy Spirit. Both the command and the promise of Christ, our Lord, then, should move us to partake of the sacrament frequently.

"The pronouncement of Linus and Diotrephes in this regard run counter to the love which is ours in Christ. No one is to be coerced to receive the sacrament, and one person does not have the authority to dictate new human rules concerning this. It should be realized, however, that whenever individuals absent themselves from the Lord's Table for an extended period of time, they are thereby self-excommunicating themselves and should no longer be considered a member of Christ's body."

"I want to assure you, John," said Gaius, "that your detailed explanation of your thoughts on the celebration of the Lord's Supper is highly valued. Is there any more you wish to add?"

"Yes, there is," answered John. "Two other items need mentioning. We must always bear in mind that the Sacrament of the Lord's Supper, together with Holy Baptism, and the Word, is one of the 'Means of Grace.' The Word 'sacrament' means 'a sacred act.' God instituted both of these sacraments Himself. God's grace and blessing in His presence in the sacraments must always be uppermost in our minds.

"Our bodily eating and drinking in the sacrament does not bring about these blessings received in the Lord's Supper. The power of the Lord's Supper is contained in these words, 'Given and shed for you for the remission of sins.'[24] 'It is not the eating and drinking indeed that imparts the forgiveness of sins.'[25] 'The words "for you" require all hearts to believe.'[26]

"When Christians participate in the Lord's Supper primarily for the purpose of not missing out in receiving a blessing as Linus and Diotrephes insist, they are ritualizing the sacrament. Any ritualization of the sacrament is also celebrating the sacrament unworthily and brings damnation to those who do so. We are not to forget, however, that by eating Christ's body and drinking His blood in a worthy manner, our faith is strengthened and renewed.

"Finally," said John, "I want to comment on what Paul wrote to the Corinthian congregation. He said, 'This cup is the new covenant in My blood.'[27] Matthew, Mark, and Luke say the same thing in their Gospels. A new covenant presupposes an original covenant. We know that the original covenant relates to Christ's dying for our sins, and will forever be true and in effect. The new covenant does not supersede or supplant the original covenant. The new covenant supplements the original covenant.

"The original covenant is a covenant of grace, and is what is known as 'Justification.' The new covenant is a covenant of love which includes the sending of the Holy Spirit, and is what is known as 'Sanctification.' There are those who say that this new covenant is Jesus Christ's last will and testament. Whatever term is used, God the Holy Spirit, the third person of the Holy Trinity, is the executor of the new covenant.

"'Justification' and 'Sanctification' are separate church doctrines and must remain that way. They are not to be combined or comingled in any way whatever."

As John finished, Gaius asked whether the celebration of the sacrament is restricted to the gathering of the whole congregation. He was thinking of himself and the fact that he was bedridden. John said that there was nothing to hinder him from receiving the sacrament privately. Whereupon Gaius indicated that he so desired. Apphia, Onesimus, and Marci also indicated their desire to participate with him. John then proceeded with the private celebration of Holy Communion.

The service was opened in the name of the Father and of the Son and of the Holy Spirit. John then read Psalm 51, after which he exhorted them:

> "Dearly Beloved: Forasmuch as we purpose to come to the Holy Supper of our Lord Jesus Christ, it becomes us diligently to examine ourselves, as St. Paul exhorteth us. For this holy Sacrament has been instituted for the special comfort and strengthening of those who humbly confess their sins and hunger and thirst after righteousness.

"But if we thus examine ourselves, we shall find nothing in us but sin and death, from which we can in no wise set ourselves free. Therefore, our Lord Jesus Christ has had mercy upon us and has taken upon Himself our nature that so He might fulfill for us the whole will and Law of God and for us and for deliverance suffer death and all that we by our sins have deserved. And to the end that we should the more confidently believe this and be strengthened by our faith in a cheerful obedience to His holy will, He has instituted the holy Sacrament of His Supper, in which He feedeth us with His body and giveth us to drink of His blood.

"Therefore, whoso eateth of this bread and drinketh of this cup, firmly believing the words of Christ, dwelleth in Christ, and Christ in him, and hath eternal life.

"We should do this also in remembrance of Him, showing His death, that He was delivered for our offenses and raised again for our justification, and rendering unto Him most hearty thanks for the same, take up our cross and follow Him, and, according to His commandment, love one another even as He hath loved us. For we are all one bread and one body, even as we are all partakers of this one bread and drink of this one cup."[28]

They then proceeded with the confession of sins which was followed by the announcement of the forgiveness of sins. John then led them in praying the Lord's Prayer, and continued with the consecration of the elements.

With distribution following, John said, "Take, eat; this is the true body of our Lord and Savior Jesus Christ, given into death for your sins. May this strengthen and preserve you in the true faith unto life everlasting!" and "Take, drink; this is the true blood of our Lord and Savior Jesus Christ, shed for the remission of your sins. May this strengthen and preserve you in the true faith unto life everlasting! Depart in peace!"[29]

Having finished the distribution, they sang a song of praise.

Gaius lived only another week. He was buried in a crypt on a knoll overlooking the sea.

Chapter 21
Fall 72

Sometime after Gaius had died and John had returned to Philadelphia, Onesimus was confronted by Diotrephes. Diotrephes approached in a conciliatory manner, as if he did not wish to alienate him any more than he already had. Acting on behalf of Linus in Rome, Diotrephes spoke about Gaius' collection of the writings of the apostles and evangelists. He was aware that most of the writings in Gaius' library were the original writings.

Diotrephes thought that perhaps Onesimus might not be as committed to the separation in the church at Ephesus as Gaius and John were. But Onesimus was not taken in by the smooth talking Diotrephes, and knew the purpose behind his actions was to obtain these writings and that Linus had probably convinced Diotrephes that their place was with the church in Rome.

Onesimus flatly refused to let them go. Diotrephes accepted the decision amicably, and left quietly.

Onesimus discussed his talk with Diotrephes with his mother. They were not overly apprehensive. However, a week later when Marci reported seeing several strange men lurking about the property, they became more concerned.

Apphia and Onesimus decided they should protect the collection of the apostolic writings. They took them from the library, and placed them in jars, and hid them in Gaius' burial crypt. A week later, as they returned home from visiting friends, they found the library ransacked. Thus, the estrangement between Onesimus and Diotrephes became permanent.

As time passed and their family grew, Onesimus and Marci grew more at home in Ephesus. Whereas, since Apphia was now more active in the business affairs of Gaius' commercial interests, and was on the move more often, Onesimus and Marci confined their traveling to short trips to various nearby places such as Laodicea, Colossae, and Smyrna. Their young children prevented them from going farther.

Marci's brother, Pepe, had been staying in Ephesus throughout this period. His sister's in-laws impressed him favorably, and he became a member of the church. As time went by, his interest in the Christian religion increased. He became well versed in its doctrine.

Onesimus continued to host many visitors to Ephesus just as Gaius before him had done. John occasionally came from Philadelphia. So did Archippus, who was now living in Hierapolis. Others who came to Ephesus for visits were Silas and his wife, and Tychicus and Carpus. Visitors from Jerusalem were Jude and Joses, brothers of Jesus. Actually, they were no longer at Jerusalem, but were now in Pella across the River Jordan; having fled the Roman sack of Jerusalem a few years previously.

About five years after the trip to Gaul, Barnabas stopped in Ephesus on his return to Cyprus. He felt that his missionary work in Gaul had been very rewarding, and now that he was getting up in years, he longed to go home. He considered his work in Lugdunum to have been particularly fruitful. The Word had been planted. He also reported that in Luca, he learned that Mark had been killed on his visit to Alexandria as he was witnessing to the Gospel.

Barnabas was happy to learn that Pepe had become a Christian. Although he taught several men in Ludgunum and Lutetia to take charge of the churches in Gaul, there was a need for more preachers of the Word. Barnabas and Onesimus discussed the possibility of Pepe's return to Gaul. Pepe liked the idea.

Summer 75

Diotrephes had not forgotten about John and what he had done to him. Periodically, he arranged for someone to harass John in little ways. This harassment grew. John decided to move back to Ephesus and once again he stayed in Gaius' residence. Onesimus was pleased with this arrangement, for it provided the opportunity for Eusebius and Polycarp to receive instruction from John.

Onesimus had read John's letters and his Gospel many times, but did not yet fully understand everything in them. John mentioned the coming of antichrist, so Onesimus asked about this person. He was wondering if he was the same as the person that Paul spoke of in his second letter to the congregation at Thessalonica. The one whom Paul called the lawless one.

"I am surprised that you call antichrist a person, Onesimus," answered John. "Antichrist is of the devil, the father of lies. Antichrist is, therefore, also a liar. It is as Paul writes, 'The coming of the lawless one is according to the working of Satan with all power, signs, and lying wonders, and with all deception of unrighteousness in those who perish, because they did not receive the love of the truth, that they might be saved.'[1] and 'And for this reason God will send them strong delusion, that they should believe the lie, that they all might be condemned who did not believe the truth but had pleasure in unrighteousness.'[2]

"Paul and I were writing of one and the same thing. Satan would very dearly have us believe that antichrist is a person. It is just another one of his tricks. However, believing that antichrist is a person does not in itself condemn us. It just facilitates his evil scheming.

"What really condemns us is denying that Jesus is the Christ. I'll repeat what I have written, 'He is antichrist who denies the Father and the Son.'[3] By denying that Jesus is the Christ, you are also denying the relationship which exists between the Father and the Son. This is vitally important. The relationship between the Father and the Son is that they are <u>One</u>.

"In my Gospel I try to stress this, not only for the enlightenment for the Jews, but also for the instruction and benefit of the Gentiles. I will quote a few passages: 'And the Word became flesh and dwelt among us, and we beheld His glory, the glory as of the only begotten of the Father, full of grace and truth.'[4] and 'Then Jesus answered and said to them, "Most assuredly, I say to you, the Son can do nothing of Himself, but what He sees the Father do; for whatever He does, the Son also does in like manner. For the Father loves the Son, and shows Him all things that He Himself does; and He will show Him greater works than these, that you may marvel. For as the Father raises the dead and gives life to them, even so the Son gives life to whom He will. For the Father judges no one, but has committed all judgment to the Son, that all should honor the Son just as they honor the Father. He who does not honor the Son does not honor the Father who sent Him.'[5]

"'You judge according to the flesh; I judge no one. And yet if I do judge, My judgment is true; for I am not alone, but I and the Father who sent Me. It is also written in your law that the testimony of two men is true. I am One who bears witness of Myself, and the Father who sent Me bears witness of Me.' Then they said to Him, 'Where is Your Father?' Jesus answered, 'You know neither Me or My Father. If you had known Me, you would have known My Father also.'[6]

"'Jesus said to him (Thomas), 'I am the way, the truth, and the life. No one comes to the Father except through me. If you had known Me, you would have known My Father also; and from now on you know Him and have seen Him.' Philip said to Him, 'Lord, show us the Father, and it is sufficient for us.' Jesus said to him, 'Have I been with you so long, and yet you have not known me, Philip? He who has seen Me has seen the Father' so how can you say, 'Show us the Father?' 'Do you not believe that I am in the Father, and the Father in me?'[7]

"And also, 'My sheep hear My voice, and I know them, and they follow Me. And I give them eternal life, and they shall never perish; neither shall anyone snatch them out of My hand. My Father, who gave them to Me, is greater than all; and no one is able to snatch them out of My Father's hand. I and the Father are one.'[8]"

John went on to tell Onesimus more. "As the Father and the Son and the Holy Spirit is incorporeal, so therefore, is also antichrist, who opposes Christ and His Father, incorporeal, and not a person.

"The devil was incapable of becoming incarnate in the same manner as Christ became incarnate, so he created the delusion that antichrist is a person. By believing that antichrist is a person, we are more easily confused as to the true nature of his evil intentions. And then we unwittingly fall into his snares and do precisely what he wants us to do, and do exactly the opposite of what we should be doing."

Then John directed Onesimus to Jesus' prayer for Himself, for His disciples, and for all believers: "Jesus spoke these words, lifted up His eyes to heaven, and said, 'Father, the hour has come. Glorify Your Son, that Your Son also may glorify You, and You have given Him authority over all flesh, that He should give eternal life to as many as You have given Him. And this is eternal life, that they may know You, the only true God, and Jesus Christ whom You have sent. I have glorified You on the earth. I have finished the work which You have given Me to do. And now, O Father, glorify Me together with Yourself, with the glory which I had with You before the world was.

"'I have manifested Your name to the men whom You gave Me out of the world. They were Yours, You gave them to Me, and they have kept Your word. Now they have known that all things which You have given Me are from You. For I have given to them the words which You gave Me; and they have received them, and have known surely that I came forth from You; and they have believed that You sent Me. I pray for them. I do not pray for the world but for those whom You have given Me, for they are Yours. And all Mine are Yours, and Yours are Mine, and I am glorified in them.

"'And now I am no longer in the world, but these are in the world, and I come to You. Holy Father, keep through Your name those whom You have given Me, that they may be one as We are. While I was with them in the world, I kept them in Your name. Those whom You gave Me I have kept; and none is lost except the son of perdition, that the Scripture might be fulfilled.

"'But now I come to You, and these things I speak in the world, that they may have My joy fulfilled in themselves. I have given them Your word; and the world has hated them because they are not of the world, just as I am not of the world. I do not pray that You take them out of the world, but that You keep them from the evil one. They are not of the world, just as I am not of the world. Sanctify them by Your truth. Your word is truth. As You have sent Me into the world, I also have sent them into the world. And for their sakes I sanctify Myself, that they also may be sanctified by the truth.

"'I do not pray for these alone, but also for those who will believe in Me through their word; that they all may be one, as you, Father, are in Me, and I in You; that they also may be one in Us, that the world may believe that You have sent Me. And the glory which You gave Me I have given them, that they may be one just as We are one: I in them, and You in Me; that they may be made perfect in one, and that the world may know that you have sent Me, and have loved them as You have loved Me.

"'Father, I desire that they also whom You have given Me may be with Me where I am, that they may behold My glory which You have given Me; for You loved Me before the foundation of the world. O righteous Father! The world has not known You, but I have known You; and these have known that You have sent Me. And I have declared to them Your name, and will declare it, that the love with which You have loved Me may be in them, and I in them.'[9]"

John continued, "The time will come when men will say and

pray that they should be <u>one</u> with each other in the church so that they may be <u>one</u> with the Father and the Son. The people who teach this are in reality denying the true <u>oneness</u> which exists between the Father and the Son. To be a true member of the body of Christ, men must first be <u>one</u> with the Father and the Son. As they are <u>one</u> with the Father and the Son, the <u>oneness</u> with each other follows. Our true <u>oneness</u> with the Father and the Son is a sure testimony to the sin-sick world.

"To be <u>one</u> with the Father and the Son here on earth means to be in communion with God. The Holy Spirit provides this true unity. Every time we partake of the Holy Supper, we should be aware of this fact. While this communion here on earth is still an imperfect state because of our sinful nature, the communion of the glorified saints in heaven with God will be perfect and everlasting.

"Those who insist that the 'communion of saints' on earth is to be comprised of an earthly organization deny this truth. Some will go so far as to say that salvation may not be procured outside of their organization. They are in effect trying to put God in a box. Trying to confine God in such a manner is another goal of antichrist. The Spirit of God cannot be confined. He extends as far as the east is from the west. His presence is like that of the wind; no one knows from where it comes, and no one knows where it goes. These people demonstrate the spirit of antichrist.

"One of the tricks Satan uses when he would have us believe that antichrist is a person is that of complacency. If antichrist is thought of to be another person, this more or less releases us from any concern. Christians should be concerned about the deception of Satan in regard to antichrist.

"To say that antichrist is a person is to say that he does not have other spheres of operation. 'For many deceivers are gone out into the world who do not confess Jesus Christ as coming into the flesh.'[10] They are all an antichrist, and combined they show antichrist's spirit.

Antichrist does not confine his operations solely in one person or in one organization. All Christians, individually or corporately, are objects of his hellish schemes. If we are lulled into believing that antichrist is somewhere else in Christendom, his job is made easier.

"Likewise, such thinking very often leads to pride – falsely. We become overly secure of our position in the Christian life. It is almost as if we tell ourselves that we already have one foot in heaven. And before we are aware of it, Satan strikes, and strikes hard. He leads us to believe that we, ourselves, have contributed to this well being of our soul.

"Gnostics are of this nature. As their spiritual knowledge increases, so does their self-esteem and self-assurance in religious matters. It can also happen in a similar manner in the matter of the celebration of the Sacrament of Holy Communion. This is especially true of those who say that as they more frequently participate in the sacrament, they are becoming more <u>one</u> in Christ; as if their actions bring this about. The Holy Spirit is He who creates our <u>oneness</u> in Christ. And there is no degree in our <u>oneness</u> in Christ, just as a person with superior spiritual knowledge does not merit special favor in God's sight.

"Such synergistic thinking is evil, and Satan rejoices when this happens. He is made happy when people forget that God alone supplies the grace for our spiritual well being. Paul expresses this very nicely in his letter to the congregation here in Ephesus: 'For by grace you have been saved through faith, and that not of yourselves; It is a gift of God, not of works, lest anyone should boast.'[11] It is a shame that Diotrephes disregarded this admonishment by Paul. A poet puts it thus:

> 'By grace I'm saved, grace free and boundless;
> My soul, believe and doubt it not.
> Why stagger at this word of promise?
> Has Scripture ever falsehood taught?

    Nay; then this word must true remain:
    By grace thou, too, shalt heav'n obtain.'[12]

"I would like to call your attention to what happened in your native Galatia," John continued. "The Judaizers came and preached a 'different gospel.'[13] They taught that it was necessary to continue the keeping of old Jewish ceremonial laws, such as circumcision. Paul, in his letter to the Galatians, rebukes such teaching, and warns these Christians not to allow themselves to be placed anew under the law. This would be just another 'yoke of bondage.'[14] Our justification before God is by faith alone in His sacrificial death.

"Paul writes about this also in his letter to the Romans, 'Now we know that whatever the law says, it says to those who are under the law, that every mouth must be stopped, and all the world may become guilty before God. Therefore, by the deeds of the law, no flesh will be justified in His sight, for by law is the knowledge of sin. But now the righteousness of God apart from the law is revealed, being witnessed by the Law of the Prophets, even the righteousness of God which is by faith in Jesus Christ to all and on all who believe. For there is no difference; for all have sinned and fall short of the glory of God, being justified freely by His grace through the redemption that is in Christ Jesus, whom God has set forth to be a propitiation, through faith, in His blood, to demonstrate His righteousness, because of the passing over of the sins that were previously committed, through the forbearance of God; to demonstrate at the present time His righteousness, that He might be just and the justifier of the one who has faith in Jesus. Where is boasting then? It is excluded. By what law? Of works? No, but by the law of faith. Therefore, we conclude that a man is justified by faith apart from the deeds of the law.'[15]

"And still antichrist comes with his bag of tricks. He twists not only what is written by the apostles and evangelists, but also what is spoken by Jesus himself, as Peter points out in his second letter. The time will come when men will be told that the good that they are to do as followers of Christ must be done to secure favor with God. That they are to be a meritorious service. Jesus, however, tells us that we are to let our light so shine before men that they may see our good works so that His name may be glorified. Our sanctified lives are to be observed, and not used as a tool for exploitation. All boasting is excluded.

"Eventually, this type of temptation will also be used in regard to Christ's command that we are to love one another even as He has loved us. Antichrist will convince many that if we but love our fellow-believers and also our neighbors, we will merit some special favor with God. Our love for each other is based solely on Christ's love for us, and must always be our response to His great love.

"It is evident as Paul says, that 'The mystery of lawlessness is already at work.'[16] And he is at work from within the church!"

The Holy Spirit placed a shadow over the mind of Onesimus after John told him these things, and Onesimus did not speak of them to any other persons. The time for full disclosure of these mysteries had not yet come.

Fall 82

Diotrephes became more relentless in his pursuit of John as more years passed. He eventually contrived with the provincial Roman officials to have him arrested and convicted of sedition. John was banished to the island of Patmos to live in isolation. He was to be allowed but one visitor a year. At his sentencing, John designated his yearly visitor to be Onesimus.

Patmos was a well-known prison colony in the Roman Empire. Most prisoners confined there were put to hard labor. But because of John's age and the nature of his crime, he was spared that. Instead, he was placed in solitary confinement.

Onesimus knew how lonely a life John was enduring. At the time of his first visit, he wanted somehow to help alleviate John's tedium, so he took along some writing material and paper in the hope that these things could be given to John. Happily the prison officials allowed it.

Fall 92

The prison visits continued for some time, and Onesimus always contributed some small item for John's use. John was forever grateful to Onesimus for everything. On one visit, the Roman prison officials told Onesimus that John, because of his age, was no longer required to stay in prison. John went home with Onesimus, taking with him a number of scrolls. He requested that the scrolls not be opened until after his death.

John lived two more years. Onesimus buried him in Gaius' crypt. After the burial and a period of mourning, Onesimus opened the scrolls and began to read, "The Revelation of Jesus Christ, which God gave Him to show His servant – things which must shortly take place. And He sent and signified it by His angel to His servant John, who bore witness to the Word of God, and to the testimony of Jesus Christ, and to all things that he saw.

"Blessed is he who reads, and those who hear the words of this prophecy, and keep those things which are written in it; for the time is near."[17] …. "For I testify to everyone who hears the words of the prophecy of this book: If anyone adds to these things, God will add to him the plagues that are written in this book.

"And if anyone takes away from the words of the book of this prophecy, God will take away his part from the Book of Life, from the holy city, and from the things which are written in this book.

"He who testifies to these things says, 'Surely I am coming

quickly.' Amen. Even so, come, Lord Jesus. The grace of our Lord Jesus Christ be with you all. Amen."[18]

Onesimus' eyes were moist. He laid the scrolls aside and thought about the collection of the writings of the apostles and evangelists and about each of the authors. Matthew, Mark, Luke, John, Paul, Peter, Apollos, James, and Jude. He had known and had come to love them all. This final legacy of John would be the appropriate conclusion to their writings.

Onesimus then meditated on the warnings given by John. The preachers of the Gospel are given a great responsibility. They must preach everything that is contained in the Law and Gospel, neither adding anything or deleting anything. The whole Word of God must be proclaimed.

Next Onesimus focused on how John referred to himself in this final book. From the very beginning he calls himself 'Christ's servant.' And then as he fell at the feet of the angel who talked to him to worship him, how the angel said, "See that you do not do that! I am your fellow servant, and of your brethren who have the testimony of Jesus. Worship God! For the testimony of Jesus is the spirit of prophecy."[19] And then again when John wrote, "And he said to me, 'These words are faithful and true.' And the Lord God of the holy prophets sent His angel to show His servants the things which must shortly take place. 'Behold, I am coming quickly! Blessed is he who keeps the words of the prophecy of this Book.' And I, John, saw and heard these things. And when I had heard and seen, I fell down to worship before the feet of the angel who showed me these things. Then he said to me, 'See that you do not do that. For I am your fellow servant, and of your brethren and prophets, and of those who keep the words of this book. Worship God.'[20]"

We are all servants of God, thought Onesimus, together with the angels and the prophets and the apostles and all those who are believers. His heart was warmed at the remembrance of Gaius, his father, and of thinking of his dear mother, Apphia, and likewise remembering Paul and

Peter and all the rest.

In his reverie Onesimus then retraced his entire life. It began as a slave, the son of a slave. In human bondage. And set free. Freed to a life of service in Christ. Voluntarily a slave of the Lord, captivated by His love. It was entirely appropriate when the Apostle Paul so rightly wrote, "I, therefore, the prisoner of the Lord."[21]

Every true believer, too, may say, "I am a prisoner of the Lord."

SOLI DEO GLORIA

APPENDIXES

A – A Chronology of the New Testament Books of the Bible
B – Observations on the <u>Works of Josephus</u>

APPENDIX A
A Chronology of the New Testament Books of the Bible

BOOK	AUTHOR	YEAR	LOCATION (Location of Addressee)
Matthew	Matthew	33-38[1]	Jerusalem and elsewhere
James	James	36	Jerusalem (Dispersion)
Jude	Jude	46	Jerusalem (Dispersion)
Mark	Mark	42-47	Jerusalem and elsewhere
I Thessalonians	Paul	50	Corinth
Luke	Luke	50-51	Troas and Jerusalem (Athens)
I Timothy	Paul	52	Troas (Ephesus)
I Corinthians	Paul	53	Ephesus
Titus	Paul	53	Ephesus (Crete)
II Corinthians	Paul	55	Thessalonica
Romans	Paul	56	Cenchrea and Athens
Philemon	Paul	56	Caesarea (Colossae)
Colossians	Paul	56	Caesarea
Philippians	Paul	56	Caesarea
Galatians	Paul	56[2]	Caesarea
John	John	58-60	Ephesus
Ephesians	Paul	59	Rome
II Timothy	Paul	59	Rome (Philippi)
II Thessalonians	Paul	60	Rome
Acts	Luke	53-61	Troas and Rome (Athens)

Hebrews	Apollos	60-61	Rome and elsewhere in Italy (Corinth, and Ephesus)
I Peter	Peter	62	At Sea and Rome (Various Churches)
II Peter	Peter	64	Rome (The Church at Large)
I John	John	69	Philadelphia (Ephesus)
II John	John	70	Philadelphia (Ephesus)
III John	John	70	Hierapolis (Ephesus)
Revelations	John	83-92	Patmos

COMMENTARY

MATTHEW

The phrase 'to this day' or 'until this time' is used by Matthew twice in his Gospel. It is by nature a relative phrase, and the length of time span cannot be stated absolutely or with any certainty. This phrase is often looked upon as representing a longer time frame (ten or twenty years), but this is not always necessarily true. As used by Paul and in the Old Testament, it covers generations. A shorter time frame, however, is not entirely implausible. One interpreter (Beck) even replaces the phrase in 27:7-8 with the phrase 'ever since.'

MARK

Many Bible observers maintain that Mark's Gospel was addressed to a Roman audience. They say, therefore, that Mark wrote it after Peter arrived in Rome in the middle 60s.

Peter ministered to a Roman family twenty years earlier. Luke writes about it in the 10th Chapter in the Book of Acts. Cornelius and his family believed and were baptized. Two chapters later Luke tells of Herod's violence to the Church in 44, and relates the story of the imprisonment of Peter and his miraculous escape. Peter went to the home of Mary, the mother of John Mark. And Peter departed and went to another place. It is conceivable that Mark may have gone with Peter. It is also conceivable that Mark and Peter, at the request of Cornelius, may have begun to put the story of the life of Christ into writing. In speaking of Mark's Gospel in his book, 'The Word of the Lord Grows,' Martin H. Franzmann writes that the resemblance of the structure of the Gospel is akin to that of Peter's sermon in the house of Cornelius.

I THESSALONIANS

Five of Paul's letters can be accurately placed in a chronology of New Testament books. Without a doubt, I Thessalonians was written during his second journey. Without a doubt, I and II Corinthians, I Timothy, and Romans were written during his third journey. II Timothy can also be fairly accurately placed. Without a doubt, this letter was written not long after Paul first arrived in Rome. (See comments under I Timothy.) The placing of the rest of Paul's letters and Hebrews and Luke's Gospel revolve around these five letters.

Paul writes in Romans (15:19), "So that from Jerusalem and round about to Illyricum (Dalmatia) I have fully preached the gospel of Christ." Since Paul established the church in Dalmatia before going to Rome, and since Titus departed for Dalmatia before Paul wrote II Timothy, it is evident that everything relating to Titus took place before Paul went to Rome.

Scripture does not state positively that Paul established the church in Crete. It is possible, then, that Titus may have established this church himself. We hear nothing of his whereabouts from the time of the Jerusalem Council in 49 until Paul indicates in II Corinthians that he showed up in Corinth in 55. In the meanwhile, Paul had written him a letter. This letter was delivered by Apollos and Zenas, the lawyer, as they journeyed. Paul was apparently in Ephesus when he wrote this letter and Apollos had just returned there from Corinth. Paul indicated that Apollos was at that time not willing to return to Corinth (I Cor. 16:12). He also indicated that he had visited Titus in Crete (Titus 1:5), and was now advising him how to conduct his ministry. Paul's visit would had to have taken place some time during his 18-month stay in Corinth in his second journey. He could easily have gone there, for Crete is only about 250 miles south of Corinth. Titus was apparently eager to leave Crete, but Paul entreats him to stay until he sends for him. Artemas or Tychicus were not needed by Paul to tell

Titus he could leave, because Titus left of his own accord and showed up in Corinth sometime in 55. It was during this time that Paul must have gone to Dalmatia, and was now arranging for Titus to be sent there.

In maintaining that II Thessalonians was not written soon after I Thessalonians was written, consideration must be given to the possibility of Silas and Timothy remaining with Paul for an extended period of five or six months. The salutation in both letters includes both men as being with Paul. Since Timothy had just come from Thessalonica, we must assume that Silas was with Paul when Timothy came. Now that Timothy had rejoined Paul, the Thessalonians were without someone to lead them. Paul wrote to them that Satan hindered him from coming to them. The return of Timothy now meant that Silas would be free to go to Macedonia. It is, therefore, entirely plausible that Silas delivered the letter which Paul had written to the Thessalonians.

LUKE

Luke's Gospel is the more chronologically precise of the three synoptic Gospels. Luke tells us that himself when he says to Theophilus that he was writing an orderly account. What Luke is also saying is that his Gospel was written after that of Mark and Matthew. Without a doubt he had read them. This means that those who assert that Mark and Matthew's Gospels were written after Paul arrived in Rome are mistaken.

It is maintained by some (including the NJKB) that Paul quotes Luke's Gospel in his first letter to Timothy (5:18), "The laborer is worthy of his wages." If this is so, then Luke would had to have written his Gospel during the time of Paul's second journey. Luke reverts from telling the story of Paul in the first person to the third person at the time of Paul and Silas' imprisonment at Philippi. It is apparent that they became separated at this point. Luke's whereabouts are not revealed again until Paul was ready to depart for Syria at the end of his third journey. Luke was at Philippi at this time. This would have given Luke from the fall of 49 to the early part of summer in 53 to write his Gospel. A trip to Jerusalem may even have taken place. Paul's first letter to Timothy was definitely written during his third journey.

The many versions of the Bible in recent times give us a wide divergence of presentation of the opening four verses of Luke's Gospel. These verses must of necessity be also viewed in the light of what Luke says in the 'Acts of the Apostles,' (16:8-10) – "And passing by Mysia they came to Troas. And a vision appeared to Paul in the night. A man of Macedonia stood and pleaded with him, saying, 'Come over to Macedonia and help us.' And after he had seen the vision, immediately we sought to go to Macedonia, concluding that the Lord had called us to preach the gospel to them."

The 'they' in verses 8 and 9 instantly becomes 'we' and 'us' in verse 10. Was Luke's conversion and commission to preach that sudden? Not too likely. He had prior knowledge of the life and mission of Christ. His meeting with Paul, Silas, and Timothy stirred this latent knowledge. 'Having had perfect understanding of all things from the very first' could well take us back to the time of Christ's ministry.

And what exactly is Luke referring to when he writes, "Those who from the beginning"? The question might well be asked, "The beginning of what?" Luke is no different a person than others; we all have to rely on recorded history to learn what has already happened in the world. Luke, therefore, could well be referring to the entire Old Testament writings as well as to writings about more recent events surrounding the birth of John the Baptist and the birth of Jesus in Bethlehem.

The first four verses of Luke's Gospel contain the first of several veiled hints about the author: "Having had perfect understanding of all things from the very first." The very first of what? Certainly he cannot mean from the very first time he heard the Gospel message. No, it would have greater meaning to say that Luke had perfect understanding of all things from the very first of Jesus' public ministry. Luke is telling his readers that the source of material for his Gospel is both from personal experience and from others more knowledgeable of certain other things than he, such as Christ's genealogy and the circumstances surrounding His birth.

The second veiled hint comes in chapter 2, verse 2, of Luke's Gospel. Luke curiously states, "This census first took place while Quirinius was governing Syria." Couldn't a more prominent Roman official have been used as a historical citation? Luke is here telling his readers that he was a Syrian.

The next veiled hint as to the identity of Luke comes from Matthew. He writes (4:23-24), "And Jesus went about all Galilee, teaching in their Synagogues, preaching the Gospel of the kingdom, and healing all kinds of sickness and all kinds of disease among the people. And His fame went throughout all Syria; and they brought to Him all sick people who were afflicted with various diseases and torments, and those who were demon-possessed, epileptics, and paralytics, and He healed them." The 'they' in verse 24 includes Luke. Thus, Luke is a Syrian physician from Damascus who came to know of Jesus and His miracles in the early part of Jesus' ministry.

The section of Luke's Gospel from 9:51 to 18:14 is noted for being the most comprehensive portion of Scripture relating to Jesus' public ministry. It is not unrealistic to suppose that Luke had first-hand knowledge of this part of Jesus' ministry, and it is entirely possible that Luke was in the company of the man who brought his son to Jesus to be healed (Luke 9:37-41, Mark 9:14-29, and Matthew 17:14-21). Luke, having seen Jesus perform the miracle the disciples could not, may very well have decided to follow Jesus from that point on.

We now turn to the book of Acts for the next veiled hint. It is the account of the coming of the Holy Spirit on Pentecost. In the middle of listing all the places from which people came to Jerusalem, Luke inserts this phrase (2:10), "Both Jews and proselytes." The emphasis here is on the word 'proselytes.' Was Luke a physician from Damascus who became a proselyte and followed Jesus on His final journey to Jerusalem and the cross?

The final veiled hint may be anticipated. Yes, it is the account of Cleopas and his friend on the road to Emmaus on Easter Sunday afternoon. Many throughout the years have speculated that Cleopas' friend was none other than Luke, himself. This, too, following the outline above, is very plausible.

After the ascension, Luke returns to Damascus where eventually he is one of the intended victims of Saul the Pharisee. The tables are turned, however, and Luke becomes Paul's benefactor. It is entirely possible that Luke was the one who engineered Saul's escape from the Jews at Damascus by letting him down in a large basket through the opening in the wall of the city (Acts 9:23-25).

When Paul and Luke meet in Troas on Paul's second missionary journey, it is not their initial meeting. It is a renewal of an old friendship; a friendship which endured another eleven years until that fateful day in 61 A.D. when Paul stood before Nero to be judged by Caesar.

Luke's sources for his Gospel, then, were historical records, stories related to him, and his own personal experiences.

I TIMOTHY

Saying that II Timothy was written by Paul not long after he first arrived in Rome means that I Timothy must have been written sometime during Paul's third journey. Since Timothy was with Paul during the latter part of the third journey, this letter must have been written in the early part of the journey. This was when Paul could have written (1:3), "As I urged you when I went into Macedonia – remain in Ephesus ..." It appears that Paul also went into Macedonia in the early part of this journey as well as in the latter part of this journey. Paul, then, would have had a chance to read Luke's Gospel.

The last time Paul was at Troas prior to his going to Rome was when he was ready to depart for Syria at the end of his third journey. He had his planned journey to Rome in his mind at that time, and was making preparations for it. To that end, he arranged to leave his cloak, the books, and the parchments with Carpus in Troas. (Cf. II Tim. 4:13). It should be noted that their ship sailed from Troas to Assos, while Paul traveled there on foot. It would be unlikely for him to travel on foot if he had taken his possessions noted above with him. Paul could have been planning to return on his trip to Rome on land via Colossae, Troas, and Philippi, and continuing on through Dalmatia. In that way, he would again be able to visit the newly established church there, which was now being served by Titus.

Paul writes in II Timothy (4:11), "Get Mark and bring him with you, for he is useful for ministry." Paul also includes Mark as greeting the people at the close of his letters to Philemon and the church at Colossae. Mark and Paul were estranged at the beginning of his second journey in 49, and about seven years had now passed. Since Mark's whereabouts are not recorded, the best possible time for a reconciliation between the two would seem to be during the first part of Paul's third journey; the same time when Paul wrote in I Timothy (1:3), "As I urged you when I went into Macedonia – remain in Ephesus." Luke in Acts (19:1) describes this time as follows: "And it came to pass, while Apollos was at Corinth, that Paul, <u>having passed through the upper regions</u>, came to Ephesus."

TITUS

Paul does not give any impression in this letter that he actually established the church in Crete. He instructs Titus to do certain things, such as appointing elders. If Paul had, in fact, established the church, the things he instructs Titus to do would already have been done by himself. The role the city of Nicopolis plays in the events surrounding Titus leaving Crete is obscure and cannot be determined.

II CORINTHIANS

Paul speaks of 'the brother' in 8:18, 'our brother' in 8:11, and 'our brother' in 12:18. Who is he talking about? In reviewing the names of those accompanying Paul to Jerusalem in Acts 20:4, one name stands out among the rest. Gaius of Derbe alone is the one who is not from the immediate area. Timothy was referred to by Paul as his son (I Tim. 1:2, II Tim. 1:2). Paul does not hesitate to call Luke by the name of 'the physician' when referring to him (Col. 4:4, Philemon 24, I Tim. 4:11).

ROMANS

Biblical scholars have ever been puzzled by much of chapter 16. Verses 3-16, containing the greetings to more than two dozen individuals, just does not seem to fit in this letter. The four persons in the Roman Church known to us by name (Cf. II Tim. 4:19) are not mentioned. None of the persons in this list are known outside of this section with the exception of Aquila and Priscilla, and their last known presence was that of being in Ephesus. Did Epaenetus (v. 5) move to Rome already within the two years that Paul first arrived in Ephesus?

Verses 17 and 20 are just plainly out of sync with the rest of the letter. The rest of the letter demonstrates Paul's pastoral concern for these Christians. He lovingly gives them instructions in the living of a sanctified life. His use of the word 'urge' in verse 17 represents a change in the tone of his message.

It is entirely possible that this section is a fragment of an entirely different epistle, the rest of which has been lost to us. It does not blend in with any of the other epistles of Paul.

PHILIPPIANS AND COLOSSIANS

The letters to the Colossians and Philippians are sometimes said to be part of the 'Captivity Letters' originating from Rome. Here we must consider the possibility of Paul returning to these places together with Ephesus. Paul intended to head west to Spain after visiting Rome. Paul told the elders at Ephesus that they would see his face no more (Cf. Acts 20:38). He wrote to Philemon in Colossae to also prepare a guest room for him. To the Philippians he wrote he also hoped to come to them shortly. There was still a good possibility for these things to happen if Paul wrote these words while in Caesarea. His stay in Rome did not afford that possibility, but while he was in Caesarea, there was still some hope. The Roman garrison in Caesarea must be viewed as an extension of 'Caesar's household' in Rome. Then, too, as Paul traveled from Colossae to Philippi, he could stop at Troas where he had left his belongings with Carpus (Cf. II Tim. 4:13).

The fact that Paul recalls the visit of Epaphroditus (Philippians 2:25) and the fact that in his second letter to Timothy written from Rome he refers to Onesiphorus and his family indicates that these two letters were not written from the same place.

In maintaining that Paul's letters to the churches at Colossae and Philippi and the letter to Philemon were written from Caesarea, a point must be made concerning the five individuals mentioned in Philemon and Colossians. They are Aristarchus, Mark, Epaphras, Luke, and Demas. When Paul writes in his second letter to Timothy from Rome, he states emphatically, "Only Luke is with me." This letter also says that "Demas has forsaken me." Paul writes that he wants

Timothy to "Get Mark and bring him with you." Epaphras, a man from Colossae, apparently returned to his hometown. We learn from Acts 27:2 that "Aristarchus, a Macedonian from Thessalonica, was with us" when we sailed from Caesarea. We hear nothing more of him.

Had Colossians, Philemon, and Philippians been written from Rome, all this information would have been turned upside-down.

GALATIANS

The phrase 'so soon' is also a relative phrase. To some it may mean something entirely different than it does to others. When Paul and Silas left Antioch on the second journey, they wanted to see how the brethren in the churches visited in the first journey were doing. A year and a half passed; they had had no word. We read in Acts 16:4-5, "And as they went through the cities, they delivered to them the decrees to keep, which were determined by the apostles and elders at Jerusalem. And so the churches were strengthened in the faith and increased in number daily." The Galatians, therefore, were first receiving the decrees of the Jerusalem Council at the beginning of Paul's second journey in late summer of 49.

At the beginning of Paul's third journey some three years later, Luke records (Acts 18:23), "And after he spent some time there (Antioch), he departed and went over the region of Galatia and Phrygia in order strengthening all the disciples." The absence of some statement in regard to what the Judaizers were up to in Galatia indicates that they had not yet arrived.

Paul's letter to the Galatians does not contain any reference to the 'collection for the saints' (Cf. I Cor. 16:1). The orders given to the churches of Galatia about this must have been verbal. Had Paul's letter to the Galatians been written sometime during his third journey, Paul would have missed an excellent opportunity to remind them again about this in his letter. In addition, because Paul still speaks of the churches of Galatia positively, it indicates that they were still in his good graces.

From the time Paul left Galatia on his third journey to his imprisonment in Caesarea, a period of approximately four years passed. This was time enough for the Judaizers to come into Galatia to defile them.

Paul's reference to his two visits to Jerusalem was in the context of his truly being one of the apostles. This does not, therefore, cover the full range of his trips to Jerusalem. Paul's trips to Jerusalem from the time of his conversion to the Jerusalem Council may be summarized as follows:

    1 – 35 – Acts 22:17-21 – Saul is overcome by a trance in the temple.
    2 – 38 – Gal. 1:18 – Saul visits Peter.
    3 – 40 – Acts 9:26-31 – Barnabas introduces Saul to the disciples.
    4 – 45-46 – Acts 11:27-30 – Relief is sent to Judea through Saul and Barnabas at the time of famine.
    5 – 49 – Acts 15 and Gal. 2:1 – Paul goes to the Jerusalem Council.

EPHESIANS

Tychicus, the bearer of this letter, was also the bearer of Paul's letter to the church at Colossae written from Caesarea in 56. He must have traveled from Colossae to Rome on his own, perhaps knowing full well that Paul intended to go there, for he had traveled with Paul from Troas to Syria.

II TIMOTHY

There is a sense of urgency in this letter. Paul left his things with Carpus at Troas in 56. He needed them when he got to Rome in 59. He, therefore, could not wait until 64 or 65 to get them as has been suggested by some.

II THESSALONIANS

Paul concludes this letter with the remark that his salutation is with his own hand, which is a sign in every epistle. This is a reference to more than one epistle. Most commentators place the writing of both of Paul's letters to the Thessalonians close together in the year 50. I Thessalonians is Paul's very first letter, so what he says at the end of his second letter is hard to reconcile with this arrangement. What, in fact, he does say at the end of his second letter must be regarded as a statement after the fact.

Since Paul, Silvanus, and Timothy are mentioned in the greeting of both of these letters, the time and place when these three are together is very limited. They are together in Corinth when the first letter was written. It is unsure whether they were ever together in Ephesus. They may have been together some time in Macedonia, but the need of writing would not be present.

Silas was there in Rome at the time when Peter penned his first letter; he was, no doubt, to deliver it. For how long a time Silas was in Italy prior to his assisting Peter with his letter is not certain. It is possible that when Paul asked Timothy to 'get Mark,' Mark was not available, and thus, Timothy had to persuade Silas to go with him.

Another consideration that must be made is that the topic of antichrist is not a very appropriate one in the initial preaching of the Gospel to non-Christians. Paul must have told the Thessalonians about this during a subsequent visit.

Note the final remarks in the comments on I Thessalonians. Had Silas returned to Paul to report to him the events taking place in the church at Thessalonica, Paul would have noted that in this letter, in much the same manner as he noted the coming of Timothy in his first letter.

APPENDIX B

Observations of The Works of Josephus
Conclusions reached in the Study of The Works of Josephus

A – Inconsistencies

There are contradictions in the dating of events in Josephus' works. 'The Wars of the Jews' (Chart 2 – Figure 1) contains a very obvious error. Book IV carries the time to the fall of 68. Vespasian did not become emperor (see Chart 3) until December 69, and Titus did not begin the siege of Jerusalem until early 70. A review of Books III and IV (Chart 4) reveals that the time covered in Book III is, indeed, about one year, but that the time covered in Book IV is closer to 28 months, rather than 'about one year.'

Another inconsistency is contained in the chronology of 'The Antiquities of the Jews' and 'The Wars of the Jews.' Josephus' timing is off by three years. This is shown by the chronological years indicated in the heading of each book, and is illustrated in Charts 1 and 2.

The data given in the 'Antiquities' indicates that Herod the Great died in 1 B.C. Chart 1, taken from 'Antiquities,' places the death of Antigonus in 35 B.C., while the naming of Herod King of Judea by Antony and Augustus is set in 38 B.C. The data give in 'Wars' indicates that Herod the Great died in 4 B.C., and is shown in Chart 2. Most historians accept the timing in 'Wars' unequivocally. They contend that Herod's reign as King of Judea should be dated from the time that Herod kills Antigonus, and maintain that this happened in 38 B.C. They say, then, that the actual naming of Herod king by Antony and Augustus would fall three years earlier in 41 B.C. on the 184th Olympiad (Antiq. 14-14-5).

An Encyclopedia Britannica Micropaedia[1] article on Flavius Josephus includes the following paragraph: "Book XVIII of the 'Antiquities' contains a celebrated reference to Christ. But the implication in the text of Christ's divinity could not have come from Josephus, and the passage undoubtedly represents the tampering (if not outright invention) of a later Christian copyist." An 'assessment' of Josephus in this same article states, "As a historian, Josephus shares the faults of most ancient writers: His analyses are superficial, his chronology faulty, his facts exaggerated, his speeches contrived."

What all this is saying is that in the writings of Josephus, there is much that is left to be desired. It also might be said that much of what is in his work is not exactly immune from tampering. This is especially true in regard to what pertains to Christianity, including the dating of the death of Herod the Great. Specifically, this includes the number of the Olympiad in which Herod was named King of Judea by Antony and Augustus (Antiq. 14-14-5), and also the number of years covered in Book II of 'Wars.' The difference of three years here could be a significant change (Chart 2 – Figure 2). According to <u>The New Standard Jewish Encyclopedia</u>,[2] the year in which Antiochus Epiphanes plundered the temple in Jerusalem was 168 B.C. Josephus' timing in 'Wars' places this event in 171 B.C. (Chart 2 – Figure 1).

The question may be raised as to why anyone would want to tamper with the writings of Josephus. At the end of the 5th century and the beginning of the 6th, there lived in Rome a canonist monk by the name of Dionysius Exiguus. He apparently had a low beginning and had been befriended by Gothic monks. Dionysius came to have a perfect knowledge of Greek and Latin as is proved by his many translations. There was a division in the church regarding the determination of the date of Easter. Dionysius recommended one cycle of dates as opposed to another, and used the year of the Incarnation as the point of departure. He was the first to date the Christian era by the birth of Christ, and is credited with devising the historical dating of B.C. and

A.D. Since he had opponents in this controversy and since he undoubtedly used the works of Josephus in coming to his conclusions, it may be possible that his opponents thus tampered with the works of Josephus in order to discredit him. Other such controversies may also have occurred.

The plundering of the temple in Jerusalem by Antiochus Epiphanes points to another inconsistency in Josephus. He writes (Antiq. 12-5-3 and 4), "King Antiochus returning out of Egypt, for fear of the Romans, made an expedition against the city of Jerusalem, and when he was there, in the 143rd year of the kingdom of the Seleucidae, he took the city …. Now it came to pass, after two years, in the 145th year, on the 25th day of Chasleu … in the 153rd Olympiad, that the king came up to Jerusalem, and, pretending peace, he got possession of the city by treachery…."

The chronology of Josephus in 'Wars' indicates that Antiochus Epiphanes took Jerusalem in 171 B.C. (Chart 2 – Figure 1). The 153rd Olympiad extends from 167 to 164 B.C. The adjusted chronology of 'Wars' (Chart – Figure 2), showing the taking of Jerusalem by Antiochus Epiphanes to be 168 B.C., which agrees with The New Standard Jewish Encyclopedia, allows for the 145th year of the kingdom of the Seleucidae (166 B.C.) to fall on the 153rd Olympiad. The dating of the taking of Jerusalem by Antiochus Epiphanes in Josephus, therefore, does not agree.

Conclusions reached in the Study of The Works of Josephus
B – Concerning the Life of Jesus Christ

The accurate timing of the life of Jesus Christ hinges on two facts that Josephus relates in his 'The Antiquities of the Jews' and 'The Wars of the Jews.' They are the fact that Tiberius Caesar reigned 22 years, 5 months, and 3 days (Antiq. 18-6-10), and the fact that Archelaus was banished to Vienna in Gaul in the ninth year after he had become king at the death of his father, Herod the Great (Antiq. 17-13-2, Wars 2-7-3).

That Tiberius Caesar died in A.D. 37 is a universally accepted fact, as is the rest of the chronological information regarding Roman Emperors (Chart 3). Thus, Tiberius became emperor in A.D. 14. This means that when the word came to John the Baptist in the 15th year of the reign of Tiberius (Luke 3:2), that this happened in A.D. 29. Jesus was about 30 years old at this time. This, in turn, means that Jesus would had to have been born in 2 B.C.

Josephus starts to bring his 'Antiquities' to a close by saying, "Since it was this Florus who necessitated us to take up arms against the Romans, while we thought it better to be destroyed at once, than by little and little. Now this war began in the second year of the government of Florus, and the twelfth year of the reign of Nero" (Antiq. 20-11). The twelfth year of the reign of Nero is A.D. 66. Counting the years furnished by Josephus in Chapters 18-19-20 from the time of Florus back to the banishment of Archelaus is 57-1/2 years. This puts the banishment of Archelaus somewhere in A.D. 9. This means that since Archelaus was banished in the ninth year of his reign, his father, Herod the Great, would had to have died in the year 1 B.C.

Herod died in Jericho, having gone to the baths at Callirrhoe for treatment for his various ailments (Wars 1-32-5 to 8). Herod reigned 37 years after having been made king by the Romans, and 34 years after the slaying of Antigonus (Antiq. 17-8-1). Herod, therefore, was made king by the Romans in 38 B.C. (14-14-5), and Antigonus was slain in 35 B.C. (Antiq. 15-1-1). This agrees with Josephus' chronology.

However, when Josephus states that Herod was made king by the Romans on the 184th Olympiad (Antiq. 14-14-5), a discrepancy occurs. Saying that Antigonus was slain in 35 B.C., and that Herod was made king in 38 B.C., places the latter event in the 185th Olympiad. This points to another possible instance of tampering in the works of Josephus. Changing CLXXXV (185) to CLXXXIV (184) would not be too difficult.

Caesar Augustus died at the age of 77 in A.D. 14, having reigned 57 years, 6 months, and 2 days (Antiq. 18-2-2, Wars 2-9-1). Of this time, he ruled together with Antony for 12 years. His reign, then, began in 43 B.C. when he was about 20 years old. In 31 B.C., he, then known as Octavian, defeated Antony in the battle of Actium, and then ruled by himself for 45 years. This happened in the 7th year of Herod's reign (Antiq. 15-5-2). Antigonus is beheaded in 35 B.C.

Herod began rebuilding the temple in Jerusalem in the 18th year of his reign or in 20 B.C. (Antiq. 15-11-1). Josephus writes (Antiq. 15-11-6), "But the temple was built by the priests in a year and six months." This work was finished in 17 B.C. (Chart 1). The entire job of restoring the temple, however, took 8 years and was finished in 12 B.C.

The 15th year of the reign of Tiberius is, then, A.D. 29. John the Baptist preaches several months, and then Jesus, who is about 30 years old, is baptized in the River Jordan by John. Jesus thus begins his ministry early in the year A.D. 30. After a three-year ministry, Jesus is crucified in A.D. 33 when he is 33 years old.

Writing in <u>Christianity Today</u>, Ernest L. Martin, in giving an account of the astronomical phenomena in 3/2 B.C., states in his final paragraph, "The astrological <u>interpretations</u> I have suggested in this article may or may not be correct, but the occurrence of these astronomical phenomena in 3/2 B.C. is certain." He then adds, "Those exhibitions no doubt caused a great deal of excitement and wonder. They may well indicate that the early Christian historians were correct when they said Christ was born sometime in the period 3/2 B.C."[3]

CHART 1
THE ANTIQUITIES OF THE JEWS
Chronology

Book	Event	Interval of Years	Accumulative years	Time
	From the Creation			4616 B.C.
I	To the death of Isaac		2953	1883 B.C.
II	To the Exodus out of Egypt	220	2953	1663 B.C.
***************************				
XII	Death of Judas Maccabeus	170	4467	149 B.C.
XIII	Queen Alexandra's death	82	4549	67 B.C.
XIV	The death of Antigonus	32	4581	35 B.C.
XV	Finishing of the Temple by Herod	18	4599	17 B.C.
XVI	The death of Alexander and Aristobolus	12	4611	5 B.C.
XVII	The Banishment of Archelaus	14	4616 4625	---------- A.D. 9
XVIII	The Departure of the Jews from Babylon	32	4657	A.D. 41
XIX	Fadus the Roman Procurator	3 ½	4660 ½	A.D. 44 ½
XX	To Florus	22	4682 ½	A.D. 66 ½

CHART 2 – Figure 1

THE WARS OF THE JEWS
Chronology

Book		Interval of Years	Time
	From Antiochus Epiphanes taking Jerusalem		171 B.C.*
I	To the death of Herod the Great	167	4 B.C. fall
II	Till Vespasian was sent to subdue the Jews by Nero	69	A.D. 66 fall
III	To the taking of Gamala	About 1	A.D. 67 fall
IV	To the coming of Titus to besiege Jerusalem	About 1ä	A.D. 68 fall
V	To the great extremity to which the Jews were reduced	½	A.D. 69 spring
VI	To the taking of Jerusalem by Titus	One month	A.D. 69 spring
VII	To the sedition of the Jews Jews at Cyrene	3	A.D. 72

* - Antiochus Epiphanes plundered the temple at Jerusalem in 168 B.C.

ä – This interim of time is erroneous. Titus did not besiege Jerusalem until early in A.D. 70 after his father, Vespasian, became emperor in December of A.D. 69. The time covered by Book 4 of the 'Wars' is approximately 28 months.

CHART 2 – Figure 2
THE WARS OF THE JEWS
Chronology (Adjusted)

Book		Interval of Years	Time
	From Antiochus Epiphanes taking Jerusalem		168B.C.¶
I	To the death of Herod the Great	167	1B.C. fall
II	Till Vespasian was sent to subdue the Jews by Nero	66¶	A.D.66 fall
III	To the taking of Gamala	About 1	A.D.67 fall
IV	To the coming of Titus to besiege Jerusalem	28 months	A.D.70 early
V	To the great extremity to which the Jews were reduced	½	A.D.70 summer
VI	To the taking of Jerusalem by Titus	One month	A.D.70 Aug/Sep

(On the 8th day of Elul in the second# year of the reign of Vespasian – 'Wars' 6-10-1)

VII	To the sedition of the Jews at Cyrene	3	A.D.73

¶ - A change of three years.
\# - The Second Jewish Regnal Year.

CHART 3
ROMAN EMPERORS

Emporer	Years Ruled	Time
Julius Caesar (c100 B.C.-44B.C.)	c56	to 44B.C.

Antonius (83?-30B.C.) to 43B.C.
(An interim rule of ten months or so by virtue of the imperium he already possessed)

Antonius (Mark Antony) Together with   12 plus   to 31B.C.
    Augustus until the Battle of Actium.

Caesar Augustus (Called Octavian   45   to A.D.14
    until 27 B.C.) 63B.C.-A.D.14 – Died August 19
    Total years reigned by Caesar Augustus - 57 years plus a one month hiatus; Tiberius was co-regent with August us for two years.

Tiberius Caesar (from September 17)   22 year 5 months   to A.D.37
    42B.C.-A.D.37 – Died March 16

Gaius Caesar (Caligula)   3 years 8 months   to A.D.41
    A.D.12-41 – Died January 24

Claudius I   13 years 8months   to A.D.54
    10B.C.-A.D.54 – Died October 13

Nero   13 years 7 months   to A.D.68
    A.D.37-68 – Died June 9

Galba – Died January 15	7 months plus	to A.D.69
Otho – Died April 15	3 months	in A.D.69
Vitellius – Died December 20	8 months plus	in A.D.69
Vespasian	10 years	to A.D.79

CHART 4
Synopsis Books III and IV

Book III of 'The Wars of the Jews' begins approximately three months after the closing of Book XX of 'The Antiquities of the Jews;' in the twelfth year of the reign of Nero and in the second year of the government of Florus (Antiq. 20-11-1).

Oct 66 – Vespasian is sent into Syria by Nero.
- Vespasian besieges Jotapata and is opposed by the forces under Josephus.
- Josephus flees Jotapata in its second siege to escape harm.
- Trajan goes against Japha; Titus comes to assist Trajan.

Jun 67 – Japha falls on the 25th day of Sivan.

Jul 67 – Jotapata is taken in the 13th year of the reign of Nero on the 1st day of Tamuz; Vespasian returns to Ptolemais.
- Josephus is mistakenly mourned in Jerusalem, and the Jews are vehemently angry when they learn that the death of Josephus was fiction and that he was with the Romans. Josephus advises Vespasian.
- Taricheae is taken, and there is fighting in Galilee.

Sep 67 – Prisoners are taken on the 8th day of Elul. Gischala and Gamala are besieged.

Oct 67 – Gamala is taken on the 23rd day of Tisri, and Gischala surrenders. Mischief is done by John of Gischala and Ananus. The Idumeans fight back. There is much cruelty. There is trouble at Masada.
- Vespasian marches against Gadara in Perea.

Mar 68 – He enters the city on the 4th day of Adar.
- There is commotion in Galatia. Men of power revolt from Nero.
- Vespasian foresees civil wars coming. He makes haste to finish the Jewish wars. There are campaigns on Great Plains and around Jericho.
- Vespasian fortifies places round about Jerusalem.
- As Vespasian was returned to Caesarea and was getting ready with all his army to march directly to Jerusalem, he was

Jun 68 – informed that Nero was dead. Nero had reigned 13 years and 8 (days?) months.
- The war in Galatia ended. Galba is made emperor and returned from Spain. He is accused by soldiers as being a pusillanimous person.
- Vespasian suspends operations against Jerusalem, and sends Titus to go to Rome to hail Galba and receive his commands. Agrippa goes, too.

Jan 69 – As Titus and Agrippa were sailing along the coasts of Achaia, they hear that Galba is slain. He reigned 7 months and 7 days.
- Otho is made emperor. Agrippa continues on to Rome, while Titus returns to Caesarea to his father.
- They are in suspense over the fluctuating conditions, and cancel their expedition against the Jews.
- There is Jewish turmoil surrounding Jerusalem and Masada. Sedition and civil war prevails not only in Judea, but also in Italy. Otho fights against the forces of Vitellius. He kills himself. He had reigned 3 months and 2 days.

Apr 69 – Vitellius is made emperor. Otho's army goes over to him.
- Vespasian meanwhile removes himself from Caesarea and marches

Jun 69 – against those places not yet overthrown on the 5th day of Sivan.

Jun 69 – That Vitellius is made emperor is reported to Vespasian. After overthrowing those places, he returns to Caesarea. Vitellius' being made emperor produces indignation in Vespasian. He could not with any satisfaction own him as his lord. He restrains anger, but is prevented from returning to Rome.
- Commanders and soldiers declare Vespasian as their emperor.

They round up support to dethrone Vitellius.

– Vespasian desires to obtain the government, and tries to consolidate his position. Mysia and Pannonia are glad to take an oath of fidelity to Vespasian.

– Vespasian is declared emperor of the east, and he goes to Berytus. Embassages (emissaries) come to him from Syria. Josephus is remembered for his good advice and is released.

Nov 69– Vespasian goes to Antioch, but is undecided upon his next move. Mucianus, because it is winter, marches on foot through Cappadocia and Phrygia instead of going by sea.

– Antonius Primas takes a third of the legions of Mysia and hurries to fight against Vitellius. Vitellius sends Cecinna to face the threat. Cecinna is overawed with the forces of Antonius and goes over to his side. This greatly diminishes the reputation of Vitellius. After being rescued from a betrayal, Cecinna is sent by Antonius to tell Vespasian the good news.

Dec 69 – Sabinus, together with Domitian, Vespasian's other son, revolt in Rome. In the resulting tumult in Rome, Sabinus is slain.

– Antonius comes with his armies to Rome and the challenge is met by Vitellius and his forces. Vitellius is beheaded on the 3rd day of Casleu. He reigned 8 months and 5 days.

Dec 69 – Vespasian is made emperor while he was still in Alexandria, where he had gone with Titus.

Conclusions reached in the Study of The Works of Josephus
   C – The Rebuilding of the Temple by Herod the Great

The timing and dating of the rebuilding of the temple at Jerusalem is slightly confusing, to say the least. Reference dates do not always have the same meaning for everyone. This is especially true in regard to the answer of the Jews when Jesus remarked, "Destroy this temple, and in three days I will raise it up" (John 2:19). They said, "It has taken forty-six years to build this temple, and will You raise it up in three days?" (v. 20).

Perhaps the proper way to analyze the rebuilding of the temple is to divide it into various phases. These phases might be described as follows:

    A. Preparing the site.
    B. The building of the inner temple by the priests.
    C. The building of the remainder of the temple.
    D. The ongoing construction.

The rebuilding of the temple by Herod was begun in the 18th year of his reign, or in other words, 20 B.C. Josephus states (Antiq. 15-11-3), "So Herod took away the old foundations, and laid others, and erected the temple upon them."

The building of the inner temple was the responsibility of the priests alone. Herod did not participate in this phase of the building, as Josephus relates. This phase was completed by the priests in a period of one year and six months, and Josephus indicates that this phase was completed in 17 B.C. Apparently, then, the phase of preparing the site also took about eighteen months.

Josephus also states (Antiq. 15-11-5), "However, he (Herod) took care of the cloisters and the outer enclosures; and these he built in eight years." It is not clear whether this was eight years after the priests completed their work or not. If it is calculated from the time the priests were finished, then this work was finished in 9 B.C. If not, then 12 B.C. At this time, however, the temple was functional, that is to say, ready for use.

From the conversation of the Jews and Jesus recorded by John, it is clear that construction on the temple continued in subsequent years, and that it was still going on during the time of Christ's ministry. It has been said by some that the temple was not finally finished until A.D. 64.

Determination now has to be made as to which date the Jews were referring to when they talked with Jesus. 9 B.C. or 12 B.C. can safely be ruled out altogether. To say that they referred to 20 B.C. is not entirely accurate. This would put the time of the conversation in A.D. 26, much too early in Jesus' life. For the Jews of that time, the building of the temple may not have started until the priests began their work. The work of the priests did not begin until at least 18 B.C. Forty-six years from that time would be A.D. 28.

There is still some question, however, if this is what these Jews were referring to. The activity of the priests and the rest of the Jews was something that was set apart. Since Josephus makes this differentiation, it is quite possible that these Jews were referring to the time when the priests were finished with their work. This was, as stated above, in 17 B.C. Forty-six years from this time places the conversation of Jesus and these Jews in the spring (the Passover) of A.D. 30, in the early part of Jesus' ministry.

The translator of The Works of Josephus – William Whiston (1667-1751)

The introduction of this volume states, 'that he was a rather diversified individual, having noteworthy accomplishments in the areas of mathematics, philosophy and theology.'[4] He was brought up in a Presbyterian atmosphere with very meager financial resources. His father died while Whiston was in his late teens, leaving a widow and seven children. As a child, he was somewhat of a loner. He managed to continue his education only after a great struggle, and was plagued with a continuous shortage of funds.

He eventually came to Cambridge. In 1708, he declared that the doctrine of the Trinity was erroneous, and could not be persuaded otherwise by his peers. When he would not relent, he was banished from this institution. This stance alienated him from many of his associates. As a person he was characterized as a man with absolute honesty and simplicity. Newton was a contemporary of his and in his later association with him, Newton likewise shunned him, because he became afraid of him.

The translation of Josephus appeared in 1737. During this time, he attended the Church of England, but when he became uncomfortable with the Athanasian Creed, he gave up communion and joined the Baptists. He was enamored with eschatological things, and in 1746, announced that the millennium would begin in 20 years.

Two interesting footnotes appear in Antiq. 18-3-3 and 18-4-6. "He was (the) Christ; and when Pilate, at the suggestion of the principal men amongst us, had condemned him to the cross (A.D. 33, April 3), those that loved him at the first did not forsake him, for he appeared to them alive again the third day (A.D. 33 April 5), as the divine prophets had foretold these and thousand other wonderful things concerning him; and the tribe of Christians, so named for him, are not extinct at this day."

"About this time it was that Philip, Herod's brother, departed this life, in the twentieth year of the reign of Tiberius*, after he had been tetrarch of Trachonitis, and Gaulonitis, and of the nation of the Bataneans also, thirty-seven years."

> * This calculation is exactly right; for since Herod died about September, in the fourth year before the Christian era, and Tiberius began, as is well known, August 19, A.D. 14, it is evident that the 37th year of Philip, reckoned from his father's death, was the 20th of Tiberius, or near the end of A.D. 33 (the very year of our Savior's death also), or, however, in the beginning of the next year, A.D. 34.

Likewise, the footnote in Antiq. 15-5-2: "At this time it was that the fight happened at Actium, between Octavius Caesar and Antony, in the seventh year of the reign of Herod:#"

> # It is here to be noticed, that this seventh year of the reign of Herod, and all the other years of his reign, in Josephus, are dated from the death of Antigonus, and never from his first obtaining the kingdom at Rome, above three years before.

The calculations do not agree with the chronology of Josephus! Josephus twice (Wars 1-33-8, Antiq. 17-8-1) records the death of Herod, and in each instance states that Herod reigned 34 years since he caused the death of Antigonus (in 35 B.C. according to the chronology of Josephus) and 37 years since he had been made king (in 38 B.C.). This places the death of Herod the Great in 1 B.C.

Whiston, in apparently agreeing that Herod the Great died in 4

B.C., and also stating in the footnotes that the crucifixion of Jesus took place in A.D. 33, puts the age of Jesus at the time of his death at 36. Perhaps the reason why the conclusion of Whiston that Jesus was crucified in A.D. 33 was not taken seriously by anyone was because of this very thing, in addition to the animosity which was held against him.

Addendum

1 – Early Church History and Projection
2 – St. Paul's Third Missionary Journey and Projection

EARLY CHURCH HISTORY and PROJECTION (**)
Derived primarily from the Book of Acts
33 – Acts 1:9 – Christ ascends into heaven.
  Acts 1:15 – At the upper room prayer meeting, Matthias is chosen as an Apostle.
  Acts 2 – The Holy Spirit comes on the day of Pentecost in a mighty rushing Wind. Peter preaches a sermon. A vital church grows.
  Acts 3 & 4 – Peter and John enter the temple. They heal a lame man, and are arrested. They are let go. They spoke the Word of God with boldness.
  Acts 4 & 5 – The multitude of those who believed shared their possessions, and all things were held in common. Barnabas, having land, sold it and gave the proceeds to the Apostles. Ananias and Sapphira lied to the Holy Spirit about their giving and were struck dead.
34 – Acts 6 – 8 – Seven men are chosen to serve in the church. Named as assistants to the Apostles were Stephen, Philip, Prochorus, Nicanor, Timon, Parmenas, and Nicolas. Stephen is accused of blasphemy. He defends himself vigorously, but becomes the first martyr. Saul, a devout Pharisee, witnesses the event with approval.
  Acts 8 – Saul begins to persecute the church. The church is scattered. Philip preaches Christ in Samaria. The people heeded those things which Philip spoke. Peter and John are sent to Samaria. They pray for the people, but Peter chastises Simon the sorcerer. Philip also preaches to an Ethiopian eunuch who had great authority under Candace the Queen of the Ethiopians.
35 – (Fourteen years before The Jerusalem Council in 49) – Gal. 2:1
  Acts 9 – Saul takes his persecution to Damascus. Saul meets the Lord on the road to Damascus and is converted. Ananias

baptizes Saul.

Galatians 1:16-17 – Paul, formerly Saul, later relates that he did not immediately confer with flesh and blood, nor did he go up to Jerusalem to those who were apostles before him; but went to Arabia, and returned again to Damascus.

Acts 9 – Saul preaches Christ immediately in Damascus. The Jews hear about it and plot against him, but Saul escapes when the disciples took him by night and let him down through the wall of the city in a large basket.

35 – Acts 22:17 & 21 – Luke relates that Paul later recalled that when he went to Jerusalem and was praying in the temple, that he was in a trance. The Lord appeared to him and told him to leave the city immediately because his testimony would not be accepted, and said, "Depart, for I will send you far from here to the Gentiles."

38 – Galatians 1:18-19 – Paul later relates that after three years, he went up to Jerusalem to see Peter, and remained with him fifteen days. He did not see any of the other apostles, except James, the Lord's brother. Afterward, he came into the regions of Syria and Cilicia, and was unknown by face to the churches of Judea which were in Christ (v. 21).

40 – Acts 9:26-31 – Saul comes to Jerusalem to try to join the disciples, but they were all afraid of him. But Barnabas took him and brought him to the apostles. Saul was received by the church at Jerusalem. Then the churches throughout all Judea, Galilee, and Samaria had peace and were edified.

40 – Acts 9:32-41 – Peter passes through all parts of the country including Lydda and Sharon. He heals Aeneas, who had

been paralyzed. At Joppa, Peter restores Dorcas to life.

Acts 10 – Cornelius, a centurion of the Italian Regiment at Caesarea, sees clearly in a vision an angel of God coming in and speaking to him. As a result, he sends a delegation to Joppa to find Peter. Peter also has a vision, and eventually goes to Caesarea to meet Cornelius. Peter preaches to the household of Cornelius, and they are baptized.

Acts 11 – The disciples at Jerusalem heard of the Gentiles receiving the Holy Spirit as Peter was speaking to them, and when Peter came up to Jerusalem, he explained his experience with Cornelius.

41 – Acts 11:22-26 – The church at Jerusalem sends out Barnabas to go as far as Antioch to learn about the ministry to the Hellenists that was taking place there. Many people were being added to the Lord. Barnabas then departs for Tarsus to seek Saul. He brought him to Antioch and for a whole year, they taught many people. And the disciples were first called Christians at Antioch.

42 – ** – Peter continues to minister to the family of Cornelius. Cornelius expresses to Peter his wish to have the story of the life of Jesus Christ put into writing. Peter discusses this wish with Mary, the mother of John whose surname was Mark, at whose home he often stayed. Mark was agreeable to assist Peter with this project, and they began immediately.

44 – Acts 12 – Herod brings violence to the church. He kills James the brother of John with sword. He also seizes Peter, and puts him in prison. The Lord miraculously rescues Peter, and he comes to the home of Mary, the mother of Mark. Later Peter goes to another place. Herod, how-

ever, goes to Caesarea, and dies a horrible death.

** – John Mark goes with Peter, and together they decide to go to Antioch to visit Mark's cousin Barnabas. They continue to work on the project of writing the story of the life of Christ.

44 – Galatians 2:11 – While at Antioch, Peter readily associates with the Gentiles and eats with them. This was observed by Saul. But when certain men from James came, Peter, together with other Jews and Barnabas, withdrew and separated themselves, fearing those who were of the circumcision. Saul withstood Peter to his face on this matter, because he was to be blamed.

45 – ** – Peter and Mark then return to Jerusalem. Their work on Mark's Gospel continues.

45 – Acts 11:30 – Agabus, a prophet from Jerusalem had come to Antioch and foretold of a great famine to come in the world. The famine was now upon them. (See also Josephus Antiq. XX-II-5.) The church at Antioch determined to send relief to the brethren in Judea. They sent it to the elders at Jerusalem by the hands of Barnabas and Saul.

46 – Acts 12:25 – Barnabas and Saul returned to Antioch when they had fulfilled their ministry. They also took with them John, whose surname was Mark.

** – Peter, however, stayed close to Jerusalem, but also went to Caesarea to deliver Mark's not quite completed Gospel.

47 – Acts 13:1-3 – The church at Antioch sends Barnabas and Saul out to the work for which the Holy Spirit called them. Mark accompanies them. They came first to Cyprus, but when they continued on from Paphos to Perga in Pamphylia, John Mark departed from them and returned

to Jerusalem.

** – Mark realized that if he continued with them he would be gone for too long a time, for he promised Peter that he would return to help him finish their project to write the story of the life of Christ at the request of Cornelius. Mark did not think to mention this to either Barnabas or Saul.

47 – Acts 13 & 14 – Barnabas and Saul's travels took them to Antioch in Pisidia, Iconium, and Lystra and Derbe, cities in Lycaonia.

48 – Acts 14:21-26 – They return to Antioch in much the same way as they had come.

49 – Acts 15 – Barnabas and Saul, now called Paul, stayed in Antioch a long time. After a while, certain men came from Judea and taught things concerning circumcision which caused dissension among them. The decision was made to go up to Jerusalem to see the apostles and elders about this question. Paul and Barnabas left for Jerusalem, and took Titus, a Greek, with them. And the apostles and elders came together to consider this matter. Simon Peter also participated in the discussion. Titus was not commanded to be circumcised.

49 – Acts 15:22-29 – Judas and Silas, themselves being prophets, also went with Paul and Barnabas as they returned to Antioch. Judas returned to Jerusalem after a time, but Silas remained there. Paul and Barnabas carried with them a letter prepared by the Council. The letter concluded with the statement, "That you abstain from things offered to idols, from blood, from things strangled, and from sexual immorality; if you keep yourself from these, you will do well."

49 – Acts 15:40-41 – After some days, Paul and Barnabas decided to go back and visit the brethren in every city where they had gone to see how they were doing. A difference of opinion arose when Barnabas wanted to take Mark along with them. Paul objected. So Barnabas took Mark and sailed to Cyprus, but Paul chose Silas and departed. They went through Syria and Cilicia, strengthening the churches.

** – The subsequent whereabouts of Peter are not recorded. A reference to his being at Corinth at some time is made by Paul in his first letter to the church at that place. In his first epistle, Peter gives an indication that he ministered to the pilgrims in Pontus, Galatia, Cappadocia, Asia, and Bithynia. Peter also indicates in this letter that Mark was with him.

– Mark is also mentioned as being with Paul when he wrote a letter to Philemon, as well as when he wrote a letter to the Colossians. In Paul's second letter to Timothy written from Rome, Paul asks that Timothy get Mark and bring him to Rome when he comes. Timothy was apparently in Macedonia (Philippi) at this time. Whether or not Mark was actually in the area at that time is not known.

– Titus is not heard from again until he came to Corinth in 55, as recorded by Paul in his second letter to the church at that place.

ST. PAUL'S THIRD MISSIONARY JOURNEY and PROJECTION (**)

52 MAR – ** – Apollos arrives in Ephesus at the invitation of Gaius of Derbe. John Mark also arrives in Ephesus.

Acts 18:26 & 27 – Aquila and Priscilla meet Apollos at the synagogue, and explain to him the way of God concerning baptism more accurately. Apollos goes to Achaia.

** – Mark leaves Ephesus for Colossae in the hope of finding Peter.

52 MAY – ** – Paul comes to Colossae on the way to Ephesus. He learns that Mark was recently there, and that he had left for Troas and Macedonia. Paul is eager to have a reconciliation with Mark. This causes a problem for Paul. Paul decides to go to Troas to look for Mark.

I Tim. 1:3 – Paul sends a short note to Timothy in Ephesus telling him to stay there.

I Tim. 1:1 & 2 – Paul writes to Timothy from Troas. "Paul, an apostle of Jesus Christ, by the commandment of God our Savior and the Lord Jesus Christ, our hope, To Timothy, my true son in the faith."

** – Paul goes to Macedonia and finds Mark who is with Peter. Paul and Mark are reconciled.

52 JUN – Acts 19:1 – Paul arrives in Ephesus, having passed through the upper regions. Apollos is still in Corinth.

Acts 19:2-5 – Paul finds some disciples, and explains to them baptism in the name of the Lord Jesus.

Acts 19:8 – Paul speaks boldly in the synagogue for three months but when some would not believe, he withdrew. He then reasons daily in the school of Tyrannus, which continues for two years.

53 MAR – I Cor. 1:10 – Paul learns from the household of Chloe that there are contentions in the church at Corinth.

** – Apollos also returns to Ephesus and corroborates the story.

53 APR – I Cor. 1:1 & 2 – Paul writes a letter to the church at Corinth. "Paul, called to be an apostle of Jesus Christ through the will of God, and Sosthenes our brother, To the church of God which is at Corinth." He also says that he strongly urged Apollos to return to them, but that he was unwilling to do that at this time. He extends a hearty greeting to them from Aquila and Priscilla.

53 JUN – ** – Apollos plans a trip to Rome, and intends to take Zenas the lawyer along to accompany him. When Paul discovers this, he writes a letter to Titus in Crete. Paul had visited Titus there while he was in Corinth several years earlier. Apollos agrees to deliver this letter.

Titus 3:13 – Paul writes to Titus, "Send Zenas the lawyer and Apollos on their journey with diligence, that they may lack nothing."

53 AUG – Acts 19:10 – As Paul continues reasoning daily in the school of Tyrannus, all who dwelt in Asia heard the word of the Lord Jesus, both Jews and Greeks.

Acts 19:20 – So the word of the Lord grew mightily and prevailed.

** – Others who heard the word were men from Dalmatia. They talked with Paul about the possibility of someone coming to their country with the word. Paul was thinking of this when he wrote to Titus, 3:12, "when I send Artemis to you or Tychicus, be diligent to come to me to Nicopolis, for I have decided to spend the winter there." Paul thought of going to Dalmatia by sea from there.

53 OCT – ** – Paul's plan to go to Dalmatia was upset when he was told that going there by sea was an unwise idea. These men suggested going overland, for the Roman government had greatly improved the roads.

54 MAR – ** – Timothy returns to Ephesus.

54 JUN – Acts 19:22 – Paul sends Timothy and Erastus into Macedonia, but he himself stayed in Asia for a time.

54 JUL – Acts 19:29 – As Paul stayed in Asia for a time, a riot erupted in Ephesus and the whole city was filled with confusion. Paul's travel companions, Gaius and Aristarchus, men of Macedonia, were seized. Paul was also in danger because of his preaching.

Acts 20:1 – After the uproar had ceased, Paul called the disciples to him, embraced them, and departed to go to Macedonia.

** – Onesimus, a slave who had run away from Philemon (Philemon 15), made a connection with Paul and went with him.

54 AUG – ** – Paul catches up to the men from Dalmatia and goes with them to their home country. Erastus went with him, together with Demas, a man from Thessalonica, and also Onesimus. Paul stayed in Dalmatia for three months. He told the people he would send someone to stay for a longer time.

54 DEC – Acts 20:2 – When Paul had gone over that region and given them much encouragement, he came to Greece.

** – Paul was not received in Corinth with open arms, so he soon returned to Macedonia and Troas.

55 JAN – ** – Paul sends Artemas to Crete to tell Titus to come to Troas.
　　　　** – Paul was able to minister to the Christians at Philippi, Thessalonica and Berea, and he also gave support to Silas.
　　　　II Cor. 8:17 – Titus arrives in Corinth of his own accord, and he stays there for a while.
55 FEB – II Thess. 2:3 & 4 – Paul tells the church at Thessalonica, "Let no one deceive you by any means; for that Day (the Day of Christ) will not come unless the falling away comes first, and the man of sin is revealed, the son of perdition, who opposes and exalts himself above all that is called God or that is worshiped, so that he sits as God in the temple of God, showing himself that he is God."
55 MAR – II Cor. 2:12 & 13 – When Paul came to Troas to preach Christ's gospel, a door was opened by the Lord. Paul does not find Titus.
　　　　** - Titus arrives in Troas shortly before Paul's arrival.
　　　　II Cor. 7:6 – Titus and Paul meet. Timothy is with Paul.
　　　　** – Paul was now able to send one of his helpers to Dalmatia.
55 APR – II Cor. 1:1 – Paul writes a second letter to the church at Corinth. "Paul, an apostle of Jesus Christ by the will of God, and Timothy our brother, To the church of God which is at Corinth, with all the saints who are in all Achaia:" It is to be delivered by Titus.
55 APR – II Cor. 8:6 – Paul sends Titus back to Corinth. "So we urged Titus, that as he had begun, so he would also complete this grace in you as well."
　　　　II Cor. 12:18 – Paul sends 'our brother' (Gaius of Derbe) with

Titus.

55 JUN – ** – Titus returns to Macedonia as agreed to with Paul. Titus then departs for Dalmatia, accompanied by Demas and Onesimus.

** – Paul again leaves for Corinth. Erastus goes with him.

55 SEP – Acts 20:3 – Paul stays in Corinth three months. And when the Jews plotted against him as he was about to sail for Syria, he decides to return through Macedonia.

55 OCT – ** – Paul stops off at Cenchrea.

Romans 1:7 – Paul writes a letter to the church at Rome, "To all who are in Rome, beloved of God, called to be saints: Grace to you and peace from God our Father and the Lord Jesus Christ."

55 OCT – Romans 16:1 & 2 – Phoebe, who is a servant of the church in Cenchrea, will deliver Paul's letter to the Romans.

55 DEC – ** – Paul makes arrangements to continue on to Macedonia.

56 JAN – II Cor. 8:19 – 'The brother' (Gaius of Derbe) who accompanied Titus back to Corinth was chosen by the churches to travel with Paul with the gifts for the Judean saints. They will administer the gifts.

56 FEB – ** – Gaius of Derbe and Paul then leave for Macedonia.

56 MAR – ** – Arriving in Philippi, Paul learns that Demas and Onesimus, who went to Dalmatia with Titus, had returned to Thessalonica and remained there. As Paul wanted to continue on to Troas, he instructed Luke, who was in Philippi, to stay behind and wait for those two as the rest of them leave.

56 MAR – Acts 20:4 – "And Sopater of Berea accompanied him to Asia – also Aristarchus and Secundus of the Thessalonians, and Gaius of Derbe, and Timothy, and Tychicus and Trophimus of Asia."

56 MAR – Acts 20:5 – "These, going ahead, waited for us at Troas."
56 MAR – Acts 20:6 – Luke and his companions sailed away from Philippi after the Days of Unleavened Bread, and in five days joined the others at Troas, where they stayed seven days.
56 MAR – Acts 20:7-12 & 13 – Paul ministers at Troas, and departs the following day for Assos on foot.
56 MAR – II Tim. 4:13 – Paul leaves his cloak, and his books and parchments with Carpus.
    ** – In leaving his belongings with Carpus, Paul's plans were that after going to Jerusalem, he would go overland to Rome by way of Colossae, Troas, Macedonia, and Dalmatia. He wanted to visit Titus to see how he was doing. From Rome, he then would continue on to Spain.
56 MAR – Acts 20:13 – After seven days at Troas, the sailing ship leaves Troas for Assos, there intending to take Paul on board.
56 APR – Acts 20:15 – They then came to Mitylene, Chios, and Samos, and they stayed at Trogyllium; and the next day they came to Miletus.
    II Tim. 4:20 – Trophimus left the ship sick at Miletus.
    Acts 20:17-18 – Paul exhorts the Ephesian elders, and tells them, "that they would see his face no more."

NOTES:

Chapter 1

1 – Acts 2:36
2 – Acts 2:37
3 – Acts 2:38, 39
4 – Matthew 9:11-13
5 – Joseph Klausner, From Jesus to Paul, New York, N.Y., The MacMillan Co., 1943, p. 393.
6 – Matthew 28:18-20

Chapter 2

None

Chapter 3

1 – Matthew 9:9
2 – Matthew 2:1-2

Chapter 4

None

Chapter 5

None

Chapter 6

1 – Klausner, p. 198
2 – Acts 5:27-32
3 – Acts 7:51-53
4 – Acts 9:4
5 – Acts 9:5
6 – Acts 9:6
7 – Acts 9:6
8 – Acts 9:6
9 – Acts 9:17
10 – Galatians 1:17
11 – Acts 22:18
12 – Acts 22:21
13 – Galatians 1:19
14 – Galatians 1:21, 22
15 – Acts 9:31
16 – Acts 11:19-24
17 – Acts 11:26
18 – Acts 11:29-30
19 – Acts 12:1, 2
20 – Acts 13:2
21 – Acts 15:1
22 – Acts 15:19

23 – Acts 15:29

1 – Acts 16:9
3 – Acts 18:6

Chapter 7
2 – Galatians 6:9
4 – Acts 18:21

Chapter 8
1 – Acts 18:23
3 – Acts 19:1
5 – Romans 15:13

2 – Acts 18:25, 26
4 – II Corinthians 2:1
6 – Luke 9:51

Chapter 9
1 – Acts 23:1
3 – Acts 24:22
5 – Galatians 5:1
7 – Acts 25:10
9 – Acts 25:12
11 – Acts 26:31

2 – Acts 23:11
4 – Philemon 22
6 – Galatians 6:18
8 – Acts 25:11
10 – Acts 26:28
12 – Acts 26:32

Chapter 10
1 – II Peter 1:16-19
3 – Acts 25:12
5 – I Peter 3:19
7 – Luke 24:50, 51
9 – Mark 13:13
11 – Matthew 16:21-23

2 – Acts 25:10, 11
4 – Luke 2:14
6 – Mark 16:15, 16
8 – Mark 13:13
10 – Matthew 16:13-20

Chapter 11
1 – Galatians 3:28

2 – Galatians 3:29

Chapter 12
1 – Matthew 16:18
3 – Matthew 10:28
5 – Ephesians 4:3
7 – I Corinthians 1:10
9 – Matthew 10:34

2 – Matthew 10:32, 33
4 – Luke 9:48
6 – Ephesians 4:4-6
8 – Matthew 16:17
10 – Matthew 10:37-39

11 – Luke 4:26
12 – C. S. Lewis, The Four Loves, New York & London, a Harvest/ HBJ book, p. 171
13 – Luther's Small Catechism, the First Commandment, Par. 30, p. 52
14 – C. S. Lewis, p. 172
15 – Ephesians 6:12
16 – John 10:30
17 – Colossians 2:9
18 – John 14:6
19 – John 3:16
20 – John 17:11
21 – John 17:21
22 – John 17:22
23 – John 13:34, 35
24 – John 4:24
25 – Amos 3:3
26 – The Nicene and Post-Nicene Fathers, Second Series – Volume IV – Athanasius, P. Schaff & H. Wace, Editors, Grand Rapids, Eerdmans Publ., Four Discourses Against the Arians, Discourse III, Par. 21, p. 405ff.

Chapter 13

1 – Klausner, p. 588
2 – ibid., p. 203
3 – ibid., p. 203
4 – ibid., p. 140
5 – ibid., p. 198
6 – ibid., p. 461
7 – ibid., p. 463
8 – ibid., p. 518
9 – ibid., p. 393
10 – Acts 1:6
11 – Klausner, p. 211, 212
12 – Galatians 1:11-16
13 – Hebrews 7:26, 27
14 – Hebrews 11:1
15 – II Thessalonians 2:1-12

Chapter 14

1 – II Thessalonians 2:3
2 – II Thessalonians 2:7
3 – Mark 1:17
4 – II Thessalonians 2:3
5 – II Thessalonians 2:7
6 – II Peter 3:10-18
7 – II Timothy 3:16-17

Chapter 15

None

Chapter 16

1 – II Peter 1:15 – cf. Malachi Martin, <u>The Decline and Fall of the Roman Church</u>, New York, G. P. Putnam's Sons, p. 19
2 – John 14:26
3 – Luther's Works - American Edition, Jaroslav Pelikan and Helmut T. Lehmann, General Editors, St. Louis, Mo., Concordia, and Philadelphia, Pa., Muhlenberg/Fortress, 1957-1974, 31:344.
4 – I Corinthians 1:10
5 – The Lutheran Hymnal – Statement 34, The Athanasian Creed, p. 53
6 – Hebrews 2:11
7 – Ephesians 4:3
8 – Ephesians 4:1, 2
9 – John 15:9-12
10 – John 15:5
11 – Luther's Small Catechism, St. Louis, Mo., Concordia, 1943, Par. 315, p. 200
12 – I Corinthians 12:13

Chapter 17

1 – John 15:18-24
2 – Mark 13:13
3 – Psalm 19:1
4 – Isaiah 7:14
5 – Micah 5:2
6 – Matthew 28:18-20
7 – Hebrews 11:1
8 – Luther's Small Catechism, Explanation of the Third Article of the Apostle's Creed, p. 123
9 – Matthew 6:9-13
10 – Luther's Small Catechism, Par. 244, p. 170
11 – ibid, The Nature of Baptism, p. 170
12 – ibid, The Blessings of Baptism, p. 174
13 – Mark 16:16

Chapter 18

1 – Matthew 28:19
2 – I Corinthians 15:20-28
3 – I Corinthians 15:54
4 – I Corinthians 15:57
5 – II Corinthians 5:17-21
6 – I Corinthians 15:58

Chapter 19

None

Chapter 20

1 – I John 5:18-21
2 – John 13:34, 35
3 – I John 2:15
4 – I John 4:7, 8
5 – I John 5:1-4
6 – I Corinthians 13:4-8
7 – I John 4:17-19
8 – Galatians 5:22, 23
9 – Revelations 3:19
10 – Matthew 28:20
11 – Luther's Small Catechism, The Sacrament of the Altar, Par. 302, p. 197
12 – I Corinthians 11:26
13 – Matthew 5:23, 24
14 – Matthew 26:29; Cf. Mark 14:25 and Luke 22:18
15 – Luther's Small Catechism, Note in Section IV, p. 35
16 – I Corinthians 11:28, 29
17 – John 20:22, 23
18 – Luther's Small Catechism, The Sacrament of the Altar, Par. 324, p. 204
19 – Luther's Works, American Edition, 31:25. Ninety-Five Theses – Thesis 1
20 – Acts 2:42
21 – I Corinthians 11:20
22 – I Corinthians 11:25
23 – J. B. Phillips, <u>The New Testament in Modern English</u>, Rev. Ed., New York, N.Y., The MacMillan Co., p. 358-9.
24 – Luther's Small Catechism, The Sacrament of the Altar, Section III

- The Power of the Lord's Supper, p. 201.
25 – ibid., Par. 316, p. 201.
26 – ibid., Section IV – The Salutary Use of the Lord's Supper, p. 202
27 – I Corinthians 11:25
28 – The Lutheran Hymnal, The Order of a Confessional Service, The Exhortation, p. 47
29 – The Lutheran Hymnal, The Distribution, p. 29

Chapter 21

1 – II Thessalonians 2:9, 10
2 – II Thessalonians 2:11, 12
3 – I John 2:22
4 – John 1:14
5 – John 5:19-23
6 – John 8:16-19
7 – John 14:6-10
8 – John 10:27-30
9 – John 17
10 – II John 7
11 – Ephesians 2:8, 9
12 – The Lutheran Hymnal, Hymn 373, v. 1
13 – Galatians 1:6
14 – Galatians 5:1
15 – Romans 3:19-28
16 – II Thessalonians 2:7
17 – Revelations 1:1-3
18 – Revelations 22:18-21
19 – Revelations 19:10
20 – Revelations 22:8, 9
21 – Ephesians 4:1

Citations from the Works of Josephus

<u>Antiquities</u>
  12-5-3 & 4
  14-14-5
  15-1-1
  15-5-2
  15-11-1
  15-11-3
  15-11-5
  15-11-6
\# 17-8-1
¶ 17-13-2
* 18-2-2
  18-3-3
  18-4-6
  18-6-10
  20-11-1

<u>Wars</u>
\# 1-33-5 to 8
¶ 2-7-3
* 2-9-1
  6-10-1

\# - ¶ - * = Parallel

APPENDIX A

1 – Martin Chemnitz, in his <u>Examination of the Council of Trent</u>, Volume 1, Translation by Fred Kramer, St. Louis, Mo., Concordia, 1971, cites the reckoning of Theophylact, a Byzantine prelate, d. c1108, "that Matthew wrote in the eighth year after the ascension of Christ," p. 78. Neither Chemnitz nor the person he cites approves the reckoning of Theophylact.
2 – Martin Chemnitz writes in his <u>Loci Theologici</u>, Translation by J. A. O. Preus, St. Louis, Mo., Concordia, 1989, Volume II, p. 535, "For the Galatians had been converted to the faith at least six years before Paul wrote this epistle (Galatians) as Theodoret suggests."

APPENDIX B

1 – 15th Edition, 6:623.
2 – Garden City, N. Y., Doubleday & Co., 1977, p. 118.
3 – 'The Celestial Pageantry Dating Christ's Birth,' by Ernest L. Martin, <u>Christianity Today</u>, December 3, 1976.
4 – The remainder of the information about Whiston is from the <u>Dictionary of National Biography</u>, New York and London, MacMillan & Co., 1900, Volume 61.

SUPPLEMENT
The Antichrist Puzzle

The names of antichrist are:
- II Thess. 2:3 – "The man of sin."
- II Thess. 2:3 – "The son of perdition."
- II Thess. 2:7 – "The mystery of lawlessness."
- II Thess. 2:8 & 9 – "The lawless one."

Definition of perdition:
1. A state of final spiritual ruin; loss of soul; damnation.
2. The future state of the wicked.
3. Hell.
4. Utter destruction or ruin.

Evaluation of sin and lawlessness:

I John 3:4 & 8a – "Whoever commits sin also commits lawlessness, and sin is lawlessness." "He who practices sin is of the devil."

The traits of antichrist:

He is under the influence of Satan.

II Thess. 2:9 & 10 – "The coming of the lawless one is according to the working of Satan with all power, signs, and lying wonders, and with all deception of unrighteousness in those who perish."

He is a liar.

I John 2:22a – "Who is a liar but he who denies that Jesus is the Christ."

He will cause a great apostasy.

I Thess. 2:3 – "Let no one deceive you by any means; for that Day (the day of Christ) will not come unless the falling away comes first."

Matthew 24:11 – "And many false prophets will rise and deceive many."

Matthew 24:24 and Mark 13:22 – "For false christs and false prophets will arise and show (great) signs and wonders so as to deceive, if possible, even the elect."

He will arise from within the church.

I John 2:18 & 19 – "Little children, it is the last hour: and as you have heard that the Antichrist is coming, even now many antichrists have come, by which we know that it is the last hour. They went out from us, but they were not of us; for if they had been of us, they would have continued with us; but they went out that they might be made manifest, that none of them were of us."

II Thess. 2:4 – "(The man of sin, the son of perdition), who opposes and exalts himself above all that is called God or that is worshiped, so that he sits as God in the temple of God, showing himself that he is God."

He was already working at the time of the apostles.

II Thess. 2:7 – "For the mystery of lawlessness is already at work."

I John 4:5 – "And even now it (the spirit of antichrist) is already in the world."

The characteristics of the victims of antichrist are:

II Thess. 2:10 – "They (those who perish) did not receive the love of the truth."

II Thess. 2:11 & 12 – "God will send them (those who perish) strong delusion, that they should believe the lie, that they all might be condemned who did not believe the truth but had pleasure in unrighteousness."

Matthew 24:10 – "And then many will be offended, betray one

another, and hate one another."

A description of an antichrist:

> II John 7 – "For many deceivers have gone out into the world who do not confess Jesus Christ as coming in the flesh. This is a deceiver and an antichrist."

A description of the spirit of antichrist:

> I John 4:3 & 5 – "And every spirit that does not confess that Jesus Christ has come in the flesh is not of God. And this is the spirit of antichrist, which you have heard was coming, and even now it is already in the world." "They are of the world. Therefore they speak as of the world, and the world hears them."

A description of antichrist:

> I John 2:22b – "He is antichrist who denies the Father and the Son."
>
> I John 2:23a – "Whoever denies the Son does not have the Father either."

How to avoid the antichrist:

> I John 3:10 – "In this the children of God and the children of the devil are manifest: Whoever does not practice righteousness is not of God, nor is he who does not love his brother. For this is the message that you heard from the beginning, that we should love one another."
>
> I John 5:2 & 3a – "By this we know that we love the children of God, when we love God and keep His commandments. For this is the love of God, that we keep His commandments."
>
> II John 6 – "And this is love, that we walk according to His commandments."
>
> II John 9 – "Whoever transgresses and does not abide in the doctrine of Christ does not have God. He who abides in the doctrine of Christ has both the Father and the Son."

A restraining force presently is preventing the revealing of the

antichrist:
> II Thess. 2:6 & 7b – "And now you know what is restraining, that he may be revealed in his own time. Only He who now restrains will do so until He is taken out of the way."

The antichrist will be revealed:
> II Thess. 2:8 – "And then the lawless one will be revealed, whom the Lord will consume with the breath of His mouth and destroy with the brightness of His coming."

What is the doctrine of Christ?

The Eternal Word – John 1:1-4
> "In the beginning was the Word, and the Word was with God, and the Word was God.
>
> "He was in the beginning with God.
>
> "All things were made by Him, and without Him nothing was made that was made.
>
> "In Him was life, and the life was the light of men."

The Word Becomes Flesh – John 1:14
> "And the Word became flesh and dwelt among us, and we beheld His glory, the glory as of the only begotten of the Father, full of grace and truth."

God's Supreme Revelation – Hebrews 1:1-4
> "God, who at various times and in different ways spoke in the time past to the fathers by the prophets,
>
> "Has in these last days spoken to us by His Son, whom He has appointed heir of all things, by whom also He made the worlds;
>
> "Who being the brightness of His glory and the express image of His person, and upholding all things by the word of His power, when He had by Himself purged our sins, sat down at the right hand of the Majesty on high,
>
> "Having become so much better than the angels, as He has by inheritance obtained a more excellent name than they."

+ + + + +

The Athanasian Creed (29-35)
> "For the right faith is that we believe and confess that our Lord Jesus Christ, the Son of God, is God and Man;
> God the substance of the Father, begotten before the worlds; and Man of the substance of His mother, born in the world;
> Perfect God and perfect Man, of a reasonable soul and human flesh subsisting.
> Equal to the Father as touching His Godhead and inferior to the Father as touching His manhood;
> Who, although He be God and Man, yet He is not two but one Christ;
> One, not by the conversion of the Godhead into flesh, but by taking the manhood into God.
> One altogether; not by confusion of Substance, but by unity of the Person."

The Augsburg Confession III 1-2
> "It is also taught among us that God the Son became man, born of the Virgin Mary, and that the two natures, divine and human, are so inseparably united in one person that there is one Christ."

Luther's Small Catechism – Second Article of the Apostles Creed – The Office of Christ
> "Christ was appointed to be my Prophet, Priest, and King.
> A – As my Prophet, He revealed Himself by word and deed, and by the preaching of the Gospel still reveals Himself as the Son of God and the Redeemer of the world.
> B – As my Priest, Christ fulfilled the Law in my stead perfectly (active obedience), and sacrificed Himself for me (passive

obedience), and still intercedes (pleads) for me with His Heavenly Father.

C – As my King, Christ with His almighty power rules over all creatures, governs and protects His Church, and finally leads it to glory."

What does it mean to deny the Father and the Son? It means:
1. A denial of the Trinity of God – Father, Son, and Holy Spirit.

   I John 5:7 & 8 – "For there are three who bear witness in Heaven: the Father, the Word, and the Holy Spirit; and these three are one. And there are three that bear witness on earth: The Spirit, the water and the blood; and these three agree as one."
2. A denial that Jesus Christ sent the Holy Spirit into the world at the request of His Father.
   John 15:26 – "But when the Helper comes, whom I shall send to you from the Father, the Spirit of truth who proceeds from the Father, He will testify of Me."
3. A denial of the relationship of the Father and the Son. The relationship of the Father and the Son is that they are One; and this relationship is an incorporeal relationship even as is the Holy Trinity.
   John 10:30 – "I and the Father are one."
   John 14:11 – "I am in the Father and the Father in Me."
   John 17:22 – "We are one."

How do we deny the oneness of the relationship of the Father and the Son?
1. By saying that we can be one with each other without being one with the Son.
   John 15:5 – "Without Me, you can do nothing."
2. By saying that by our own efforts we can be of assistance to

the Holy Spirit in the working of our own salvation.

Eph. 2:8 & 9 – "For by grace you have been saved through faith, and that not of yourselves: it is a gift of God, not of works, lest anyone should boast."

3. By confusing the work of each of the members of the Holy Trinity, including the intermingling of the "The Means of Grace."

John 14:26 – "But the Helper, the Holy Spirit, whom the Father will send in My name, He will teach you all things, and bring to your remembrance all things that I said to you."

4. By not keeping the unity of the Spirit in the bond of peace.

Eph. 4:1-3 – "I, therefore, the prisoner of the Lord, beseech you to walk worthy of the calling with which you were called, with all lowliness and gentleness, with longsuffering, bearing with one another in love, endeavoring to keep the unity of the Spirit in the bond of Peace."

What is the unity of the Spirit? It is described in the next four verses:

Eph. 4:4-6 – "There is one body and one Spirit, just as you were called in one hope of your calling; one Lord, one faith, one baptism, one God and Father of all, who is above all, through all, and in you all."

What does 'Unity of the Spirit' signify?

It signifies the Triune Godhead, and its gifts and graces to men.

One body – The Sacrament of the Lord's Supper

One Spirit – The Third person of the Holy Trinity

One hope – A gift from God – Sanctification (The new covenant of love and the sending of the Holy Spirit)

One Lord – The Second person of the Holy Trinity

One faith – A gift from God – Justification (The original covenant of Grace)

One baptism – The Sacrament of Holy Baptism

One God and Father of all, who is above all, and through all, and in you all – The First person of the Holy Trinity

Endeavoring to keep the unity of the Spirit is an ongoing process. Human beings, being what they are, are on their own incapable of achieving the keeping of the unity of the Spirit perfectly. Jesus Christ is the only 'One' capable of doing this. The church must solely look to Him for guidance.

When the Christian church interprets Ephesians 4:4-6 as a charter and guide for itself as it wrestles with the problem of ecumenical unity, it takes these verses out of context. Verses 4-6 must remain connected to verse three. St. Paul is not writing about a physically visible church in these verses.

Any claim that the church can achieve oneness with each other apart from its Lord and Savior Jesus Christ exhibits the spirit of antichrist. Those making such a claim are in reality usurping for themselves a position of authority in the church; a position Christ reserves for Himself.

Ephesians 4:4-6 may also be used as a basis for the doctrine of the Holy Trinity. The 'one body' spoken of by Paul is the "holy Christian Church, the communion of saints" (The Apostles' Creed, the Third Article). The holy Christian Church, the communion of saints is that group of true believers known by God alone.

One of the attributes of God is that He is eternal. He is the Alpha and Omega. He is the Beginning and the End (A to Z). He is past, present, and future.

In a certain sense, each member of the Holy Trinity takes care of one of these facets of time. God, the Father, has taken care of the past. To Him is ascribed the work of Creation. He created all things well. God, the Son, has taken care of the future. To Him is ascribed the work of Salvation. The believer's place in heaven is secure. God, the

Holy Spirit, takes care of the present. To Him is ascribed the work of Sanctification. He works faith in the hearts of men through the Word, and in the Sacrament of Holy Baptism. He strengthens men's faith through the Word, and in the Sacrament of the Lord's Supper. This is not to say that all three members of the Holy Trinity are not presently active in the world. St. John puts it this way: "I am the Way, the Truth, and the Life" (John 14:6). The Father is the Way, He holds the world in His hand; the Holy Spirit is the Truth, His Word is Truth; and the Son is the Life; He is the Lord of life. St. Matthew closes his Gospel with the saying of Jesus, "Behold, I am with you always, even to the end of the age" (Matt. 28:20).

What does it mean to say that one does not confess that Jesus Christ has come into the flesh?

1. It means a denial of the oneness of the Father and the Son.
2. It means a denial that the Son is of the same substance of the Father.
3. It means a denial that the Son was begotten of the Father from eternity, and, therefore, that He is co-eternal with the Father and the Holy Spirit.
4. It means a denial that the Son became incarnate by the Holy Spirit of the Virgin Mary.
5. It means a denial that the Son vicariously atoned for the sins of the whole world through His suffering, death, resurrection, and ascension.
6. It means a denial that the Son does not now sit in glory at the right hand of the Father in heaven.
7. It means a denial that the Son will return at the end of time to judge both the living and the dead.

In his epistles, the Apostle John not only speaks about antichrist, but also about 'an' antichrist and the 'spirit of' antichrist. The description he gives these two things is that they both do not confess that Jesus Christ has come into the flesh. This characteristic may also be applied to the antichrist, even though John does not specifically say as much.

It must be remembered that the antichrist represents total opposition to Jesus Christ and everything He stands for. This includes everything contrary to what is revealed to us about Jesus Christ in the Bible, such as the establishment of His church on earth and His oneness with His Heavenly Father to His incarnation, which encompasses His coming into the flesh. These facts are highly significant as we attempt to determine more precisely who the antichrist really is.

All the speculation that evil historical personalities such as Nero, Diocletian, Trajan, Napoleon, Hitler, Stalin, or even some latter day evil person might be the antichrist is entirely mistaken. The same may be said of individual groups such as Communists, Islam, the Jewish nation, or even various sects such as the Mormon Church or the Jehovah Witnesses. Individuals or individual groups such as these have not and do not now operate from within the church and are most assuredly not the antichrist.

In considering the Bishop of Rome as a candidate as the antichrist, it must be taken into account that even though the Pope's faults and the faults of the Roman Catholic Church are many, denying that Jesus Christ has come into the flesh is not one of them. The Pope unequivocally affirms that Jesus Christ has come into the flesh. If the Pope did deny this truth, the entire doctrine of the Roman Catholic Church concerning the Virgin Mary and her role as the mother of God would collapse. This fact in itself disproves the contention that the Pope is the antichrist. In addition, it must be remembered that the Roman Catholic Church shares the three Symbols of the Christian Faith with the rest of Christendom. All three of these creeds emphatically state that Jesus Christ has come into the flesh.

The consideration of the timing of the coming of antichrist is also important. There are some who say that the great and final antichrist will appear just prior to the end of the world. Presumably, much of this thinking is based on apocalyptical Scripture. It may also be based on what other holy writers have to say in regard to 'the end of the age,' etc. Some of these thinkers present a very plausible case as they cite the prophesies of Old Testament writers such as Ezekiel, Daniel, and others, and the writings of St. John the Divine. They very convincingly liken 'The Empire of Antichrist' to 'The Roman Empire' as they declare their vision of Armageddon, The Rapture and the millennium, and the Second Coming of Jesus Christ.

'Eschatology' is a word that has more and more taken on an intense meaning of late. While interest in 'the final things' or 'end times' has always intrigued men, this interest has heightened in recent years. This is self-evident by the number of books written on the subject and in the popularity of these books.

The diversity of opinion about what is all meant in speaking of 'the final things' or 'end times' is almost as varied as the number of books that have appeared. There is a continuing struggle going on to figure out what the Biblical writers mean, and how it applies to the antichrist. This is especially true of apocalyptical writings of Daniel and the Revelation of St. John the Divine.

There are, however, other Scripture passages which speak of these things. Matthew devotes two chapters in his gospel to it when Christ replies to the disciples' query (Matt. 24:3): "And what will be the sign of Your coming, and of the end of the age?" John speaks in his epistles (I John 1:18), "Little children, it is the last hour." St. Paul writes to the Corinthians (I Cor. 10:11): "Now all these things happened to them as examples, and they were written for our admonition, on whom the ends of the ages have come." The writer to the Hebrews states at the beginning of his treatise (1:2), "(God) has in these last days spoken to us by His son."

To understand more clearly about eschatological things, determination must be made as to what the holy writers mean by 'end of the age,' 'the last hour,' 'the ends of the ages,' and 'these last days.' A good place to begin is to look at the genealogy of Jesus Christ as given to us by Matthew (1:1-17) and Luke (3:23-28). Matthew covers from Abraham to Christ; Luke covers from Christ to Adam. The fact that Matthew includes only the time from Abraham on indicates that Abraham denotes an important separation in the division of the 'times.' The life of Jesus Christ is very naturally another division of the 'times.' The end of the final division of the 'times' is, of course, Christ's second coming.

The following chart graphically shows these divisions of the 'times' and their significance.

From Adam to Abraham	– The Age of Creation	– The Beginning of Time
From Abraham To Christ's First Coming	– The Age of Promise	– The Covenantal Time
From Christ's First Coming To Christ's Second Coming	– The Age of Fulfillment	– The End Time

Speaking in these terms, then, it may be said that the 'end time' existed already during Christ's stay on earth. The 'end time' has been going on ever since. It is apparent that the holy writers were all talking about the same thing in using these different terms. Thus, when they were writing, they were not only addressing the issues of their day, they were addressing the issues of every generation since and up to the present, including the approach of the end of the world.

The issue of the antichrist had the same meaning for the holy writers as it has had for peoples living throughout the ages, and as it has in our generation. The antichrist and the 'very'antichrist, or the 'last and final' antichrist mean exactly one and the same thing. That is not to say that the activity of the antichrist is at every moment in history as intense in one moment as compared to another. The antichrist has his ups and downs even as we do.

Nowhere is this more plain than what is demonstrated in the Reformation and in the life of Martin Luther. God spoke to Satan and said, "You have had your day for a time, now I will have Mine." Martin Luther, by God's Holy Spirit, dealt a serious blow to the work of antichrist. It did not, however finish him off. The Lutheran Church in Germany again came under heavy attack from the antichrist as its rulers attempted to combine the churches into one body. As a result, many of God's persecuted faithful left their homeland and came to America.

The antichrist followed them. He made the same old 'pitch' he always makes: "Christ's church here on earth must be one." "Christians must be one with each other regardless of their differing doctrine." Organizations were formed and soon the ecumenical era emerged. The ecumenist's watchword is the same as the antichrist's watchword. To be effective in proclaiming the gospel of Jesus Christ here on earth, Christians must unite in oneness with each other; forget about inaccuracies which separate various denominations. This is false ecumenicity.

Chapter 15 of John's Gospel is very pertinent in this regard. Verse 1: "I am the true vine, and My Father is the vinedresser."

Jesus compares The Kingdom of God to a vineyard. Verse 5: "I am the vine, you are the branches. He who abides in Me, and I in him, bears much fruit for without Me you can do nothing."

Can man really be one with each other? Yes, some say, and insist that this is what Jesus had prayed for in His high-priestly prayer, John 17:21: "That they all may be one, as You, Father, are in Me, and I in You; that they also may be one in Us, that the world may believe that You have sent Me."

There are those who believe that this should be interpreted to read: "That they all may be one 'with each other,'" They say that interpreting this verse to read: "That they all may be one 'with Me,'" is erroneous.

Can man really be one with each other without first being one in Christ? Tying together branches severed (verse 2 of John 15: "Every branch in Me that does not bear fruit He takes away.") from the True Vine (Christ) is nothing less than tying dead and dried-up sticks together. Bearing fruit means living a sanctified life as outlined in Galatians 5, and loving God above all things, and loving God above all things means being obedient to Him. "For this is the love of God, that we keep His commandments," I John 5:3. Not bearing fruit means not obeying God's laws. Matthew speaks of this in Chapter 15 of his Gospel: Defilement is from within – verse 7: "Hypocrites! Well did Isaiah prophesy about you, saying: 'This people draws near to Me with their lips, But their heart is far from Me. And in vain they worship Me, Teaching as doctrines the commandments of men.'" Isaiah 29:13.

Those favoring the first interpretation are basing their hopes for ecumenicity on a horizontal oneness. This is false ecumenicity. Our only hope for true ecumenicity is a vertical oneness with Christ. By asserting that man can be one with each other, these people are displaying the spirit of antichrist. Again verse 5: "Without Me you can do nothing."

Many Christians outside The Roman Catholic Church (even within the church that bears Martin Luther's name) have succumbed to the latest wiles of the antichrist, and Christ's true church on earth now has a real battle on its hands. Christians must first be one with Christ, even as He is one with His Father, before they can be one with each other. This is true ecumenicity. To be one with Christ means that Christians must be obedient to God and keep His commandments. This is what love is about (I John 5:2 & 3). Christ was obedient to His Father when He became incarnate to suffer and die for the sins of all men, thus becoming our Prophet, our Priest, and our King.

So then, who is antichrist? Before attempting to answer that question, further consideration should be given as to whom antichrist is not.

If, as expressed above under the question, 'What does it mean to deny the Father and the Son?' the relationship of the Father and the Son is an incorporeal relationship, it follows that the one who opposes the Father and the Son must likewise be incorporeal. Therefore, what this presupposes is that antichrist is not a man.

If antichrist were a man, this would mean that Satan would have to become incarnate; incarnate in much the same way that Christ became incarnate. Christ, in His mercy, will never allow such a thing to happen, for if He did, it would mean that He would negate His vicarious atonement. When Christ made His descent into hell, He proclaimed His victory over death and over Satan.

Satan, however, is one who never can accept defeat as long as this world stands. His fight must continue, and one of the ways he continues his fight is to try to delude men into believing that as an opponent of Christ, he will appear on earth in the form of antichrist.

In the meantime, he will attack Christ's church here on earth with all the cunning he can muster. St. Paul writes (Eph. 6:10-12): "Finally, my brethren, be strong in the Lord and in the power of His might. Put on the whole armor of God, that you may be able to stand against the wiles of the devil. For we do not wrestle against flesh and blood, but against principalities, against powers, against rulers of the darkness of this age, against spiritual wickedness in high (heavenly) places."

Another of the tricks the devil uses is that he tries to get men to believe that they truly can become one and remain one with each other in the church on earth. Such a church would be a centrally governed earthly organization with hierarchical control. He has succeeded insofar as the Bishop of Rome has been victimized by antichrist. Antichrist has set up his earthly base of operations in the Church of Rome. But antichrist is never quite satisfied. He wants to subvert all Christendom; and all Christendom is forever his target. He was quite successful for a time, but our gracious Lord sent His servant, Martin Luther, to help stem the tide. Satan has not taken such a setback lying down. He keeps hammering away at the church.

Antichrist uses many other tricks in order to deceive Christ's church here on earth, but we know that when we are one with Christ and His Father (John 17), and are obedient in His love, we will remain His servants and be one with each other.

So then, who is antichrist? The question might better be, "What is antichrist?" Antichrist is that incorporeal image created by Satan as his last desperate attempt to combat a victorious Christ. Thinking in these terms, then, all of the prophecies of Daniel and the other Old Testament prophets and the Revelation of St. John the Divine can be applied to the Bishop of Rome, who is the unwitting victim of antichrist.

When Peter came to Rome several years later than Paul, he no doubt saw and experienced many of the same things that Paul had seen and experienced. This would be true of both things in the city of Rome as well as in the church in Rome. However, he evidently was not as equally endowed by the Holy Spirit when it came to interpreting those things in a spiritual manner.

Peter writes in his second epistle, (3:14-16): "Therefore, beloved, seeing that you look for such things, be diligent that you may be found by Him in peace, without spot, and blameless; and account that the suffering of our Lord is salvation – as also our beloved brother Paul, according to the wisdom given to him, has written to you, as also in all his epistles, speaking in them of these things, in which are some things hard to understand, which those who are untaught and unstable twist to their own destruction, as they do also the rest of the Scripture."

Paul's epistles had evidently been made available to Peter for him to read and study. The letters to the church at Thessalonica were no doubt included. It is entirely possible, therefore, that Peter was referring to what Paul had written in II Thessalonians 2 when he stated, "In which are some things hard to understand." These same things are also hard for us to understand.

Foremost among things hard to understand is what Paul says in verses 6-7 and 11-12 in this chapter. "And now you know what is restraining, that he may be revealed in his own time. For the mystery of lawlessness is already at work; only He[1] who now restrains will do so until He[1] is taken out of the way." "And for this reason God will send them strong delusion, that they should believe the lie, that they all might be condemned who did not believe the truth but had pleasure in unrighteousness."

The New King James Bible boldly ventures to capitalize 'he' in verse seven, whereas most other translations use the lower case. What is evidently meant is that 'he' stands for deity. Taken one step further, the third person of the Trinity. This immediately presents another dilemma. A restraining Holy Spirit does not fit our image of what John paints in his Gospel, (16:13a): "However, when He, the Spirit of truth, has come, He will guide you into all truth;" and (15:26): "But when the Helper comes, whom I shall send to you from the Father, the Spirit of truth who proceeds from the Father, He will testify of Me."

Is it really the Holy Spirit who is restraining? Does not Paul write to Timothy? (I Tim. 2:4): "Who (God) desires all men to be saved and to come to the knowledge of the truth." This truly puzzles us. Our searching must continue, and in doing so, verses 11 and 12 must be examined; these verses are meant to help explain verses 6 and 7. Verses 11 and 12 are not the only instance in the Bible where it states that God places a hindrance before men when it comes to revealing His word. Numerous times the Bible states that the mysteries of God are hidden from men.[*]

God reveals His word to men at His good pleasure. Thus, the Kingdom of God is not always easily found. God sets obstacles in the way, or so it seems. Jesus himself says, (Matthew 10:34): "Do not think that I have come to bring peace on earth. I did not come to bring peace but a sword." It follows, then, that if the Father and the Son seem to us to set hindrances for men to come into the Kingdom of God, the Holy Spirit, too, may act in a similar manner. The second half of John 16:13 seems to corroborate this: "for He will not speak on His own authority, but whatever He hears He will speak; and He will tell you of things to come." When the time comes for the Holy Spirit to tell of things to come, then will be the time when "He is taken out of the way" (II Thess. 3:7).

[1] or, he (NKJB)

[*] e.g., Matthew 11:25, Luke 9:45, Luke 18:34, I Cor. 2:7